NOTHING BUT WORDS
Dustin Hoiseth

NOTHING BUT WORDS
Dustin Hoiseth

POLYVERSE PUBLICATIONS · SANTA BARBARA

Contents

PROLOGUE

The back of Ethan's head pulsed with pain as he rubbed at it to check the damage. When he pulled his hand back into the dim light, it was covered in blood. The pain made everything hazy, including his memory. He struggled to remember how he'd ended up in the dark cave he now found himself in. The only source of light trickled in from an opening directly above. Had he fallen into the cave, hitting his head in the process? It seemed the only logical explanation.

By the time Ethan had acquainted himself with the limited space of the subterranean cave, his memory had begun to return. He'd been searching for answers. Answers that he'd found but had been unable to accept. It had all led him to a pounding headache in a small dark cave. A small dark cave that he couldn't possibly have been to before. Yet, as Ethan took notice of the stack of papers lying at the far end of the cave, he knew that wasn't true. An even deeper memory, obscured by far more than a simple head injury, returned. The memory poured into him the longer he stared at the papers. It seemed to whisper in his ear, "You've been here before, and there are even more unpleasant answers to be found. Answers to questions you didn't even know to ask."

Ethan knew there was only one path forward, and it wasn't up through the hole he'd fallen through. He could see words printed on the paper and moved to get a closer look. The top page had only a title and an author, inviting even wilder curiosity.

Ethan knelt to pick up the small manuscript sitting before him. The only answers that mattered were in those pages.

CHAPTER 1

Ethan looked out the window of Ashley's old station wagon as they drove through Northern California. The road they were on cut straight through an ancient redwood forest. The seemingly unending forest seemed so powerful. A place that had yet to be beaten by the devouring machine of society. A place where the magic of nature still existed. Ethan had always respected the forest. To him, it was a place of mystery, where fantastical things could still happen.

As the station wagon flew down the highway, the trees passed through Ethan's vision in a blur. The writer in Ethan stirred as he looked out at the trees. It was like each tree was a word in a greater story the forest was trying to tell him. But the story was written in the language of the forest. An ancient language Ethan didn't know.

Of course, it was all in Ethan's head. They were just trees, and he was just a writer with an overactive imagination. Ethan wasn't just any writer, though. He was one of sixteen contestants invited to participate in the Known Poets and Authors Writing Festival. The festival was held every year in the small Northern California town of Ustumah City. It hosted anyone who wished to come for the seven days of festivities, each day with a different focus or theme. The central piece of the festival was the writing contest. Eight poets and eight fiction writers were invited to compete against each other to see which poem and which novel would be crowned that year's best. Ethan had been chosen for his fiction novel, *"In Despair."*

Ethan was joined by his girlfriend Ashley and his best friend, Marcus. The three of them saw the festival as a vacation and a much needed one at that. Ethan and Ashley's relationship had been put through the wringer that past year, and they hoped to use the break to rekindle it. Not only that, but Ethan had grown distant from his lifelong friend Marcus as well. The trip was a chance to fix their friendship too.

The radio struggled to pick up the local radio station that Ashley had tuned in to a few miles back, but nobody complained. In fact, no one had said anything for the past hour of driving. It had been a tough year for the three friends, and this had been far from the first silent car ride they'd shared.

Ashley was laser-focused on the road, her jet-black hair fluttering as the breeze blew in from her open window. Marcus sat in the back, playing a game on his phone. All the while, Ethan continued to stare out at the trees.

It wasn't long before Ashley turned the car off the highway, and the group was heading down a two-lane road toward their destination. The road sloped downward, and from above, they could make out Ustumah City sitting among the surrounding forest like an insignificant speck.

"I knew this was a small town, but I wasn't expecting this small. This is going to be a cramped vacation," Marcus said as they spotted Ustumah.

Ashley looked back at him, "You'll be alright, city boy." Marcus laughed at that, "You grew up in the city too."

"Yeah, but you don't hear me complaining."

Marcus just sighed and sat back to continue with his phone game. "Ethan, you there?" Ashley asked, noting his silence.

Ethan had been completely distracted since the moment Ustumah City had appeared in front of them. Looking out at the small town, Ethan had an overpowering feeling that he'd been there before. Despite the feeling, Ethan was sure he had never actually been to Ustumah. He'd seen it in pictures, but this feeling went well beyond that. It was as if he'd been there recently. He just couldn't remember.

"Ethan?" Ashley asked again.

It broke Ethan out of his trance, and he turned to her. "Sorry, I'm here," he said. "I just had the strangest feeling that I've been here before."

"Deja vu," Marcus offered from behind his phone.

"Yeah," Ethan agreed, and just as quickly as the feeling had come on, it disappeared. Eventually, they arrived in Ustumah City. There were a staggering number of tourists wandering the streets of the small town. Ashley had some difficulty navigating the car through the people-flooded streets.

"Damn, this festival is no joke," Ashley said.

Ethan smiled, "It's nice to see so many people that still care about a good book."

It took longer than it should have due to all the people, but Ashley finally parked the car outside the Ustumah City Visitor's Center. It was there that Ethan was supposed to meet with his publisher's representative at the festival, Sarah. Ethan had met Sarah once before, and they'd spoken on the phone a few times the previous week. She was a no-nonsense kind of person, and Ethan was intimidated by her.

Once they had parked, the three friends exited the car. Ethan looked around at all the tourists and realized he was overdressed. He liked to wear a sort of business casual kind of look. His blazer and button-up made him stick out like a sore thumb among the casually dressed tourists. With Marcus walking next to him, he felt like he stuck out even more. Marcus was a good few inches taller than Ethan, in much better shape, and wore a tight shirt that showed off his muscles. Ethan felt that he must've looked like the nerd standing next to the jock. Ethan's only saving grace was Ashley to his other side. She had on tight black jeans, a small leather jacket, and a fashionable scarf around her neck. Anyone would look cool walking next to her, Ethan told himself.

The group entered the Visitor's Center, and Ethan immediately spotted Sarah. She seemed to have been impatiently waiting and jumped up as she saw them enter. "About time," she said.

"Sorry if we're a little late," Ethan offered.

Sarah just shook her head. "It's my job to wait here for you. Even if it's only for a five-minute meeting," she said, rolling her eyes. "This shouldn't take long."

"We couldn't have done this over the phone then?" Ethan asked.

"No, because I'm supposed to deliver this to you personally," Sarah said, handing Ethan a key and a small piece of paper with an address. "The Ustumah City Book Club insists that contestants stay in their private cabins just outside of town for the duration of the contest.

You've been given the keys to the Chekhov Cabin."

"Oh, we get to stay in a cabin. Cute," Ashley said, rubbing Ethan's back. "Wait, why is a book club giving out free cabins?" Marcus asked.

Ethan and Ashley looked at Marcus in shock. "Don't you ever pay attention?" Ethan asked.

Sarah butted in. "The Ustumah City Book Club are prominent members of the community here. They host this festival and pretty much run this entire county. Try and act like you know who they are. If you don't, it'll make Ethan look bad. And that makes me look bad. And that makes Cardinal's Nest Publishing look bad. So don't say anything like that again," she said, glaring at Marcus.

Marcus just nodded silently.

Sarah shook her head and turned back to Ethan. "Why don't you three get settled at the cabin. Maybe head back into town and familiarize yourself with the area afterward," she said.

"Yeah, sure thing. I'd love to see some local sights," Ethan said.

"Do whatever you want," Sarah said, rolling her eyes again. "Just make sure that you're here around four. You need to meet me at the Ustumah City Book Store for the Meet the Writers Event; I'll text you the details."

Ethan nodded. "You got it."

There was an awkward moment of silence as no one said anything. Sarah looked at them, seemingly confused before she shooed them away. "Well, go on. Get situated at the cabin."

The three turned around and headed out toward Ashley's car. "She's fun," Marcus joked once they were out of earshot.

CHAPTER 2

Back in the car, Ashley followed the directions Sarah had given them, and they eventually made a turn onto a dirt road deep in the forest. The further they went, the more the redwoods seemed to close in around them until the road was just wide enough to fit the car.

Together the towering redwoods cast a large shadow that blanketed the road. An almost ominous feeling took hold of the silent car.

Finally, Marcus broke the silence, "And I thought Ustumah City was in the middle of nowhere… This cabin is so deep in the woods; it gives the middle of nowhere a new meaning."

Ethan let out a sigh without even realizing, "Forest, Marcus. This is a forest, not woods."

"What?" Marcus asked, confused.

"A wood is similar to a forest, but it could just be a few trees. A forest like this is much larger," Ethan explained. He wasn't sure why he'd said that, but lately, everything Marcus said rubbed him the wrong way. He felt a tinge of guilt for trying to belittle his friend like that, but he knew if he apologized now Marcus would just rub it in his face later. So instead he said nothing.

Marcus shook his head silently, "Okay…" He paused, "Thanks for the lecture, Professor Garland…"

Ashley bit her lower lip and looked at Marcus in the rear-view mirror. He made eye contact for a moment before shaking his head again and looking out the car window. For a moment Ashley considered saying something to try and change the subject and give the two something positive to talk about, but she knew the two men well enough to keep the silence. They both needed it to clear their heads. They'd talk when they were ready.

For a long while, there was nothing but the steadied breaths of the car's occupants, and the sound of gravel crunching beneath the tires along the dirt path. Finally, the car took a turn up a hill and a small cabin came into view. The cabin was completely surrounded by an old wooden fence that met in the front of the cabin to form a wooden archway. Ashley guided the car through the archway and parked the car directly in front of the cabin's porch.

"Well, we're finally here," Ashley said smiling at Ethan. "It's a cute little place," She added.

Ethan forced a smile. He was upset with Marcus over something so pointless, while Ashley was doing nothing but try to be positive. "Yeah, looks cozy. Only cabin I've ever stayed in was four times this size," he said, leaning in for a kiss.

Ashley kissed him back, but something in the back of Ethan's head told him that she had hesitated for the briefest moment before doing so. *She loves you, it's all in your head,* Ethan told himself. The past year and a half had been a constant internal battle. One side was convinced he'd already lost his girlfriend, and the other was desperately trying to stop his lack of confidence from sabotaging the relationship any further.

Inside the cabin, Ethan and Ashley unpacked their things in the larger bedroom, while Marcus unpacked his in the cramped guest room. Marcus passed Ethan in the hall and gave him a friendly smack on the shoulder.

"I didn't think it was possible, but this room is smaller than our dorm back at school," Marcus chuckled, pointing into the guest room.

Ethan laughed, Marcus was extending an olive branch and Ethan intended to take it. "At least you have the room to yourself this time. Now I won't have to listen to you greasing the pipe every night," Ethan smirked.

"I told you, man! I just fidget a lot when I sleep!" Marcus blurted defensively.

Ashley laughed from inside her bedroom, "How long are you going to try and use that excuse, Marcus?"

Marcus opened his mouth to respond, but he thought better and instead gave Ethan a playful punch in the arm. "Who the hell says 'greasing the pipe?'" Marcus asked as he continued on his way to the car for the rest of his things.

"I'm a writer!" Ethan called after him, "I can't just say 'jerking yourself off,' I've got to at least try to be more creative than that."

Inside the bedroom, Ashley smiled as she unpacked her things. She and Ethan had been together for about three years, and recently they'd had their fair share of issues. But all of their problems were below the surface. They'd been distant from each other, but they'd been working on it. Ethan and Marcus, on the other hand, had been friends forever. They'd always had a trouble-free friendship, but right around the same time Ashley and Ethan's issues began, Ethan and Marcus started to have problems too. Their problems were much more surface-level.

They'd argue about anything, almost like they were looking for excuses to fight. Sometimes when Ashley thought about it, it made her sick to think that she was what had caused a rift between them. She had hoped that this trip would be a nice relaxing chance for them to mend their friendship. So far it had not gone well, but their conversation in the hallway had just given her hope.

Ethan and Marcus finished grabbing the rest of the bags out of the car, and as they walked back into the cabin something caught Ethan's eye that he hadn't noticed before. Mounted above the mantle of the fireplace was an old rifle. A satisfied grin crept onto Ethan's face.

"Hey, Ash! What did Sarah say this cabin was called again?" Ethan asked.

Ashley appeared from out of the hallway, Marcus right behind her. "The Chekhov Cabin, I think. Why?" Ashley said curiously.

Ethan let out a calm laugh. "Yeah, I thought so. That's really funny. Or really clever I should say," Ethan said pointing to the rifle hanging on the wall.

"Why's that?" Marcus chimed in, a spark of curiosity in his voice.

"Well," Ethan started, excited to explain, "Anton Chekhov is a famous writer from the late 19th century. He was well known for his short stories, but he is better known for coming up with the dramatic principle known as Chekhov's Gun." As Ethan began explaining, Ashley and Marcus' curiosity deflated knowing Ethan was about to go on one of his rants. Ethan too wrapped up in what he was saying failed to notice their lack of enthusiasm and continued, "Chekhov's Gun states that everything mentioned in a story must be relevant to the story, otherwise they should not be included. Basically, elements of the story should not make 'false promises' by never having any importance. This is of course not counting red herrings, which would be an exception to this rule. But that's a conversation for another time." Ethan let out a satisfied snicker as he moved to his conclusion, "I didn't find it clever just because they put a gun in 'The Chekhov Cabin,' but because the entire invention of Chekhov's Gun is based on a quote by Chekhov where he stated something along the lines of, 'If in the first act you have hung a rifle on the wall, then in the following one it should be fired. Otherwise, don't put it there.'"

Ethan smiled proudly at Ashley and Marcus who didn't respond right away, so Ethan continued nervously, "I mean, that had to have been on purpose on their part, considering Ustumah City's connection with writing. I just think that's pretty cool."

Ashley forced a smile and nodded, "Of course. That is super cool, babe. I would have never noticed that, you're such a little writer." She walked up to Ethan and kissed him on the cheek.

Once again, Ethan fought his internal battle, She doesn't find you interesting. Nothing you say interests her.

No, she's just not a writer like me. She doesn't find these kinds of things as exciting as me, but at least she thinks it's interesting that I do, Ethan told himself.

"Ethan, buddy, I gotta tell you. You are my best friend for an uncountable number of reasons, but 'nerdy writing stuff' like that is just not one of them. Sorry man," Marcus said smirking.

Ashley hid a grin on her way back to the bedroom.

Ethan's skeptical side cringed, these interests define who you are. Your best friend doesn't appreciate them and neither does she. You're going to lose them both just for being yourself. Ethan did his best to shake the doubt.

Ethan faked a playful grin, "Don't forget, my nerdy writing stuff is why you're on this free vacation in the first place."

Marcus caught on and laughed, "Since when is being dragged out to Nothing Happens, USA, and being shoved into a cabin two sizes too small, a vacation?"

"Hey, you can leave whenever you want. I can call you a cab right now," Ethan joked.

"Yeah, if the driver can ever find their way out here, sure thing," Marcus said as he walked back into his room.

A while later, Ethan and Ashley finished unpacking their things and Ashley looked at the clock. "It's almost one o'clock. Sarah said we had to meet her in town for the Meet the Writers event around four. We should leave soon. Give ourselves some time to check out the town before the event," Ashley said.

"You're right," Ethan agreed, "I did want to check things out, and get a little lay of the land before diving into the festival events." Ethan called into Marcus' room, "You ready yet?"

Marcus dumped one of his bags out onto his bed. "Not really, but I am so ready to get out of here. It feels like the walls are closing in around me," he replied.

Ethan grabbed his favorite blazer, favorite button-up, and a pair of jeans. "I'm gonna get changed real quick, then we can go."

Ashley walked up to him and mussed his hair and the two shared a quick moment. She kissed him and said, "I'll meet you in the car." Winking at him as she left the room.

Marcus called in as Ethan was shutting the door, "Let me guess, business casual? Same thing you were just wearing but different articles of clothing? Oh, and don't forget to muss your hair like you always do."

Ethan called back as he closed the door shut. "Hey, there's nothing wrong with business casual. I'm about to meet my only fans, I should look my best right? Besides, at least I don't wear my shirts two sizes too small," he laughed.

"How else can I show off these guns?" Marcus yelled out a little too seriously.

A few minutes later they were all back in the car, headed back into Ustumah City. "How about a little local radio?" Ashley suggested as they pulled out onto the dirt path.

CHAPTER 3

Back in town, the chaos of the festival had picked up. There were now at least twice as many tourists wandering the streets. In contrast with the quiet retreat of the Chekhov Cabin, the disarray was even more noticeable for Ethan, Ashley, and Marcus. Ashley navigated the car through the flood of people to the first open parking spot she could find.

"I had no idea it got this crazy at the 'Kay Poff,'" Ethan commented as the car came to a stop.

Marcus grabbed Ethan's seat pulling himself forward, leaning between Ashley and Ethan. "The hell is 'Kay Poff,'" he asked. Ashley shook her head, just as confused.

"Y'know, 'Kay Poff.' K. P. A. W. F," Ethan said looking at the others expectantly. He got nothing but blank stares in return. "Known Poets and Authors Writing Festival," Ethan clarified with a sigh.

Ashley and Marcus looked at each other and smiled, letting out a shared, "Ooooohhh, yeah." Ashley opened her door and slapped Ethan playfully on the leg as she got out, "C'mon Kay Poff, let's have a look around."

Ethan watched her for a moment as she smiled at him and stepped out of the car. Her genuine smiles had a way of doing that to him. He'd sit there admiring her beauty and her grace. Even the way she gracefully exited the car made him feel like the luckiest guy on earth. Sometimes he wondered how he had gotten so lucky. A guy like him rarely ended up with a girl like her.

Ashley led the way through town, confidently stepping around the large groups of tourists swarming the ragtag of booths set up along the small-town streets. Marcus and Ethan followed along like lost puppies. At one point Ethan spotted a booth that hadn't been set up earlier. It was run by Cardinal House Publishing, and they were selling copies of '*In Despair.*'

How interesting, Ethan thought, his book was being bought and sold just a few feet away and he had had no idea. Eventually, the three emerged from the thick crowd of people onto Ustumah City's Main Street, which had remained open and free of people to prevent traffic issues. There were still plenty of tourists wandering around on the main street, but it was minuscule compared to the crowd that filled the other streets.

Ashley turned to the two men and pointed down the street. "I figured we could check out some local places here. Probably give us a better feel for the town than the feeding frenzy going on back there," Ashley said, pointing back toward the crowd.

Ethan took a moment to look down Main Street. The view was really something when you stopped to appreciate it. The three of them were at the top end of the street, which sloped down until it eventually turned into a lonely road that disappeared into the thick forest that stretched on far beyond Ustumah City. It was lined with buildings that looked like they were straight out of an old western movie. Ethan was sure that most, if not all, of the building were originals that had been there since the founding of Ustumah City. Though clearly refurbished, they still had a certain charm to them. Each building was a different shade of blue, white, or brown, and together they created an almost patchwork-like look to the town. One building in particular stood out to Ethan as he contemplated the history of Ustumah. It was smaller, with plaques and pictures out front. A hanging sign read 'Ustumah City Museum.'

"How about we go take a look at the museum?" Ethan asked.

"Of course you'd pick a museum," Marcus complained.

Ashley put a gentle hand on Marcus' shoulder and looked to Ethan, "As far as I'm concerned this is your trip babe. We'll do whatever you want."

Marcus visibly relaxed as Ashley's hand touched him, "Yeah, of course. You know I'm just messing with you man. Museums aren't my thing, but I'm all about it if you are."

Ethan knew Marcus meant what he said. They'd been friends forever, and while Marcus has always enjoyed more physical activities like sports, Ethan had always been into more nerdy things like chess or museums. The reason they were such great friends is that they pushed each other to try different things, and were both better for it. Ethan knew he wouldn't be anywhere near as in shape as he was if it weren't for Marcus.

"Learning a little something won't hurt you," Ethan joked, "I know you've got plenty of room up there." Marcus rolled his eyes but grinned at Ethan as he and Ashley followed him toward the museum.

Out front of the museum, a large picture hung on the wall depicting Main Street back in the early days. There were a fraction of the buildings that currently lined the street and they all looked much more fragile in the picture than their present-day counterparts. Nothing but a dirt road sat between them as the redwoods rose up in the background. The plaque below the picture read, 'Doe Creek (now Ustumah City), March 3rd, 1851. One week after the discovery of one of the largest gold deposits in Northern California was found only a few miles away. Only a few short months from the time this picture was taken, Doe Creek would be transformed forever from a quiet lumber town to a booming gold town.' Ethan waved Ashley and Marcus over.

"Check this out. I knew Ustumah had its roots as an early western settlement, but I didn't know anything about this huge gold deposit being discovered here," Ethan explained.

Marcus feigned interest, but Ashley played along. "Says it was originally named Doe Creek. Wonder what that's all about," Ashley asked.

Ethan hurried over to another picture hanging on the opposite side of the Museum entrance, motioning for his companions to follow. The picture depicted a group of solemn-faced Native Americans standing amongst a collection of weathered huts.

Ethan read the description on the plaque beneath aloud, "Pictured above is the Ustumah tribe, a Native American people that inhabited the local area for many years before Doe Creek (now Ustumah City) was settled. This picture depicts the Ustumah tribe after they were peacefully relocated by early settlers who then founded Doe Creek." Ethan continued reading an even larger plaque that rested below, "Conflict between the Ustumah people and the Doe Creek settlers started not long after, when the settlers went back on their promise not to cut down the nearby redwoods. The Ustumah regarded the forest itself as a magical deity with the power to turn stories and legend into reality. In fear of upsetting this great power, the Ustumah started violent attacks on Doe Creek settlers. The conflicts ended when the United States Army intervened, massacring the entire Ustumah tribe. To this day no full-blooded Ustumah have been located, and only distant relatives remain. In an attempt to make up for this tragedy, Doe Creek was later renamed to Ustumah City, all logging was halted, and a grant was set up to financially support any living descendant with even the smallest fraction of Ustumah blood." Ethan stepped back and there was a moment of silence.

Marcus was the first to break the silence, "I had no idea this place had such a crazy history."

Ethan nodded, "Yeah, I bet there's even more interesting stuff inside." Ethan moved to enter the museum, but Ashley stopped him, pointing to a small, framed piece of paper hanging just to the side of the Ustumah tribe picture.

"What's that?" Ashley asked.

Ethan walked over to see. It was a small piece of paper the size of a note card. On it was a small poem.

> *"All fear the lover,*
> *Most dangerous beast of all.*
> *Its greed knows no end."*
> *-Unknown Poet*

The three companions contemplated the poem in silence. After a moment Ashley read the plaque below aloud, "Little is known about The Unknown Poet other than that they lived in Ustumah City, and their work is highly regarded. They have written many poems, usually haiku, and many short stories that are still studied today. Every November, Ustumah City holds its world-renowned Known Poets and Authors Writing Festival, to put a face to the most talented writers of the year. The hope behind the festival is that never again will such a great artist remain anonymous and unremembered." Ashley looked at Ethan. "So that's why they call it the 'Known' Poets and Authors Writing Festival," she said with a hint of excitement.

Ethan nodded, happy to see his girlfriend excited about such a thing and wishing he had shared it with her himself earlier. He was about to respond when a woman's voice broke in from behind the group.

"Yup, makes sense when you hear the story behind it. But otherwise, it is a terrible name for a festival if you ask me. Doesn't exactly roll off the tongue," the woman chimed. "Ironic for a celebration based around words."

The others turned around to face her. She was a slender blonde with glasses, wearing a blazer over her top, with jeans and boots.

Business Casual, Ethan thought, feeling more confident in his choice of attire, especially considering the way this woman pulled it off. She stood confidently, and she was the only woman Ethan had seen all day that could rival Ashley's beauty.

"Sorry to just butt in like that, but I was just passing by, and your excitement drew me in," the mystery girl explained nodding at Ashley. "I felt the same way when I first found out why they named it the 'Known' festival. Y'know, a little relieved there was a reason behind the terrible name. By the way, I'm Claire," the woman finished, holding a hand out to Ashley.

Ashley took her hand and shook it, "Ashley, nice to meet you. And yeah, that's pretty spot on. Pretty much exactly my reaction just now."

Marcus eagerly took a step forward and introduced himself. "Marcus, nice to meet you," Marcus said, hand outstretched.

Claire turned from Ashley and accepted Marcus' hand, "A pleasure Marcus."

Feeling impolite Ethan moved forward to introduce himself as well, "Hi Claire, I'm-"

Claire's eyes went wide for a moment, and before Ethan could finish she interrupted, "Ethan Garland, right? Author of '*In Despair*.'"

Taken aback, Ethan nodded. "Yeah, that's me. How did you-"

Again, Claire interrupted, "I recognized you from your picture on the cover. I'm actually a pretty big fan, *In Despair* was a welcomed addition to the mystery genre. Modern mysteries are chock full of plot twists, but it's hard to find one with such emotion."

Ethan tensed up awkwardly. He was not used to receiving such praise and wasn't sure how to react. "Th-thank you," he stuttered.

Noticing his reaction Claire raised her hands apologetically, "Oh, I'm so sorry. Here you are trying to enjoy the museum and I'm probably the twentieth person to bother you like this." Claire put her hand on her chest, "I really am sorry, it's probably bad enough to be bothered by your fans here at the festival, but to get it from another contestant… That's probably worse."

Another contestant, Ethan thought for a moment. Then he realized what she meant. She was another nominated writer attending the festival. He felt terrible for not knowing who she was.

"No need to apologize, I'm just not used to the praise to be honest. I should be the one that's sorry. You have me at a disadvantage. I hate to admit my ignorance, but I don't recognize you," Ethan explained.

At that Claire relaxed. "Oh, oh good. I thought you were annoyed. And don't worry, I only recognized you because I happened to read your book. I guess I shouldn't have expected you to recognize me," Claire elaborated. "We are both the new kids on the block."

Understanding her meaning, Ethan replied, "Nice to hear I'm not the only one. It's a little intimidating coming to compete against all these famous authors when this is the first thing I've written that anyone's even recognized. What did you write?"

"Just a little poem," Claire answered, "It's a sonnet I wrote when I was coming out of a tough time. It's called 'The Human Journey.'"

Realizing she was a poet and not competition, Ethan relaxed a little. "Well, I'll have to read it soon," Ethan said smiling.

Claire moved to say something else, but she was interrupted by Ashley who suddenly threw herself around Ethan with a side hug. "You two are adorable, I'm so proud of my cute writer," Ashley said squeezing Ethan. "We'll have to read her poem together in bed tonight, babe."

A disappointed look flashed on Claire's face for the briefest moment. "Well, for now, I should let you guys enjoy the museum. I'm sure we'll be seeing each other around anyways. It was really nice to meet you guys though," Claire said with a polite wave.

"So nice to meet you too. Good luck in the contest," Ashley said waving. Ethan and Marcus both said their goodbyes as Claire began to walk away.

Ashley looked up at Ethan. "Let's look for something to eat, we can always check out the inside of the museum later. I'm starving," she said. Ashley hurried off down the street.

Ethan and Marcus followed, and when Ashley was a bit out of earshot, Ethan turned to his friend. "What was that all about?" Ethan said nodding to Ashley. "She never acts like that in front of people. Honestly, she's never that possessive."

Marcus just shrugged, "She's your girlfriend. Don't look at me. Definitely weird though."

CHAPTER 4

At lunch, Ethan had to bite his tongue to refrain from mentioning the incident with Claire. He didn't want to risk pissing Ashley off. There were enough underlying issues as it was. But that didn't stop the thought of it from running around in Ethan's head. Part of him was proud to know Ashley could get so jealous. It temporarily muzzled the part of his mind that wanted to constantly remind him that she didn't love him anymore. On the other hand, it was driving him crazy to think that she could have thought that he had been flirting with Claire. She was attractive, yes, and a fellow writer at that. But Ashley had nothing to worry about, Ethan had never fallen for a girl as hard as he'd fallen for Ashley, and he wasn't about to start with a wandering eye just because of one bad year. He just hoped she knew that. After all, he had only been trying to be friendly to Claire. Especially after her kind words about his book.

After lunch, Ethan had little time to worry anyways. Sarah had called and demanded they meet her across town before the Meet the Writers event began so that she could prepare Ethan for what was about to happen. They hurried through the crowded streets to the other side of town. Sarah then ushered them into a building that was currently off-limits to the public.

Once inside Ethan realized they were in the Ustumah City bookstore. It was an incredibly large bookstore considering the small size of the city, but it made sense, all things considered.

Sixteen custom booths had been set up throughout. One for each contestant and their poem or novel. All of the booths varied in their impressiveness. Some drew you in with powerful imagery, like the booth for the poem, *No Escape,* by Trent Richards, which depicted a man in agony as a swirl of toxic-looking vapors swirled around his head. Some were grand in scale like the booth for David Kowalski's novel, *Temptation Ablaze*, the third installment in the *Temptation's Spark* series. Others were both grand in scale and featured eye-catching images, like Robert Mitchelson's, *The Pack,* which featured a large display of yellow wolf's eyes staring out at the store, as well as multiple cardboard cutouts of large wolves surrounding the booth.

Then there was Ethan's booth. Smallest in the store, displaying the title *In Despair*, and featuring a picture of the hardcover of his novel, his profile picture from the cover, and the Cardinal's Nest Publishing logo.

"What gives Sarah? You guys couldn't get me an awesome booth like all the others?" Ethan said, turning to Sarah.

Sarah waved a dismissive hand in front of her face. "I'm not in charge of those kinds of decisions. My job is only to act as a liaison of sorts for you here at the festival. Probably just the higher-ups being stingy. You know how it is," she explained.

Not buying it, Ethan pointed to David Kowalski's huge display, plastered with multiple Cardinal's Nest Publishing logos. "They had no problem splurging on *Temptation's Ablaze*," Ethan asserted.

Sarah hesitated for a moment and then looked at Ethan sternly. "Listen, you're a big boy. I'll tell you the truth. The company has a set amount of funding they put aside each year to support the authors that are nominated for the festival. This year it was both you and David. *In Despair* is a wild card and they're not sure what to expect, but I think we all know that *Temptation's Ablaze* has a good chance of winning this thing," Sarah paused, letting it sink in. "Winning here at the festival will increase sales tremendously. It's a risk vs reward scenario and you got the short stick. Sorry Ethan, but you shouldn't take it personally," she finished.

"Well, you know what Sarah, I kind of do take it personally," Ethan said walking toward his booth ahead of everyone else.

Ashley hurried to catch up to him. "Ethan, it's a huge honor to even be at this festival. Don't let something dumb like this ruin your mood," Ashley suggested.

Ethan stopped to turn to her, "Oh yeah, I shouldn't get upset about something dumb like this. Instead, I'll just be passive-aggressive to the next friendly stranger that tries to talk to us." He regretted the words as soon as they left his mouth. Ashley was right that the display was a dumb thing to be upset about, and it wasn't the right time to bring up the situation with Claire. But he'd been so stressed lately, and he'd let his temper get the best of him.

Ashley didn't need a moment to realize what Ethan was talking about. She felt her frustration boiling up and she knew she was about to say something she would really regret. "You know what, enjoy your fucking event. I'll meet up with you afterward," she said, quickly turning around and heading toward the entrance.

Ethan was about to call out to her but thought it may be better to give her some space for now. He'd wanted her at his side when he was meeting any potential fans that might wander over to his booth, but he realized he'd screwed that up. Marcus tried to say something to Ashley, but she blew past him, and he just gave Ethan those "well, you fucked up" eyes that he would do in these types of situations. When Ashley had passed, Sarah and Marcus caught up to Ethan.

"Can we handle this like professionals now?" Sarah asked bluntly.

Watching Ashley leave through the bookstore entrance, Ethan nodded at Sarah, and the three of them continued to Ethan's booth. As they arrived Ethan noticed Claire across the way under her own booth, which depicted a person with a walking stick climbing a mountain, which slowly blended into a forest, then a city skyline, and finally space. The words, *The Human Journey, a poem by Claire Donaghue,* were displayed prominently.

Claire noticed him looking and waved with a smile. He waved back, glad she seemed unnerved by the encounter with Ashley earlier. Claire pointed at his booth and gave him a thumbs-up, mouthing the words "good luck."

Ethan returned the gesture and mouthed, "you too."

Sarah's voice cut in from behind him, "Alright, starting in twenty minutes you're going to be doing nothing but sitting in this booth for the next four hours, so be ready for that." Ethan gave her a look which she ignored and continued, "Some of the people that approach you might be some of your biggest fans, some might just be people curious about your book or as I like to call them, prospective buyers. Others will just be looking to take a picture or get you to sign something. Some of these people do it with all the writers. That way whoever wins, they can say they met them, and have proof. This festival is a real circus."

Marcus pulled up a folding chair near Ethan's booth and sat down. He looked down at his watch, and then back at Ethan, giving him a thumbs up.

Ethan smirked at him and turned back to Sarah. "Alright, well I'm not used to getting any attention for my book, so this might be a welcome change," Ethan said, trying to be positive.

Sarah huffed. It was the closest thing to a laugh he had ever seen from her. "Tell me that in four hours," she said plainly. "Listen, just be on your best behavior and try to sell the book. Building hype at this festival can be a big deal if you want to win. But most importantly, kiss the asses of the Ustumah City Book Club. They're the ones that are going to be deciding your fate. At least a few should stop by, maybe even before they open the doors to the public," Sarah explained.

Ethan nodded. "Do I have time to step away for a second before then?" Ethan asked, looking over at Claire. He'd promised to read her poem, and he wouldn't get a better chance than while Ashley was gone.

"Sure," Sarah said, "but try and hurry. You're going to want to be here if one of the Book Club members stops by."

Marcus chimed in, "If they come by, I'll stall 'em and shoot you a text."

"Perfect," Ethan said looking at Sarah expectantly.

"Yeah, go, hurry," Sarah urged impatiently.

Ethan moved to leave, but just as he was about to, he was approached by a gray-haired man with a thinly trimmed beard. He was completely casual, wearing an off-brand sweatshirt and cargo pants. Ethan recognized him immediately as David Kowalski, the famous writer Ethan's publishing company favored.

"Hello Mr. Garland. I wanted to take a moment to introduce myself before the chaos begins. I'm David," he said, stretching out his hand.

Surprised, Ethan stuttered a bit. "N-no introduction necessary Mr. Kowalski. You're a legend. I can only hope my work is as good as yours someday," Ethan said eagerly.

"Nonsense," David insisted, "your work is already up to par. I've read *In Despair,* and its no mistake that you are here competing against me at this year's writing festival."

Ethan was taken aback. He had expected a famous author like David to look down at newer authors like himself, who only had one successful novel to date. "It's an honor to hear you say that sir."

David laughed. "Oh please, don't call me sir. It makes me feel old," David said, pointing to his gray hair. He winked and continued, "but really, I just want you to know that I find it very inspiring to see young authors like you make it to a prestigious event like this. I hope you will not let this be the pinnacle of your career. Instead, look at it as a beginning."

Ethan's heart fluttered. He couldn't believe it. "Th-thank you sir. I mean, thank you David," Ethan managed.

David nodded politely, "I'm sure you'll understand, but I must get back to my booth before things get underway. I just wanted to take a moment to wish you well in the coming days."

Ethan nodded, "You too. I hope we both make it far."

At that, David nodded again and turned back toward his booth.

As he walked away, Sarah called out to him. "Much appreciated David. Kind words," she said flatly but sincerely.

Without turning back David called back to Ethan, "watch out for that one Mr. Garland. I think she may be a vampire or an advanced artificial intelligence."

Marcus laughed, and Sarah set a glare on him. Then she looked back to Ethan. "Hurry and do whatever it was you were about to do," Sarah reminded him.

Ethan hurried off toward Claire's booth, passing by a few people he was pretty sure were Ustumah City Book Club members. They didn't even notice him as they moved toward David's booth.

When he arrived at Claire's booth, she greeted him warmly.

"Came all the way over here just to say hi?" she asked.

"That, and I figured I'd take a moment to read your poem. It's the least I can do after your kind words about my book," Ethan explained.

Claire smiled and pulled a beautiful piece of parchment paper from a large stack sitting next to her. "That's good of you, but you could have done this at any time," she said, handing him the parchment.

"Nope. I'm not sure I could bear another moment knowing you'd read my work and silently judged it, and I haven't read yours," Ethan joked.

Claire gave a quick laugh and pointed to the parchment, "Well, now you can silently judge my work and we'll be even at last."

Ethan looked down at the parchment paper in his hand. It was decorated with the same mural-like picture of the person hiking featured on Claire's booth. Ethan began to read.

The Human Journey

Nothing so familiar as the concepts of ourselves.
No mystery greater than that of me.
A threat if left unchecked, overwhelms.
The path to the solution, now plain to see.
To begin to understand we look to our past.
From there we face demons with those we call friend. Perhaps our
answers line in a place where things were stashed.
Yet, there will always be others who cannot comprehend.
When the winds of change come, we must be ready.
Next, we stumble upon the crimson beast we know not about.
Now finally we realize we've had the answers already.
The next place we go will fill us with doubt.
Seeking help from another we pay visit to a death approved.
Finally, we venture to a place, expectation removed.

Written by Claire Donaghue

Ethan looked up at Claire who seemed to be eagerly awaiting his response. Ethan wasn't sure what he had expected, but he was very impressed. "To be honest, I don't read much poetry. Usually, because I just don't get it. I'd rather read a good story," Ethan admitted.

Claire frowned a bit, but Ethan continued, "But this is really damn good Claire. I'd probably read more poetry if you wrote all of it. There's obviously a reason you're here."

Claire's frown evaporated. "Thanks, it means a lot to get a compliment from someone whose writing you respect."

"I'll have to keep reading it so I can try and find something to silently judge. We're still not even," Ethan joked again. Inside his pocket, he felt his phone vibrate.

Pointing to the parchment in Ethan's hand, Claire said, "Go ahead and hang onto that. I'm sure you'll find plenty to judge."

Ethan pulled his phone out of his pocket, switched on the screen, and saw a text from Marcus. The text read, 'CODE RED, report IMMEDIATELY!!!!!!!!!' with a bunch of siren emojis. Ethan turned back to his booth where a man and woman were standing talking to Marcus who made desperate eye contact.

"Really though Claire, great poem. Sorry to cut this short, but I gotta get back over there," Ethan said, already moving away.

"Totally understand," Claire said, shooing him away.

Back at his booth, Ethan interjected into Marcus' conversation.

"Speak of the devil and he shall come," Marcus said gesturing toward Ethan with an awkward laugh.

The woman looked to Ethan with a warm smile. "Ah there you are Mr. Garland. I feared we would miss you before the public swarms the place," she said politely, "My name is Pamela Hurshman. I'm a member of the Ustumah City Council, but more relevant, I'm a member of the Ustumah City Book Club." Before Ethan could respond she gestured to the man standing with her and continued, "This is my fellow book club member, as well as the owner of this wonderful store, Keith Sanders."

Keith nodded at Ethan. "It is good to meet you Mr. Garland," Keith said.

Ethan nodded nervously at both of them. "It's a pleasure to meet you both. I'm honored to even be here in Ustumah and to be part of such a renowned event," Ethan declared.

"Oh no need to be modest," Keith said, holding up a hand, *In Despair* sets a new bar for the mystery genre. You deserve to be here as much as anyone else."

Pamela interjected, "I couldn't agree more. In fact, I was the one who initially nominated you. No one else in the club had heard of your book, but once they read it we were all in agreement to bring you here."

Ethan smiled sincerely. "That is high praise. You have no idea how nice it is to hear that." He finally let himself relax a bit. As he did, the doors to the bookstore opened and a flood of people began to enter and wander toward the booths eagerly.

"Well, that's our cue to escape," Keith joked, "Until next time Mr. Garland."

Pamela waved a quick goodbye following behind Keith, "Good luck, I hope we will get a chance to talk more later," she said.

"Of course, me too. Pleasure meeting you." Ethan replied as she walked away.

Moments later a larger group than Ethan had expected formed a line at his booth. Ethan took a seat and shot a surprised look at Marcus who responded with an impressed nod of his own. One by one people came up to Ethan asking for photos, signatures in their copies of '*In Despair*,' and asking questions about the story or characters. Some of the questions Ethan had never even thought of an answer for, and he found it slightly entertaining.

A couple hours passed, and there was no sign of the crowd letting up. At one point Marcus approached Ethan after waiting patiently through all of it.

"Gonna be honest with you bro, I'm glad you're getting all this attention, but I'm gonna go crazy if I have to sit quietly in that chair for another two hours," Marcus explained. "Mind if I go get some air? Maybe check on Ashley?" he suggested.

Mid signature, Ethan looked up at Marcus. "Of course man, cool of you to even sit through the first two hours. Good idea with Ashley. Cool her down for me, eh?" he said.

Marcus patted Ethan on the back. "I'll do my best Romeo."

Outside the bookstore Ashley pulled out a cigarette from the stash she hid in her make-up kit. Desperately she fumbled around in her purse looking for a lighter. Every second she spent searching flared her temper more and more until she threw her purse to the ground.

"Fuck, fuck, fuck," Ashley cursed as a few tourists looked on as they passed by. "Fuck off," she mumbled under her breath.

Just then, from her side a lighter flicked on in someone's outstretched hand. Ashley turned to see Marcus with worried eyes but a welcoming grin. "How did you know?" Ashley asked as she put the cigarette in her mouth and leaned forward.

Marcus held the flame up, and the cigarette ignited as Ashley inhaled. "C'mon Ash, you think I don't know you well enough by now?" Marcus replied.

Ashley felt her entire body relax as she took her first drag. She let out a long sigh, as if to push all of her stress out. "I guess so. I didn't realize I was that obvious," she admitted.

Marcus flashed his perfect white teeth. "Maybe not to Ethan, but I pay a little more attention. Sometimes I think he only sees what he wants to see when it comes to you. He doesn't see you for who you really are. That might be part of the problem," Marcus explained.

Ashley frowned at the thought and took another drag. "So, who am I really?" she asked.

Thrown off by the question, Marcus hesitated a moment. "Honestly, that's a deep fucking question Ash. I can't answer that yet," he paused, "But I can tell you that I'm impressed with the results of my investigation so far." Marcus grinned with confidence, clearly proud of his answer.

Ashley took a step toward her friend and placed a hand on his chest. "You're cheesy. But you're a good friend," she said as she met his eyes.

There was a moment of silence and Marcus sighed, taking the smallest step backward and Ashley removed her hand. "Listen, Ethan is like a brother to me, and you're one of the most amazing people I've ever met. I really want it to work out with you guys, but he needs to stop romanticizing you like you're some character in a story. And you need to stop trying to fill that role."

Ashley took a long drag of her cigarette and looked down at her feet. She looked back up and met Marcus' eyes again. "Is that what we're going to blame it on now?" she asked defiantly.

Not knowing how to respond, Marcus said the only thing he could think of, "Can I bum one of those cigarettes?"

CHAPTER 5

As the Meet the Writers event came to a close, Ethan watched as the other writers packed up their things and left. Meanwhile, he was stuck in a conversation that he would do anything to be out of. Much to Ethan's misfortune, the last person in line to meet with him had been a slightly older woman who seemed like she hadn't slept in weeks. At first, she seemed nice enough, complimenting his skill as a writer multiple times. However, eventually, she began rattling on about how similar some of the characters in his book were to people she knew in real life. She even went so far as to begin telling stories about the people she was referring to. Ethan didn't see how these people were in any way similar to any of his characters, but he politely nodded all the same. Ethan kept expecting the woman to stop, but she continued on and on.

Not wanting to be rude to a fan, Ethan endured.

Finally, Sarah walked up. "Excuse me ma'am, but I'm afraid the event has been over for twenty minutes. Mr. Garland has a busy schedule this week and really needs to be heading off."

"Oh, of course, such a fine Author is a busy man, I'm sure," the woman chimed happily. "It was so nice to meet you, I can't wait for your next book Mr. Garland," she finished.

Relieved Ethan stood up from the chair he'd been sitting in for hours. "No, thank you. Always nice to hear from a fan," Ethan said.

At that, the woman smiled, turned, and left. Just like that, the nightmare was over. Ethan turned to Sarah. "Thanks for that, I owe you one," he said.

"Actually, I'm not technically supposed to leave until you do. I was just tired of waiting, otherwise, she could've talked your ear off all night for all I care," Sarah said plainly.

"Man, you really are a robot or a vampire," Ethan mumbled.

Sarah ignored him and walked away without even a goodbye. Ethan followed her out and left the bookstore. Outside it was drastically different than when they had entered. A surprisingly chilled breeze sent a shiver through Ethan. The sun was nowhere to be seen and the night sky was blanketing the small town in darkness. A few lone streetlamps lightly illuminated the streets.

Realizing that Ashley and Marcus were nowhere to be seen, he reached into his pocket for his phone. He had a text from Ashley a little over two hours ago. "Me and Marcus are going back to the cabin to escape the frenzy, call me when you need a ride." Followed by a heart emoji.

"Dammit," Ethan said aloud, catching Sarah's attention. "Is there a problem," Sarah asked.

"Marcus and Ashley took the car back to the cabin. They expect me to wait for them to come pick me up, but it's like a forty-five-minute drive into town from the cabin," Ethan explained.

Sarah's face showed no change in emotion. "Oh, I see. Do you need a ride from someone else, or are you going to wait for them?" Sarah asked.

Ecstatic that he wouldn't have to wait in the cold dark for an hour, Ethan jumped at the offer, "Yeah if it's not too much trouble I'd love a ride."

Sarah's eyes widened. "No, no. I wasn't offering you a ride. That's much too far out of my way. I was just curious how you were going to get home. It's my job to keep track of you. At least until the week is over," Sarah corrected.

Ethan laughed. "I've never heard you make a joke. Maybe you're human after all," Ethan quipped.

Sarah stared at Ethan, a bewildered look on her face. There was a long silence as they waited for each other to say something.

Realizing she had been serious, Ethan broke the silence. "Oh. Okay. Um, yeah. I'll just wait for them here then," he said awkwardly.

"Ok, good to know. I'll see you here in town bright and early tomorrow. The Book Club announces which contestants will be paired up for the first round of voting first thing in the morning," Sarah declared as she turned to walk toward her car.

"Bright and early," Ethan confirmed, "Good night, Sarah." He watched as she kept walking, half expecting her to turn around and laugh at him for believing she would leave him there. He kept waiting for it, but she got into her car, turned it on, and drove off.

Finally, Ethan called Ashley. She didn't pick up which drove a spike into his nerves. He left her a voicemail asking for a ride. He tried not to seem upset, because he knew she was probably still mad at him for earlier. But she had a way of seeing right through him, and he knew as soon as she heard the voice mail she'd know. All he could do was hope it didn't turn into another fight.

Ethan reflected on his relationship. He cared about Ashley so much, but simply caring about her was not enough. Their relationship was crumbling, and it had everything to do with him.

He'd always felt that he was unworthy of a girl like her, but in the beginning at least, he hadn't let it interfere with enjoying every second they spent together. However, as time went on, a nagging feeling began to creep up more and more—he had started to feel like he didn't deserve Ashley. It was a strange, guilty feeling that he never expected. Like he had cheated fate and was living life in fear of discovery.

Because of that nagging feeling Ethan slowly became distant, though he hadn't meant to. At first, Ashley hadn't noticed. After a while though, Ethan noticed a change in her. She was still the same, but different in some way that he couldn't identify. Ever since he'd noticed that change, everything became worse. He couldn't help but feel like Ashley secretly wanted out of their relationship. Eventually, he began to feel the same way about Marcus. That caused a rift between them for the first time in their lifelong friendship. Rather than realize that this was all being caused by his own lack of confidence, Ethan distanced himself even more from the two of them. The two people that meant most to him. He retreated into his writing, which ironically caused him to write the only novel he'd ever had published. Not only that, but a novel that was somehow so good it was nominated as one of the eight works of fiction for the Known Poets and Authors Writing Festival. Still, Ethan would have given up all the success to have things with Ashley and Marcus back to the way they used to be. He'd hoped this trip would be a chance to make things right, but his emotions still seemed to betray him at every turn. There were still six days remaining in the festival. Plenty of time to make things right.

After only a few minutes of waiting outside the bookstore, Ashley sent Ethan a text letting him know she was on her way. He looked around and noticed that the streets were completely empty. It was a strange sight to see the town so empty, in contrast to the chaotic swarm of people that filled it during the day. A calming wave passed over Ethan as he took in the silence of the night. He hadn't realized how much the constant noise and movement of the festival had been adding to his stress until just then. He looked off into the forest beyond and listened to the breeze pass through Ustumah City.

After some time waiting, Ethan noticed a noise in the distance. A woman was sobbing quietly somewhere down the street. At first, Ethan ignored it. As the sobbing continued, Ethan could hear the pain in her voice. He grew concerned and started toward the sound.

He reached the end of the street and looked down a road to the left. He noticed a woman standing underneath one of the street-lights, holding a stack of papers in one hand and taping a flier to the lamppost with the other. Ethan noticed that the same flier had been posted multiple times on every building on the street, as well as the telephone poled and other streetlamps. In fact, a flier flapped quietly in the breeze, on the stop sign right next to him.

He lightly grabbed it in both hands and looked it over. The words 'MISSING GIRL' were displayed prominently at the top of the flier. A picture of a young girl happily posing with a golden retriever dominated the center. Below the picture were three bullet-pointed sentences: 'Ella Schaeffer, missing since October 26th, was last seen playing at Tree-line Park. Any information, please contact Elisa or Hue Schaeffer, at 565-555-2468. Please bring our little girl back to us.'

The last line should have twisted at Ethan's heart, if not for the strange spark of intrigue. He looked up from the flier and at the sobbing woman. She was still underneath the streetlamp. Her cries had become even more desperate, and she was struggling to hold the stack of fliers as she taped one to the streetlamp. Ethan looked back to the flier, and then back to the woman again. The scene unfolding in front of him, he realized, was a complete reenactment of a scene from *In Despair*. Ethan had struggled with editing the scene and remembered it well. He could see the words in his head now.

There was not a soul to be seen as Martha moved through the dark streets. There was almost pure silence, but for a quiet breeze and Martha's pained cries. The desperate mother moved with all the purpose she had left in her, posting Margaret's face on every surface in town. At first, she'd tried to hide her cries, but every time she had to face Margaret's smiling face her heart ached and the cries escaped despite her best efforts. In the picture Martha had chosen for the posters, Margaret was holding Buddy. The family had just finished enjoying an amazing day at the park, and Margaret had practically begged to take the photo. It was such a happy memory, but in light of current events, it only made the pain that much worse to think of it.

Martha would have chosen a different picture, but she had wanted something that humanized her daughter. She hoped that whatever monster was holding Margaret would see the posters and think of her as a person, not some trophy like child abductors did. To that end, the posters were just like any missing person poster, but Martha had added one special ingredient. At the bottom of the poster, the last sentence read, 'Please bring our little girl back to us.'

If only the kidnapper would read that and return Margaret to her out of some sense of guilt. Just thinking about it was too much. Finally, as she attempted to tape a poster to a lone street lamp, her despair overtook her. She fell to her knees and wailed into the night. Tears and snot rolled down her face as she fought to regain some composure. Underneath the light of the streetlamp and surrounded by darkness, Martha looked like a theater actress giving the performance of a lifetime. Only there was no one to see it, and this wasn't some fiction. Her daughter was missing, and until Martha held her in her arms again, there would be a hole in her heart that would continue to eat away at the rest of her.

Ethan recollected the scene and felt an even deeper sorrow for the woman that stood in front of him. The sorrow quickly faded as his mind began to fill with questions. He kept telling himself that the strange similarities between the reality in front of him and the story he had written could not be a coincidence. The scene was not just as Ethan had imagined it in his head when he wrote it, but it fell into the structure of what he had written almost exactly. Clearly, someone was pulling some elaborate prank on him, and he was determined to find out.

Ethan began striding toward the woman with purpose, but as he did, she collapsed to the ground. A much louder cry than before belted through the silent street. Ethan stopped and regarded the woman for a moment. This has to be a prank. It's too spot on, Ethan thought to himself. He began moving toward the woman again. The closer he got, the more real her agony appeared. If it was a prank, it was a damn good one. Doubt started to set in as Ethan realized that this woman could very well be a real mother in real distress over a missing daughter.

"Excuse me, are you alright?" Ethan asked in a soft voice, not knowing what else to say.

The woman noticed Ethan and her cries stopped. "I-I-I'm so-I'm so sorry," she managed to say as she choked back tears.

Ethan could see thick tears still streaming down the woman's face. Nobody can fake it like that, Ethan thought, realizing that this was no prank. Rather, it was the most disturbing coincidence he had ever encountered.

"Don't apologize. No, I'm sorry for approaching you like this, but I just wanted to make sure you were alright," Ethan explained.

The woman stood up and brushed herself off haphazardly, beginning to regain some composure. "Th-thank you for your concern. I just couldn't take it anymore. I shouldn't have lost control like that... But I just couldn't take it," she mumbled.

Ethan was sympathetic towards the woman, but he also felt a sense of guilt for being responsible for her embarrassment. "You shouldn't worry about that," Ethan said, placing a hand on the woman's shoulder. He hadn't meant to invade her personal space when she was so vulnerable, but he had just done it out of instinct. He felt her relax a little as his hand touched her and he continued. "Anyone would be overwhelmed when their child is missing," Ethan said.

The woman suddenly gazed into Ethan's eyes with surprise. "You know about Ella? I didn't realize you were a local. I just assumed you were a tourist," the woman exclaimed.

Ethan took his hand off the woman's shoulder, "No, I'm not a local actually. I just saw your fliers."

The woman looked embarrassed again as she stared out at the street plastered with fliers corner to corner.

"Of course," she said, shaking her head, "I should have known. Still, thank you for checking on me."

Ethan suddenly felt a strange connection to the woman. She was so similar to the main protagonist of his novel that standing here talking to her felt like talking to a person of his own creation. It gave him a strangely paternal feeling.

"Would you like some help with your fliers?" Ethan asked.

The woman donned a smile for his sake, though her eyes still showed deep despair. "No, but thank you. This is something I need to do alone," she said.

Exactly what Martha would have said, Ethan thought to himself as he recalled his protagonist. The mother in his novel had felt such a loss of control as she hoped and waited for the police to find her daughter. Posting the posters around town had been her first step in regaining that sense of control. An endeavor, Ethan knew, that she sadly failed at in the end.

The thought made his heart ache for the woman in front of him.

"I understand. I hope they find your daughter," was all he could say.

Without saying a word, the woman handed him a flier, and turned to walk away as her sobs began again. Ethan frowned and even fought back tears of his own as he walked back toward the bookstore.

When Ethan returned to the bookstore, he saw Ashley waiting for him in the car. He walked to her and hopped into the passenger seat.

"Where have you been, I tried calling you like four times to let you know I was here?" Ashley asked with some concern in her voice. She had seen the morbid look on Ethan's face and was worried.

Ethan pulled out his phone and noticed the four missed calls for the first time.

"Sorry babe. I'll explain on the way home," Ethan said staring out the passenger window.

CHAPTER 6

Back at the cabin, Marcus was lying on his bed with a storm of thoughts raging in his head. The past year had been so much more complicated than any other time in his life. The dynamic between Ashley, Ethan, and him had become so strained that it was now the main stressor in his life. He thought about Ethan, the one true friend he had always known. Ethan was like a brother to him, but now he found himself wondering if it was even possible to fix things between the two of them. As he contemplated on it, he heard Ethan and Ashley burst through the front door. They were mid conversation, and Ethan seemed very enthusiastic about something.
Marcus leaped to his feet and walked out to greet them.

"I know, I know. I know it sounds like I'm reaching, but you had to be there," Ethan said to Ashley as Marcus appeared in the living room. Ethan and Ashley looked to him as he entered. Ethan had excitement burning in his eyes.

Ashley shook her head, "Marcus, help me out here."

"What's going on?" asked Marcus.

"Ethan thinks that a character from his novel escaped from the pages and into real life," Ashley explained with a sigh.

Ethan shook his head abruptly, "When you put it like that it sounds crazy, yeah. All I'm saying is that whatever the explanation is for what I just experienced, it isn't a coincidence."

"Okay back it up for me. What happened?" Marcus urged.

Ethan's eyes lit up as he told Marcus about the woman he had encountered in town. As he explained Ethan went to his room and returned with a copy of *"In Despair,"* turning to the scene where Martha breaks down as she places the posters.

"You see, it's an exact description," Ethan exclaimed.

Marcus couldn't deny that Ethan's encounter with the woman was a strangely accurate representation of the scene from his book. Down to some very specific details.

"Yeah, there are some crazy similarities, I'll give you that," Marcus admitted.

Ashley interjected, "Yeah, but what I'm saying is that I think Ethan is just very familiar with his own story, so when he saw a similar situation, he saw it through a lens that appeared similar to his own story. I mean, eyewitnesses are found unreliable all the time. Our minds can play tricks on us that are more powerful than what we've actually experienced.

"Aw come on Ash, I know what I saw," Ethan complained.

"She does have a point, Ethan. It is kind of crazy to imagine that the scene would play out so similarly. What Ashley is saying makes more sense," Marcus offered.

Ethan frowned and pulled the flier the woman had handed him out of his back pocket and unfolded it. "Given everything else I just said, how do you explain this?" Ethan asked. He pointed to the picture of the girl with the golden retriever, and then to the line in his novel referring to the picture of the missing girl with her dog Buddy.

Marcus nodded, but then asked, "Didn't you tell me Buddy was a German Shepherd, and that your inspiration for that whole thing was a picture your little cousin took with her German Shepherd?"

"Yes, I know everything that happened isn't an exact match with what I intended when I wrote the scene. But if you think about it, it is an exact representation of the words that are on the page," Ethan clarified. "Also, this is even more undeniable," Ethan said as he pointed to the last sentence of the flier. "'Please bring our little girl back to us,' on the flier," Ethan said reading from the flier and then switching to the open page of his novel, "and 'Please bring our little girl back to us,' here in the story."

Marcus scratched his head. "Okay, I'll admit that is super coincidental. But hear me out," Marcus started. Ethan folded his arms and waited for Marcus to finish. "When you wrote this story, you wanted it to feel real. You always told me that. The whole appeal of *In Despair* was supposed to be that it was a real take on these situations, and not some fluffed-up murder mystery. I'm sure you drew a lot of real-life inspiration when you were writing this. I know it would still be a crazy coincidence for you to run into a situation that was so similar, but if it was supposed to be real it isn't so crazy to think that an extremely similar situation would play out in real life," Marcus finished.

Ethan pondered it, and for a long moment, there was silence. "I guess that does make some sense, but I'm still having a hard time shaking this feeling that something else is going on," Ethan admitted.

Ashley walked up to Ethan, placed a hand on the side of his face, and kissed him on the cheek.

"What Marcus said makes a lot of sense, babe. I mean, what else would explain it. Either someone has put an insane amount of effort into messing with you, or some kind of magic power brought your story to life. I think we can all agree that either of those would be ridiculous. Don't stress yourself out over it, you've got enough to worry about with the festival," Ashley pointed out.

Ethan reflected, maybe he was just getting worked up over nothing. "You're right, I've got an early morning tomorrow too. I should get some sleep," Ethan conceded.

Marcus sighed, "What time do we have to get up?"

"Don't worry about it. I have to be in town to meet Sarah first thing in the morning to find out what Author I'm being paired with in the contest tomorrow. You two can sleep in, and I'll head back to the cabin after I find out," Ethan offered.

"You're a true friend," Marcus said with a chuckle.

With that, Ethan said his good night and went off to bed. However, he couldn't fall asleep. His mind was racing. When Ashley finally came to bed, she noticed him still awake.

"Get some sleep babe. You shouldn't be nervous about tomorrow. You wrote a great story, and you'll beat whoever they pair you with," Ashley said.

"Thanks, Ash, it's nice to hear you say that," Ethan replied. He didn't tell her that it wasn't tomorrow's contest that was keeping him up, and instead something she had said earlier. Some kind of magic power brought your story to life, Ethan thought to himself. An insane idea at first, but then he'd remembered their visit to the museum earlier in the day. The Ustumah regarded the forest itself as a magical deity with the power to turn stories and legend into reality, Ethan recalled the words from the plaque underneath the picture of the Ustumah tribe. He couldn't honestly entertain the idea that some magic power was at work there, but it was yet another strange coincidence for him to think about.

CHAPTER 7

So early in the morning, Ustumah City was much less crowded than it had been the day before. Still, there were plenty of people wandering the streets when Ethan arrived. Ethan found a parking spot out front of the bookstore, where Sarah had texted him to meet her earlier in the morning. A small crowd was gathered outside the bookstore around a roped-off area. There was a camera crew setting up, as well as multiple teams of photographers. Inside the area, Ethan noticed Pamela and Keith from the day before, along with fourteen other people that Ethan assumed were the other members of the Ustumah City Book Club. They were standing on a makeshift stage that had been set up in front of the bookstore. On one side of the stage, Ethan noticed Claire standing amongst a group of people Ethan surmised were the other poetry contestants as well as their publishers. On the other side of the stage, Ethan saw the other fiction authors along with their publishers. Sarah was waiting amongst them.

Sarah spotted Ethan and waved him over. As he arrived, she scolded him, "You're late, Ethan."

Ethan looked at his watch. "By like fifteen minutes. Sorry, but I thought you said you wanted me here thirty minutes before anything started, so I didn't think it would be a big deal," he apologized.

Sarah shook her head. "They don't announce for another fifteen so that's not the problem. But most of the other authors got here thirty minutes early," she said emphasizing the word early. "It's nice to show up to these things with some time to spare for buttering up the book club members. It is their votes that determine the fate of you and your novel after all," Sarah finished.

"I mean, shouldn't my writing speak to whether or not I deserve to win?" Ethan asked.

At that Sarah squinted and ran her hand through her hair. "For someone who wrote a book being praised as 'sophisticatedly authentic to the nuances of human nature' you are extremely naive," Sarah said pointedly.

Not sure what to say in response, or if he should even respond at all, Ethan held his tongue. "Listen, just wait here. When they announce you and your novel just make your way to the stage. Shake hands with your opponent, share a few words, pose for the cameras, all that good stuff. Whoever is announcing will thank you both and then you're all done. Easy. Got it?" Sarah instructed.

Ethan nodded, "Got it." He figured he'd keep it short with Sarah as her patience with him seemed to be wearing thin.

A few moments later Sarah looked at Ethan as if she were about to say something. Instead, she turned and walked away to blend in with the crowd. Then Ethan was left standing with the rest of the fiction authors. David came to stand next to him.

"I hope we don't get paired against each other today. I'd prefer to see the two of us in the finals," David commented.

Ethan smiled at him. He welcomed any positive interaction after having yet another awkward conversation with Sarah. "I hope so too. And thanks again for your kind words yesterday. They really meant a lot," said Ethan.

"Don't mention it," David said simply. A moment later he gave Ethan a pat on the back and gestured at the stage. Keith, the owner of the bookstore, walked up to a microphone that had been set up center stage.

"Greetings to both the residents of Ustumah City and our welcomed guests," he said gesturing to the crowd. "And greetings to all of you at home," he continued with a gesture to the camera. "My name is Keith Sanders. I am the owner of the Ustumah City Book Store right here behind us, but more importantly, I am proudly a long-time member of the Ustumah City Book Club. It is our honor to get together every year and pick out the eight best fiction writers and the eight best poets of the year. We then host them, and all of you, here in Ustumah City for the world-renowned Known Poets and Authors Writing Festival," Keith managed in one long breath.

Keith gave a short speech on the prestige of the festival, the skill of all sixteen writers invited to attend, and ended with a quick comment about how no matter who wins, they are all winners for making it this far. Ethan found it all to be a little cheesy, but also charming.

"It is my pleasure to announce this year's pairings for the first round of voting," Keith continued. "I'll start with the magnificent poets that we have here with us," he said gesturing toward the poet's stage side.

Systematically, Keith announced the pairing for the poets. The crowd cheered as each contestant was introduced. When Claire and her poem "The Human Journey" were announced, Ethan clapped loudly. She and David were the closest things to friends he had at the event, and it just felt right to show her some support. Ethan noticed then that none of the other authors had been applauding the other contestants, and when he clapped for Claire he heard one of the authors behind him scoff.

Finally, Keith moved on to introducing the fiction authors. Ethan was the third author he introduced. "This novel has shown us that the stories closest to true life experiences can be far more thrilling than those that try to trick us with over-the-top characters and plots. The first novel of our second pairing for the fiction category is '*In Despair*,' by Ethan Garland," Keith said cheerily.

Ethan made his way to the stage where he gave an unsure wave toward the crowd, shook Keith's hand, and then took his place waiting behind him. With the cameras on him, he felt his nerves wavering. He took a deep breath and tried to relax.

Keith continued. "The novel that will be taking on *In Despair* in the first round of voting is one that took many of us by surprise. It is an action-packed adventure that at times made you more fearful for the lives of the characters than the characters themselves. There are already plans to adapt it to the big screen… '*The Pack*,' by Robert Mitchelson," Keith announced.

Ethan's heart sank. Robert was a veteran author who rivaled Stephen King's success. He had a cinematic way of writing that made for thrilling reads, and almost every book he'd written had been adapted to film. Ethan was hit with a wave of doubt in his own abilities, realizing that people would now be comparing his writing to the writing of a legend like Robert Mitchelson.

Robert marched up the stage with confidence, nodding at the crowd and the cameras. He shook Keith's hand and then turned to Ethan. He stretched a hand toward Ethan, which Ethan nervously shook. Robert regarded him with a smile that Ethan could not quite place. It was somewhere between a friendly opponent's smile and a smug smirk.

"Good luck to you. I'm a big fan of your work… it's an honor to be paired against you," Ethan managed.

Robert continued the handshake longer than Ethan had expected. He then leaned in and spoke low enough that only Ethan could hear. "Oh, thank you. But don't waste your good luck on me, you're going to need it. It is always nice to see that the book club recognizes small-time authors like yourself, but a shame that they decide to pair you against veterans like me. I suppose you'll have to enjoy the limelight while you still can," Robert said before finally releasing Ethan's hand, all the while maintaining his fake smile.

Before Ethan could process what Robert had just said to him, they were being ushered off stage. Keith continued announcing pairings for the remaining authors. Robert left the event straight from there and didn't give Ethan a second glance. Ethan watched him walk away in disbelief. After his encounter with David, he never imagined meeting one of his heroes would be quite like that.

"Hey, don't look so mortified. There are still cameras around," Sarah reminded Ethan as she approached him.

Ethan snapped out of his stupor and turned to her. "Sorry, I was just distracted by the politely rude comment he made to me on stage," Ethan admitted.

"Yeah, I've heard he is the worst kind of pain in the ass. Don't let it bother you, you need to look confident," Sarah instructed. "What are you going to do with the rest of your day? There are no official events until the results of the votes are announced later tonight, but it's a good idea to make some appearances at a few places in town throughout the day," she explained.

"Well, first I'm going to grab some breakfast and bring it back to Marcus and Ashley at the cabin. Then I'll come back into town with them," said Ethan.

"Okay, well I'll see you later then. Keep me updated," Sarah demanded as she turned to leave.

Ethan considered waiting around to watch the rest of the announcements but instead decided to head straight to the nearest cafe. Finding out *In Despair* was paired against *The Pack* had really shaken him. He wanted nothing more than to share some breakfast with his girlfriend and best friend.

At the café, Ethan had to wait in one of the longest breakfast lines he'd ever seen. The small-town cafe was packed well over its capacity. Waiting in line Ethan spotted a table with overpriced copies of all eight novels featured in the festival. Ethan realized he had never actually read Robert's "*The Pack*," and grabbed a copy. Better to lose to a great book I've read than some unknown. At least then I can feel better about it, Ethan figured.

At the register Ethan paid for his copy of "*The Pack*" and ordered three breakfast sandwiches which seemed to take forever to come out. Finally, he left the cafe toward Ashley's car with sandwiches in hand. On the way to the car Ethan passed by two officers with the Ustumah County Sheriff's Department. One of the officers seemed at least a decade older than the other. As Ethan passed, he caught wind of some of their conversation.

"It's a damn shame. I'm telling you DeMarco, I'm losing sleep over it," the older officer admitted to his partner.

"Come on Masen, we're all doing the best we can. You're the veteran around here, if you let this get you shook up then how are the rest of us supposed to cope," said Officer DeMarco.

The other officer shook his head. "If we were doing the best we could, then we would have found that little girl by now," he snapped. "If I had my way, we'd have officers from every neighboring county helping us search. But the fucking people above my pay grade don't want to draw too much attention to it. Fucking politics," the officer said with disdain.

Ethan stopped in his tracks. What he had just heard was undoubtedly word-for-word dialog from a scene in *In Despair*. The only differences were the names of the officers. In his novel, the conversation took place between Mac Richardson and his partner Tyler Deverand. Ethan swiveled around to read the officer's name tags. The older officer's name tag read 'M. Riley,' and the other officer's read 'S. DeMarco.' The names didn't match, but the name of the missing girl hadn't either. Ethan reacted without thinking, it was just instinct. He hurried over to the two officers.

"Excuse me have either of you two read my book?" Ethan interjected.

Officer DeMarco looked at Ethan with surprise, but Officer Riley regarded him with a look of disgust. "Excuse me?" Officer Demarco asked.

"Sorry," Ethan said, realizing how his interruption must seem to the two officers, "I'm an author here in town as part of the festival. It's just… Well, I overheard your conversation and-"

Officer Riley cut him off, stepping toward him aggressively. "Yeah, yeah, I recognize you now.

Ian Garfield or something like that."

"Ethan Garland," Ethan Clarified.

"Right, right. Well, Ethan, I hate to tell you but neither of us gives a damn about reading your book. Ain't that right DeMarco?" Officer Riley hissed.

Officer DeMarco replied calmly, "No, I haven't read your book."

Ethan could tell he had upset the older officer, and tried to explain himself, "It's just I overheard your conversation just now, and it was the same dialog from a scene in the book, word for word."

Officer Riley laughed and started shaking his head, turning to Officer DeMarco.

Ethan continued, "I know this sounds crazy, but this missing girl case, it shares a lot of similarities with the plot of my book. I'm starting to think there may be some kind of connection."

Officer Riley snapped at Ethan, "Listen here scribbler, this is real life. Not one of your stories. Go bring your crackpot theories to the overpriced therapist you probably see three times a week." Riley motioned to DeMarco to move on and they both began walking away.

Frustrated and still not thinking straight, Ethan called after them. "Officers! What if reading my book could help you solve the case? I know it seems crazy, but I mean-"

Officer Riley charged Ethan, grabbed him by the neck, and slammed him against the nearby wall. "Listen you piece of shit. I am so fucking tired of this god damned festival. You stuck-up writers and those self-obsessed book club members make me sick. There's a little girl missing out there, and she's likely already dead. But still, all you twats can worry about is 'my book' this and 'my poem' that. Well guess what, nobody gives a shit," Officer Riley growled, his spittle bombarding Ethan's face.

When Ethan moved to say something, Riley continued. "Next time you want to try and trick someone into buying your dumb-ass book, don't pick such a stupid lie. And think twice about who you're fucking with." He let go of Ethan. "What's your name again?" Riley asked.

"Ethan," he said catching his breath. He looked to Officer De-Marco for help, and though he was regarding Riley with a disappointed look he was making no move to intervene.

"Well, Ethan. My advice to you. Stay out of my sight with your bullshit until the festival is over," Riley threatened.

Ethan just nodded. The Officer wasn't in a good state of mind, and Ethan was truly frightened of what he might do if Ethan said the wrong thing.

With that, Riley and DeMarco left Ethan there. A few tourists were staring from across the street. Ethan noticed that he'd dropped his bag of breakfast sandwiches and scrambled to pick it up. He tried to ignore the onlookers as he made his way toward Ashley's car.

CHAPTER 8

When Ethan arrived back at the cabin, Ashley and Marcus were still asleep. They were ecstatic when Ethan woke them to relatively fresh breakfast sandwiches. While they were all sitting down to eat, Ethan figured he would bring up the incident with the officers. Surely, they couldn't just pass that off as a coincidence too.

Before he could, Ashley started in, "So babe, how did it go this morning? What book is *"In Despair"* going to beat first?"

Ethan sighed; he'd almost forgotten about the contest. But now that he remembered, all the stress came piling back on. "Robert Mitchelson's *'The Pack,'*" Ethan admitted.

Worry flashed in Ashley's eyes, but she kept a straight face. "Oh, is that the one about the wolves?" she asked, trying to play dumb.

Ethan saw through her, but understood she was just trying to make him feel better. "Damn, that's the one with the movie coming out," Marcus said, mouth full of food. Ethan deflated, "Yeah that's the one."

Ashley shot Marcus a sideways glare.

"I mean," Marcus said, swallowing, "that's bullshit that they would pair a first-time published author with a rock star like Robert Mitchelson. You know?"

Ashley scowled at him.

Marcus' eyes grew wide. "What I mean is that you totally got this. Just because Mitchelson is an extremely skilled writer doesn't mean you can't beat him," Marcus said desperately trying to fix his mistake.

Ethan sunk into his chair and pushed his plate away. Ashley, still looking at Marcus, put a hand to her forehead and then turned to face Ethan.

"You really shouldn't worry. You've written a fantastic book, and you should be proud. For all we know, they paired you against Mitchelson first because your book is the only one with any real chance of beating his," she offered.

Ethan perked up. He did it more for Ashley's sake and not because he actually felt better. "Yeah, maybe," he managed. "Man, you guys wouldn't believe how stuck-up Mitchelson is."

"A super successful and rich author is stuck up? Nah I can't believe it," Marcus chimed. "Yeah, I know," Ethan admitted, "but David Kowalski is also amazingly successful, and he's been nothing but nice to me."

"What makes you say he's stuck up?" Ashley asked.

"Oh, just what he said to me when we shook hands on stage. He acted like he was being polite, but he basically treated me like a lesser human. I mean, as far as he was concerned there was no chance I was going to beat him."

Ashley rested her hand on Ethan's back. "Don't let him get in your head. He's been to this festival before, he probably does that to everyone," she said.

Ethan nodded. "That's not even the craziest part of my morning though. There's something I have to tell you guys," Ethan said hesitantly. After how Ashley and Marcus had reacted to his run in with the mother of the missing girl, he was worried that they wouldn't see eye to eye with him on the situation with the officers either. But he needed to talk to someone about it.

Ashley and Marcus waited patiently as he told them about the word-for-word match in the dialog between the officers and his novel, and then about how Officer Riley threatened him when he confronted them about it.

Ashley rolled her eyes. "Ethan. Not this again. I don't want to be dismissive, but you need to realize you're super stressed out about the festival. You're not thinking straight. You can't go dragging other people into your wild conspiracies, especially not a couple of cops."

Ethan felt a tinge of frustration. "Yeah, but-" he started.

"But nothing," Ashley interrupted, "I'm not trying to give you a hard time. I'm trying to help you, babe. You're stressed and it's making you think things that aren't true. It happens to people all the time. It's ok."

Ethan looked to Marcus for help. Marcus just shrugged, "Sorry bud, I think Ash is right on this one. You just need to relax a bit," he said.

Ethan realized that there was no way they were going to believe him. He wasn't going crazy over a little stress; he knew what he heard. Even still, they weren't going to listen to anything he had to say about it. So, from then on, he decided he would keep it to himself.

"You're right, I just need to chill out for a bit. Then I'm sure I'll forget all about it," Ethan lied. "Why don't you guys go into town and enjoy the festival a bit. I'll stay here and relax on the couch with a book," Ethan suggested. He didn't mention that 'the book' was Mitchelson's, *The Pack,* knowing that they would advise him not to read it.

Marcus looked to Ashley expectantly, who then shrugged. "If that's what you want," she conceded.

"I think it's a good idea. Just for today. You guys can come to pick me up later and we can head back into town for the results of the votes," Ethan suggested.

Half an hour later, Ashley and Marcus were finished getting ready. They said their goodbyes to Ethan and double-checked that he didn't want to join them. After he insisted, they left, and Ethan cozied up on the couch with his new hardcover copy of 'The Pack.'

Hours passed as Ethan was sucked into the book. Every chapter was great in its own right and left him wanting more. At one point he forgot he was reading with the intent of analyzing his opponent's work and not just reading for fun.

So far, the story focused on a married couple, Matt and Jess. Matt's mother had recently passed away and had left him the family cabin. The cabin was situated on a remote mountain, but it was close enough to a popular Ski Resort that it was worth something. Matt and Jess had been staying at the cabin with plans to fix it up and sell it. There was an ominous threat of wolves that seemed to be dancing in the background of every scene as the plot progressed. The first scene where the couple encountered *The Pack* was when

Ethan knew he'd already lost. Nothing in his book could compare to the excitement. The scene itself was good, but it was the lead-up and the anticipation throughout the book to everything that ended up happening in the scene that made it amazing. Ethan read it over a few times.

"*The Pack* had Jess surrounded. She desperately spun herself around trying to maintain eye contact with the wolves, hoping that would keep them at bay. It was too late, *The Pack* was hungry, and they wouldn't wait any longer. The huge alpha lunged at Jess with a wild snarl. In fear, she closed her eyes and swung her arms up in desperation. She waited for the pain of the alpha's jaws closing around her, but instead, she heard a loud noise pierce through the air. When she opened her eyes, the alpha had spun around to face a figure approaching from the darkness. The figure was closing in fast, arms waving in the air. Jess recognized the shouts of her husband as the figure closed in. The alpha hesitated for a moment before locking eyes with Jess once again. She swallowed, taking a step back before the alpha darted into the tree line away from her savior, followed quickly by the rest of *The Pack*. As Matt reached her, he threw his rifle to the ground and embraced her.

"It's going to be alright. Now, c'mon Jess, we need to get inside."

Who is going to pick a book about a sad mother dealing with her emotions over a story with this much excitement? Ethan thought. He set the book down and closed his eyes. He'd read enough for now and it had been an early morning. He just wanted some rest.

CHAPTER 9

"Do you really think it's a good idea to leave him alone at the cabin to mope?" Marcus asked Ashley in the car.

"You know as well as I do that it's a good idea to give him some space when he gets like this," Ashley explained.

Marcus nodded. She wasn't wrong. As long as Marcus had known Ethan, he would get in these moods where he would be completely down on himself. Either for no obvious reason at all or because he was being too harsh on himself. When it happened, there was no cheering him up. In fact, just being around him in one of those moods could set him off, and the next thing Marcus knew he would be the object of Ethan's frustration. It was a quirk he didn't admire in his friend, but it was something he just knew about him and accepted. Earlier in the cabin had been one of those moods, and the best plan was to give him his space until he was ready to come back to his normal self. Marcus and Ashley discussed Ethan's recent behavior for most of the car ride into town.

When they arrived back in Ustumah City, the festival was in full bloom. There were easily almost twice as many people as the day before. Just outside of town a roadblock was set up. Ashley joined a long line of cars following a series of detour signs that eventually led to a campground just outside of the town. The campground had been converted to a huge parking area where people in neon green outfits with the word VOLUNTEER printed across their chest and backs were directing cars on where to park. Ashley was eventually guided to a spot and her and Marcus exited the car.

Outside thousands of distant conversations carried throughout the area, only interrupted by the occasional car horn.

"Ok, I thought yesterday was crazy. What the hell?" Marcus commented, looking around. "I guess most people don't show up until the second day. This must be when things really kick-off. There really wasn't a whole lot going on yesterday," Ashley explained.

Together they made their way toward town, avoiding seemingly confused tourists and frustrated drivers. The streets of Ustumah City were packed full when they arrived. Every street looked like it was in anticipation of a parade, but instead, the streets were lined with food trucks, makeshift book shops, and a whole other array of random stands.

Ashley led the way through the wall of people as she always did. However, it was so thick with people that she lost Marcus twice. After the second time, she grabbed his hand and pulled him through the crowd. She eventually yanked him into an 'air pocket' absent of people on Main Street. In front of them there stood a small make-shift wooden stage. The stage was lined with a painting of a man grabbing the sides of his head as if he were desperately blocking out a terrible migraine. Above the man swirled a collection of unpleas-ant-looking gases. A single sign read 'No Escape, by Trent Richards.'

On stage a man was sitting in a chair having a discussion with another man and woman who were leaning forward, hanging on the man's every word. Ashley couldn't make out what they were say-ing over the crowd of voices around them, but it was interesting enough. She wasn't really sure what there was to do at the festival, and this had been the first thing to pique her interest. She walked toward the stage with Marcus.

As she reached the foot of the stage with a few other onlook-ers, Ashley realized she was still holding Marcus' hand in her own. It had been a long time since she and Ethan had held hands, and she'd forgotten how comforting it could feel. Such a small gesture of human connection, but it went a long way for her. She savored the feeling a moment longer but finally disconnected herself from Marcus. She glanced at him as she did, and he just looked at her and smiled. Marcus had always had a contagious smile, and she couldn't help but smile back. There was a short silence, and then they both tried to talk at the same time.

"Sorry, you go ahead," Ashley said, raising her voice to beat out the noise of the crowd.

"No, what were you going to say?" Marcus insisted.

It was hard enough to hear each other so Ashley gave in, rather than debate over who should speak. "I was going to say, I recognize this artwork from the Meet the Writers event. Even though I was only there for a minute, this had really caught my eye," Ashley explained, almost shouting.

"I think it's one of the poems if I remember right," Marcus added. He looked around the stage expecting to find a printout of the poem to give to Ashley, but there were none.

The couple that had been on stage was just leaving, and the man sitting in the chair noticed Marcus looking around.

"Excuse me, can I help you?" the man asked.

"I'm just looking for a printed copy of the poem. Usually, these setups have them everywhere, right?" replied Marcus.

"Right indeed," the man said with a wide grin. "However, my publisher didn't bring enough, and I ran out hours ago. He was supposed to come back with more, but I haven't seen him since," he elaborated.

"Please, you and your girlfriend are more than welcome to join me on stage, and I'd be happy to recite it as well as discuss it with you," the man offered with a twinkle in his eye.

Marcus laughed and looked at Ashley who then interjected, "Oh, he's not my boyfriend. Just a good friend."

The man feigned a dramatic frown. "What a shame, you'd make a terrific couple," he said with a wink.

Marcus looked at the ground, avoiding Ashley's gaze.

"Well actually, I'm dating one of the writers here at the festival. Ethan Garland, have you met him?" Ashley asked, changing the subject.

The man's eyes lit up. "I have not had the honor, unfortunately. You're a lucky girl. I read *In Despair* only last week. Ethan is a very talented writer," he chimed.

"Oh, he'd be happy to hear that. I'll have to introduce you two," Ashley suggested. "I'm Ashley by the way. And this is Marcus."

"Trent, a pleasure to meet two fine folks such as yourselves. Now please, allow me to recite my poem to the guests of a fellow contestant," Trent insisted.

Marcus looked at Ashley with a grin on his face. He'd just now noticed the colorful way the man spoke. It was spot on with the impression Marcus would do when he was mocking writers to Ethan. Ashley knew exactly what Marcus was grinning about and let out a chuckle, waving Marcus off.

Trent was still waiting for an answer, and Ashley grabbed the side of the stage and pulled herself up. She motioned to Marcus to follow and turned to Trent, "I'd love to hear the poem recited straight from the author himself."

"Indeed, indeed. We would love to be regaled with your poem good sir," Marcus muttered as he climbed on stage.

Luckily the crowd drowned Marcus out enough that only Ashley made out what he'd said. She held back her laughter. It was funny to see someone matching Marcus' idea of an over-the-top writer so spot on, but Trent was being very friendly, and she didn't want to be rude. She turned to Marcus to give him a quick glare, but he only smirked.

Finally, Ashley and Marcus climbed into the two open chairs next to Trent. Trent smiled and leaned back in his chair, "Thank you for joining me. I wrote this poem coming out of a dark place in my life, and it means a lot to me. Having the opportunity to share it with so many people here at the festival has brightened my life in immeasurable ways."

Marcus was surprised by Trent's sudden earnestness and felt a tinge of guilt for making fun of him. "Well, thanks for giving us the live performance. Means a lot, knowing how much it means to you," Marcus said nodding at Trent.

Ashley found Marcus' change in attitude to be slightly out of character. It was a welcome change though, and she found it surprisingly mature for a man who spent most of his time cracking jokes. She put her hand on his knee instinctively, as if to silently applaud him. She didn't realize the inappropriateness of the gesture until Trent made a point to look at her hand. He said nothing, but Ashley removed her hand immediately nonetheless.

"Why don't I get started," Trent suggested, clearing the air. "This is 'No Escape,'" Trent began.

"Always, the shadow looms behind you,
Though you live in doubt of its presence,
Once seen, you must avoid its essence,
Now you must flee, for it will pursue.
Inside it contains all you wish gone,
The disease of fear that holds you back,
And evil doubt that chips till you crack,
No escape, it will find you withdrawn."

When he finished Trent leaned forward in his chair to gauge their responses. Ashley clapped and held her hands high. Marcus clapped too, and he nodded toward Trent with approval. Trent stood up with pride and gave a quick bow.

Ashley and Marcus sat with Trent for a short while discussing the poem. Eventually though other people became interested and gathered around the stage.

Marcus noticed and suggested that they move on and give Trent the opportunity to share with others. Trent thanked them both for their time and they moved on, quickly replaced by other bystanders.

"Well, that guy sure had a colorful personality," Marcus laughed to Ashley.

Ashley nodded, "He was really nice though. Super eccentric, but also really genuine. I'm glad we did that."

"Me too," Marcus smiled.

They moved on through the crowd and Ashley asked, "I wonder if Ethan has one of these set up somewhere for his book.."

"Good question. Let's have a look," Marcus suggested.

Moments later the two were navigating the crowded streets of Ustumah City, this time with Marcus in the lead. It didn't take long for them to spot the relatively small tent with the same cardboard display for *In Despair* from the Meet the Writers event. The all too familiar book cover, as well as Ethan's glum-looking portrait, would have been impossible for them to miss. It did, however, take a long moment to navigate through the crowds over to the tent.

As Marcus and Ashley arrived, they noticed an even larger tent looming right next door. The memorable cardboard cutouts of the large wolves from Mitchelson's *The Pack* seemed to guard the entrance of the tent. The cutouts almost seemed alive as they regarded Marcus with hungry yellow eyes.

"Seems a little unfair to see *The Pack* with such an extravagant setup right next to Ethan's novel. I guess it's a good thing the book club members do all the voting, and not the people visiting the festival," Marcus commented.

Ashley nodded, but before she could say anything an impatient voice called out toward her and Marcus from inside the tent of *In Despair*.

"It's about time. I was wondering if you were ever going to show," Sarah shouted as she hurried over to Marcus and Ashley. "Where's Ethan?" She asked, looking around frantically.

"Oh, he's back at the cabin resting. Is that a problem?" Ashley asked, trying to read the situation.

"It's only a problem if he wants any chance of progressing to the next round of the festival," Sarah stammered.

Ashley noticed that Sarah was visibly upset. She was not used to seeing Sarah show so much emotion and found it slightly off-putting. "We planned on picking him up and bringing him back for the winners' announcements. He was pretty stressed out this morning and I think he just wanted to relax a bit," Ashley explained.

Sarah shook her head. "He told me he'd meet me here in town after he picked you two up. He said nothing about relaxing at home. Doesn't he realize how important this is?" Sarah sputtered.

Marcus stepped in, "Listen, Ethan's not used to this kind of pressure. It's really wearing on him. What's the big deal if he just relaxes for half a day?"

Sarah threw her hands in the air. "This is why I can't stand working with new authors. I'm not going to deal with this. If you two care about his chances in the festival, call him and tell him he should be here," she said. Then she walked away back into the tent.

After Sarah had gone, Marcus turned to Ashley. "Should we call Ethan," he asked.

"No. This would just add to his stress. I'm sure Sarah is just overreacting. She seemed a little off," said Ashley.

Marcus agreed. The two had wanted to check out the *In Despair* tent, but they were reconsidering. They wanted to avoid Sarah after that confrontation. Instead, they decided to pay *The Pack* tent a visit.

"Scope out the competition. See this snob Robert for ourselves," Marcus suggested.

The inside of the tent was dominated by paperback, hardcover, and printed manuscript versions of *The Pack*. There were even still a good number of copies with special edition covers available. Among the numerous copies of *The Pack*, there were also copies of Mitchelson's other popular novels. Marcus recognized them, only because he had seen the movies they had inspired.

Ashley recognized Robert from seeing him on TV and spotted him standing in the back corner of the tent conversing with four other people. She couldn't recall how she recognized one of the people he was talking to, but somehow Ashley knew they were a member of the Ustumah City Book Club.

Ashley nudged Marcus. "Marcus, that's Robert Mitchelson," she said in a hushed tone. "I'm pretty sure he's talking with some members of the book club. Maybe we should try and listen in. We could get something interesting to tell Ethan."

"Couldn't hurt," Marcus said with a shrug.

The two made their way over toward Robert and the others. Ashley picked up a copy of *The Pack* and pretended to look it over.

"Oh, Robert you are too kind," said a woman.

"Truly, your gifts this year were overly generous. It's always great to have you here in Ustumah," added a man.

Robert waved a hand dismissively. "Think nothing of it. You are always such gracious hosts, it's the least I could do. I just hope that I can look forward to your support going forward in the festival. After all, it would be a shame to ruin the start of such a delightful week," he said pointedly.

The other four nodded silently, and a few long moments passed before the woman spoke up again. "Well, I'm sure we'd all love to see your progress in this year's festival. *The Pack* is truly one of your greatest works," she said.

Then, one of the four who had remained silent up until that point interjected. "If our 'business' here is finished, we really should be going," the man said curtly.

As the man spoke, Marcus noticed him gesture toward Ashley and himself. Ashley didn't seem to notice, and Marcus tried to get her attention, but she was focused intently on the conversation and shooed him away. Robert and the others suddenly became aware of Marcus and Ashley's proximity. They all said polite goodbyes and dispersed. Robert remained for a few moments and watched Ashley and Marcus as the two tried to seem involved in a conversation about the book.

Robert walked right up to them. "Are you two finding everything all right?" He asked politely.

"Oh yeah all good," Marcus blurted.

Robert regarded Marcus with a practiced stare, examining him. Finally, he said, "You know what, I recognize you. You were with Ethan Garland at the Meet the Writers event. Are you a close friend of his?"

Marcus hesitated. "Um, yeah. Actually, he's my best friend," he stammered.

Robert nodded. "How nice of you to come all the way here to Ustumah City to support your friend," Robert said before turning to Ashley and continuing. "I'm sorry, but I can't say I recognize you. Is this your boyfriend?" Robert asked motioning toward Marcus.

"No, I'm Ethan's girlfriend. You probably didn't see me at the event because I wasn't there for very long. I didn't want to be a clingy girlfriend and chose to give Ethan some space with his fans," Ashley lied.

"I see," Robert said. "I'm Robert Mitchelson by the way, but I'm sure you already knew that," he added, reaching out a hand toward either of them.

Marcus took his hand and shook it. "Marcus."

Robert then held his hand out toward Ashley. She made no move to shake it and said, "I'm Ashley."

Robert hesitated for a moment after Ashley rejected his handshake. "Well, it was nice meeting you both. Tell Ethan I wish him luck in tonight's voting. Make sure to let him know that there's no shame in losing tonight though. It's really saddening when struggling new authors like himself beat themselves up over such a thing," Robert explained.

Ashley felt the sudden urge to slap him or spit in his face. Instead, she let out a plain, "Mhm. I'm sure he'll feel relieved by your kind words." She turned to Marcus and motioned toward the exit of the large tent. "Let's go, Marcus," she ordered.

Marcus turned to leave with her, but Robert called out after them, "Wait, one moment." He caught up to them with two hardcover copies of *The Pack* with special edition covers. "Please take these on me. I wouldn't feel right letting such close friends of a fellow author leave empty-handed. They'll make good souvenirs at the least."

Marcus accepted his copy, but when Ashley made no move to accept hers, Marcus grabbed hers from Robert hesitantly.

"Please do tell Ethan I said hello," Robert said nodding as Marcus took the gifts.

Outside the tent, Ashley shook her head at Marcus. "Why did you accept those," she asked glaringly.

"Instinct, I guess. I didn't really think about it," Marcus admitted.

Ashley sighed and grabbed the books from Marcus, stuffing them into her purse.

"I see why Ethan said he was such a dick," Ashley elaborated as she led the way away from the tents.

"Yeah totally," Marcus agreed, "And what was up with that conversation when we walked up. If those really were book club members, was he like bribing them?"

"Sure, seemed like it," said Ashley. "Let's go find something to eat, and afterward we can call Ethan and let him know."

The two disappeared into the crowd packed streets in the direction of a group of food trucks they had passed earlier.

CHAPTER 10

Later in the evening, Ustumah City's streets died down as much of the crowd left. However, a large number of people still remained. Some walked the streets browsing what booths and tents remained while most people in town had migrated to a large park located at the bottom of Main Street. Once again, a large makeshift stage had been set up in the park. This time, however, the seats were set up in many rows in front of the stage. There were hardly enough seats for everyone, so large crowds stood all around.

Not long after eating, Marcus and Ashley had gone back to the Cabin to pick up Ethan. They'd spent most of the car ride back discussing Robert and his conversation with the book club members.

Luckily when they arrived at the stage, Ethan, Ashley, and Marcus found seats near the front row reserved specifically for them.

"I've just never heard of an author bribing one of the book club members for votes. This is a prestigious writing festival, I'd like to think it has more integrity than that," Ethan explained as he sat down. "That's why I think Sarah may have been overreacting a bit too," he finished.

"I thought the same thing at first too, but after hearing Robert's conversation, I was a little worried," Ashley said.

Ethan snapped at her, "Well what do you want me to do Ash? It's a little late to bribe them now! The votes are already in."

Marcus jumped in, "Hey man, it's ok. I think Ashley is just worried. You know, we don't want you to be bummed if you lose. Especially if it's only because you're an honest enough person to not bribe the judges."

Ethan shook his head. "Sorry, I didn't mean to react like that. It's just, this is kind of the last thing I want to hear right before I hear the results, you know?" Ethan explained.

Ashley put a hand on Ethan's leg. "I get it, you're just stressed. You should know, I have all the confidence that you can win tonight. In fact, if you lose, I think it's only because Robert is a cheater. That's all I was trying to say," she said.

Marcus laughed and pulled something out of his pocket. "Dude, I'm so confident in you I bought this before we came to pick you up," Marcus said, revealing an air horn. "I'm gonna blast it so long when they announce you've won," he chuckled.

Ethan smiled. "I don't know if I'd be more surprised I won or embarrassed that you'd be blasting the air horn."

"Have some confidence Ethan," Ashley insisted.

"I don't mean to be dramatic," Ethan admitted, "I know *In Despair* is a good book. Otherwise, I wouldn't be here. But I read a good part of *The Pack* earlier today. I just don't know if I can compete."

Ashley wasn't sure what to say and hesitated for a moment. As she opened her mouth to reply, a loud drum roll erupted from the stage and the lights brightened.

"Good evening everyone!" Shouted a short stocky woman walking across the stage with a microphone in hand. "Welcome to the announcement of the results of the first round of voting in this year's Known Poets and Authors Writing Festival!" The crowd erupted into an unexpected roar of applause.

Marcus leaned over to Ethan. "I gotta tell you, man, I had no idea how serious people took this festival," he said in a hushed tone.

Ethan nodded. "There's a lot of people that enjoy a good book. A caveman like you wouldn't understand," he said playfully.

Back on stage, the stocky woman continued. "It's been a pleasure hosting all you fine people in our little town of Ustumah City. We truly hope you have been enjoying yourselves," she said pausing for the crowd which then erupted in more applause. "Glad to hear it," she went on, "Now, I know you are all here to find out which of these eight amazing poems and these eight amazing works of fiction will be moving on to the next round and be one step closer to being this year's winner. But first, I'd like to make a quick statement. I want to thank all our contestants, poets, and authors alike, for joining us for this year's festivities. Every poem and every novel that has found its way here this year is here because it is special in its own way. I say this because I want the writers, as well as all of you here who have read or plan on reading these great works, to know that no matter what the results here tonight, these are all great works of art. Let us all remember that even those who lose here tonight, are still winners." The crowd clapped cheerily as she finished her speech.

Ethan squirmed in his seat as she spoke. Winning the festival had never been a priority for him, but now that the prospect of losing felt so real, his nerves were acting up. Ashley noticed his squirming and placed a hand on his leg to try calming him.

As the applause died down, the woman spoke up. "Well then, without further waiting, let's begin. As always, we will start with our poets," she announced.

The woman went on announcing the first two poems that had been paired against each other, announcing the number of votes each poem received. The poets made their way on stage, shook hands, and the loser walked off. The winner gave a short speech and then walked off stage as well. Another pair was announced, and the events repeated themselves. Finally, Claire's poem was announced, and Ethan tuned in with more attentiveness.

"Our next pair of poems is *The Human Journey* by Claire Donaghue, and *The Walls We Build* by James Anderson," the announcer said proudly. Claire and a man Ethan could only assume was James began to make their way on stage. The announcer continued, "In a vote of eight to eight, a tie-breaker was decided by the president of our Ustumah City Book Club, *The Human Journey* narrowly wins." The crowd cheered for Claire as she shook hands with James. "It is not often a tiebreaker is needed, so clearly these were two great works of art. But only one can go on to the next round. Congratulations to Claire Donaghue!" The woman exclaimed.

As James made his way off stage, Claire took up the mic. "Thank you all. I am still questioning if it's even real that I'm here as an actual contestant. Now I've found out I'm moving on to the next round, and I'm sure it must be a dream." Claire said pausing. She had no script and was clearly looking for the right words. "For me, poetry has always been a way to express my views of the world. Not so much to press my own views on others, but to give myself an outlet to express them in a way where I could begin to understand myself. Poetry has been as much a journey of self-discovery, as it has been a journey of discovering my ideas and my art with others. *The Human Journey* in particular is a very special poem to me. I wrote it after I learned a lot about myself, and I felt that level of self-awareness was something others could relate to if they could just be shown in the right way. Clearly, I did something right to have the honor to be standing here in front of you all. So, thank you very much for this acknowledgment that I am not just some crazy girl who thinks she can make a difference with just a typewriter," Claire finished giving a slight nod, almost a bow.

Ethan joined in with the crowd's approving applause but noticed Ashley remained unmoved in her chair. Marcus joined in with Ethan at first, but when he saw Ashley's reaction, he lowered his excitement.

The announcer finished up the last pair of poets, gave a small speech of appreciation for the poets and their poetry, and then moved on to the authors. As she was announcing the first pair of novels, a man wearing a volunteer uniform approached Ethan from near the stage.

"Mr. Garland, sorry to bother you, but I'm to inform you that yourself and Mr. Mitchelson are next to be announced. Please join me near the stage," the volunteer said leaning toward Ethan.

Ethan complied, and Ashley and Marcus wished him good luck as he left. He noticed that another volunteer was directing Robert toward the opposite end.

At the stage, the volunteer turned to Ethan and instructed him to wait there until his name was announced. Then he was to meet Robert mid-stage and shake his hand.

On stage, the winner of the first pair finished up her speech. Then the announcer woman came back over the microphone, "Our next pair of novels are *The Pack* by Robert Mitchelson, and *In Despair* by Ethan Garland."

Ethan began his stride up the stage and toward its center. On stage, the cheers from the crowd were deafening and all the lights made it hard to focus. As he and Robert approached each other they made eye contact, which Robert responded to with a smug grin. The butterflies in Ethan's stomach were threatening to burst out at any moment.

The announcer's voice rang in from the large speakers to Ethan's side. "By a vote of fifteen to one, the decisive winner is…" the voice began. Ethan felt his heart flutter, and for a moment it seemed like everything slowed down. The crowd seemed to fall to almost dead silence for a fleeting second. Ethan looked out toward Ashley and Marcus, both of whom were wearing concerned faces.

The voice went on, dragging Ethan back into reality. "The decisive winner is *The Pack*, the woman's voice announced just as Ethan and Robert reached each other.

Ethan's heart sank and he fought to contain his shame. He leaned forward and shook Robert's hand. As they shook, Robert leaned in and whispered into Ethan's ear. The applause of the crowd threatened to drown out Robert's words, but Ethan heard them clear as day.

The words dug themselves deep into Ethan's ear, "You'll never be anything but the one-off author that got lucky."

Ethan pulled back squinting into Robert's eyes. His mouth laid open, but no reply could escape his lips. Robert turned away and made his way toward the mic. Ethan wasn't sure how long he'd stayed standing there but it must have been a moment too long because a volunteer touched him lightly on the shoulder and ushered him off stage. Ethan rejoined Ashley and Marcus at his seat.

"Babe," Ashley started, hesitating as she struggled to find the right words. She could see the pain in Ethan's eyes.

Ethan waved her off, "It's alright. I never expected to win anyways." The words fell out of his mouth trembling. He had truly believed there was no chance of winning, and he'd been prepared for it. It wasn't the loss that was now eating away at him. It was Robert's words. The confirmation that the dark side of his mind needed. He was a shitty boyfriend. He was a shitty friend. He'd thought that at least he'd finally proved he was a decent writer. But the unrelenting part of his mind, filled with doubt and self-loathing, had always felt that even that wasn't true. He was a terrible writer who'd somehow managed to stumble across a great story. Now Robert had put the nail in the coffin, and he'd lost the last thing that gave him any hope.

Robert's speech poured out over the crowd, and Ashley and Marcus sat with mouths sewed shut waiting for Ethan to make the first move. He never did. The announcements ended and the event came to a close. The three made their way back toward Ashley's car along with the rest of the mob.

In the car, Ethan fought to regain control of his thoughts. He reminded himself that writing was only a small part of his life. He still had an amazing girlfriend and a loyal friend. He hadn't been sure that he'd have them for much longer, but he reminded himself that fixing things with them had been the true purpose of the trip. There is still time to make it right with them, he thought. He just needed to get out of his own head. If he could do that, he could find out what it was that was driving a rift between him and Marcus. He could figure out what it was that he needed to do to bring things with Ashley back to how they were. If I could just find those answers, Ethan yearned.

"I'm sorry guys. You've been very patient," Ethan confided into the silent car.

Ashley turned to him with a weak smile, but Marcus started in. "Hey. This was exciting for you, and I get that tonight must've been really hard," Marcus said as he leaned forward from the back seat placing his large hand on Ethan's shoulder.

Ashley chimed in, "This entire trip has been stressful for you. Tonight's been the most stressful so far, of course, you're going to shut down a little."

"Well," Ethan started, "I just want you guys to know I appreciate you. I'm not sure I've deserved so much patience from the two of you and I'm grateful. From here on out, I'm going to be better than I have."

Ashley and Marcus played Ethan's apology down, but he could tell they were grateful. He'd said exactly what they needed to hear. He was on track toward making things right. The three friends chatted happily as their car plunged deeper into the dark forest, and Ethan couldn't help but smile. It was a truly happy smile, and it was an unfamiliar yet welcome guest on his face.

As they arrived back at the cabin Ashley pulled the car into the parking spot. As she did, she noticed something glint in the tree line just outside the fence surrounding the cabin. Once they were parked, Ethan and Marcus made their way toward the cabin. The two were joking about some event from their past.

"No way, that was definitely you," Ethan insisted.

"You wish bro! I wouldn't be caught dead," Marcus shot back, gently shoving Ethan.

Ashley stood near the car and stared into the tree line. Another glint. Something bright yellow she thought.

"Do you guys see that?" Ashley asked. Marcus and Ethan kept moving toward the cabin, too engrossed in their own conversation to notice.

Ashley made her way to the edge of the fence, closer to the tree line for a closer look. As she reached the fence, she noticed rustling in the forest beyond, but it came to an abrupt stop as she arrived. Then two bright yellow objects shone out at her from beyond the dark trees. She froze, startled for a moment, before focusing in on the objects. When she realized what she was looking at, a deep fear crawled up her back to the top of her neck. Then more pairs of the glinting objects appeared. Wolf eyes, Ashley discerned too late.

Before Ashley could even consider her reaction to this revelation, easily a dozen wolves plummeted out from beyond the tree line toward her. They were far bigger than any wolf Ashley had ever seen. Some of the wolves jumped the wooden fence with ease, while others darted through the large openings between the posts. Ashley only had time to call out for the others before she was surrounded.

"Guys!" Ashley screamed in desperation.

Laughing at each other, Marcus and Ethan turned to see what had upset Ashley. Their laughter ended abruptly when they noticed the dozen or so large wolves surrounding her.

"Holy shit," Marcus muttered under his breath before darting toward the car.

Ethan hardly noticed Marcus had left his side. He was too entranced with the situation. All the odd coincidences that matched up with scenes from his book were replaying in his mind like lightning flashes. As he saw the wolves surrounding Ashley and eyeing her up patiently, he knew that this was another instance of fiction becoming reality. Only this time, it wasn't a scene from *In Despair*, it was from *The Pack*. The scene where Jess first encounters the wolves.

Ethan's mind raced as he recalled the details of what he had read earlier that day. Jess was saved by her husband when he fired a rifle at one of the wolves, injuring it.

Of course! Ethan realized. Chekhov's Gun! He turned heel and flung himself toward the cabin, fumbling for the key from his pocket. When he reached the door, he quickly unlocked it and practically crashed into the cabin's living room.

The rifle was right where it had been all along, patiently waiting above the mantle. Ethan snatched it and turned back toward the cabin entrance. He hesitated for only a moment, realizing that the rifle was likely not loaded. Please, please, please be loaded, Ethan pleaded internally. It's Chekhov's Gun for Christ's sake. He lifted the rifle's bolt handle up and slid it back. No bullet.

"Shit, shit, shit!" Ethan exclaimed. He only barely noticed the small rolled-up piece of paper that fell from the gun's open chamber and onto the cabin floor. Mind desperately racing, Ethan ran out the cabin door with the empty rifle still in hand.

Outside Ashley had been doing her best to maintain eye contact with the wolves. She thought she remembered hearing that was the right thing to do on TV. Or maybe she'd just made it up. Either way, it didn't matter. The wolves had her surrounded, and for the few she managed to maintain eye contact with, there were twice as many behind her. She spun around hopelessly trying anyways. Finally, she stopped, meeting eyes with the largest wolf of *The Pack*. It was a huge dark figure that seemed almost unnatural. She felt as if it was looking straight into her soul with its bright yellow eyes. As it snarled at her, a thick bead of saliva dripped from its mouth. Ashley instinctively raised her hands to protect herself as the large wolf took a few steps forward. The wolf let out a vicious growl and darted toward Ashley. She crouched, threw her hands up, closed her eyes, and awaited the miserable fate of being torn apart by wolves. Then, the deafening sound of an air horn rang out from behind her. She opened her eyes to see that the wolf had stopped dead in its tracks. The entire pack was now staring intently at something behind her.

Afraid to take her eyes off the wolves, she managed to glance over her shoulder. It was Marcus. He was sprinting toward the wolves waving the air horn above his head, blasting it repeatedly and shouting indistinguishably as he neared. The large wolf took one last look at Ashley before turning around and heading back into the dark forest in a blur. Almost immediately after the large wolf turned to leave, the rest of *The Pack* followed.

Marcus arrived at Ashley's side. "Are you alright Ash?" he asked, voice raised and panting.

Ashley tried to speak, but her jaw was trembling, and she couldn't produce any words through her panicked breathing. Ethan arrived only moments later with the rifle from the cabin in hand.

"Ashley are-" Ethan started.

Marcus interrupted Ethan by snatching the rifle out of his hand. He saw the empty chamber and threw the rifle to the ground. "The fuck was this going to do Ethan? Ash could have fucking died and you ran inside for an empty gun?" Marcus shouted. His fists were clenched and for a moment Ethan thought he might hit him.

Ethan tried to respond but surprise, and perhaps some embarrassment, stopped him.

Marcus wrapped his arms around Ashley and began walking her toward the cabin. "It's going to be alright Ash. Let's just get inside," he said.

Ethan watched silently as Marcus and Ashley made their way inside. Once they'd gone through the door, he turned out toward the tree line. The forest was quiet, and Ethan felt the strangest feeling that something was watching him from within. Likely just one of the wolves he thought, yet he couldn't shake the feeling that it was something more.

He picked up the rifle from where Marcus had thrown it and reflected on what had just happened. The scene had been so similar to what had happened in '*The Pack.*' He had thought for sure that he would save Ashley if he went for the rifle. He had been horribly wrong, and if it hadn't been for Marcus, Ashley would have died. He was overcome by an immense loss of confidence in himself. Crippling doubt set in as he realized he was being pulled even deeper into the rabbit hole of whatever the hell was going on. This was the third time something like this had happened. Though it didn't pan out as Ethan had expected, it only furthered his drive to understand what was happening. I need answers, Ethan thought for the second time that night. Rifle in hand he made his way into the cabin.

Inside Ashley was sitting on the couch with a blanket wrapped around her and a full glass of water beside her. Her breathing had hardly slowed, and she seemed to be staring forward at nothing in particular.

"Babe… I'm so sorry. I should have done something earlier. It's just that I thought… I thought wrong," Ethan said, stopping himself from elaborating further. He understood why he'd done what he had, but Marcus and Ashley would just pass it off as another instance of him making things up in his head. Then he'd be even more embarrassed than he already was.

Ashley looked at Ethan and nodded, but only moments later looked back forward and proceeded to stare into nothing.

Marcus was on the phone in the kitchen, and Ethan caught a glimpse of his conversation. "No, I'm not over exaggerating! There were at least ten of them, bigger than any fucking wolf I've ever seen!" Marcus yelled into the phone. He paused as the person on the other side of the line spoke, before starting again. "All I'm asking is that you do your god damned job and look into it, instead of treating me like some frightened tourist that doesn't know what he saw!" Marcus continued.

Ethan avoided Ashley's gaze as he returned the rifle to its place above the mantle. Only then did he remember the piece of paper that had fallen out of the rifle's chamber earlier. It was still lying on the ground rolled up tightly. Ethan picked it up and unfurled it gently. On the paper were three lines, twelve words, no more no less.

The heart of the woods,
fiction is reality,
there your answers lie.

There your answers lie, Ethan recited internally. A simple sentence at the end of a mysterious poem that would seem meaningless to most people. However, to Ethan the words meant everything. For the first time in over a year, he knew exactly what it was he had to do.

CHAPTER 11

The next day Ashley felt much better. The shock from the attack had hit her hard and had taken a good night's rest to wear off. When she'd woken Ethan asked her if she wanted to go home. Truthfully, part of her had wanted to say yes, but the rest of her knew that would be wrong. If they left now Ethan would be the only writer leaving. He'd look like a sore loser, and she didn't want that for him. Not only that, but Ethan had finally seemed happy last night. There were still five days of festivities left. Plenty of time for the three to really enjoy the trip and try to move on from the past. That meant more to her than some residual fear from the previous night's attack, so they agreed to stay.

That morning was the day of Poetry and Pastries in town. An early morning event where bakeries from all over the country came to show off their goods. It was a breakfast buffet all about appreciating poetry and its contribution to the world. Ethan enjoyed a good story over poetry any day. Ashley, on the other hand, was not very interested in writing, but she did enjoy poetry at times. Today's event was one she had been looking forward to. After deciding to stay in Ustumah City for the remaining five days, Ashley and Ethan quickly got dressed and prepared to head into town.

Ashley peeked into Marcus' room and caught him snoring in a deep sleep. Back out in the hallway, she stopped Ethan. "Why don't we let Marcus sleep in? You know he's not a morning person, and he had a long night arguing with the rangers about those wolves," Ashley suggested.

Ethan agreed and the two of them snuck out of the cabin toward the car. Ashley stopped partway. Ethan turned around to see her staring at the spot where the wolves had surrounded her. She looked like a deer caught in the headlights. The surrounding forest looked completely different in the light of the day, yet the contrast between the open area around the cabin and the heavily shaded tree line of the forest made it somehow seem even more ominous.

Ethan wrapped an arm around his girlfriend and kissed her on the cheek. "You sure you're ok, babe?" he asked.

"Yeah, I'm fine. I just- I just needed a second. But I'm over it," Ashley replied. Even she wasn't sure if she was trying to convince Ethan that she was alright, or if she was trying to convince herself.

Either way, the couple made it to the car. This time Ethan drove into town while Ashley relaxed in the passenger seat. Ethan was able to get the radio working once they pulled off the dirt path and onto the main road. As if by some divine intervention, 'Chamber of Reflection,' by Mac DeMarco had just started playing on the radio. It was their song. The two laughed together and shared a warm look.

"If it wasn't for this song, I'm not sure I ever would have had the courage to finally tell you how I felt," Ethan admitted.

Ashley smiled. "I always loved this song. I'd never seen you as anything but a friend. But when you came up to me that night, looked me straight in the eyes, and told me how you felt, something changed. This song was playing in the background, and it just felt so romantic. So right. I don't know what it was. I felt this spark, and I knew we had something special. Something that I didn't want to let go," Ashley explained. "It sounds so cheesy when I explain it out loud, but it was almost like there was some outside force pushing us together. I'm not really sure I ever had any choice but to fall for you. I guess it was fate."

Ethan reached over and grabbed her hand. Ashley gripped it tight, and Ethan felt closer to her in that moment than he had in over a year. "Do you remember what I said to you? Sometimes I think about it and get embarrassed. It was pretty cheesy. I almost didn't even say anything…" Ethan said, "What a mistake that would have been."

"Of course I remember," Ashley exclaimed. "You told me you were glad we were such great friends, blah blah blah, and even though you worried that what you were going to say might ruin all that, you had to say it anyway because otherwise you'd never forgive yourself. Then you just said it. 'Ashley Hollins, I love you. And the thing is, saying it isn't good enough. Saying 'I love you' is nothing but words. I want to show you. I want to show you how I feel. I want to give you how I feel. I don't think just being friends is going to cut it for me anymore.' And then you paused, for dramatic effect I'm sure," Ashley said.

Ethan interrupted, "It had nothing to do with that. I was just nervous."

Ashley let out a soft giggle and continued, "Then you said, 'I guess what I'm trying to do is ask you if you'll give me the opportunity to show you how I feel. I'm asking if you feel the same way. I'm asking if you want something more than this. Because I think we could be amazing together.' Those were your exact words. I'll never forget that."

"Jesus. It really was cheesy," Ethan sighed.

"Maybe a little," Ashley admitted, "But I'm glad you said it. We wouldn't be here right now if you hadn't." She squeezed Ethan's hand.

They spent the rest of the car ride talking about old times, sharing more than a few laughs and warm moments. It gave Ethan hope that things really could get better between them. For the first time in a long while, Ashley felt like Ethan was actually her boyfriend, as opposed to just some guy she'd been dating.

Parking was a mess again and Ethan had to find a spot just outside the city. They walked into town where the streets were surprisingly empty. Upon reaching Main Street they could see the Poetry and Pastries event taking place in the park at the bottom of the street. The same place where Ethan had suffered his loss against Robert the night before.

In the park, a couple of hundred fold-out tables had been set up in rows. They were adorned with tablecloths and thousands of chairs surrounded the tables. The stage from the night before was still set up and volunteers were moving things around on stage. On either side of the event, there were dozens of catering trucks and small food stands. It was the biggest buffet Ethan had ever seen. There were eggs, bacon, hash browns, toast on all sorts of bread, bagels, and more. Despite all the breakfast food, one item dominated the stands. Pastries. There was every kind of pastry Ethan could possibly imagine.

Upon seeing the amazing buffet, Ashley ran off toward the closest pastry stand. Ethan followed smiling as he watched the woman he loved acting like a little girl.

They both arrived at the stand, grabbed plates, and eagerly filled them with pastries. Ethan paid for them as Ashley made her way to another stand with more nutritious items. Once they had enough food, they made their way into the crowd of people circling the seating area to find a good place to eat. As they ventured down the rows a familiar voice called out to them.

Ethan turned toward it to see Claire standing from her seat and waving them over. Ethan waved back and dragged his feet as he made his way toward her, looking back at Ashley for approval. Ashley didn't seem happy but made her way toward Claire with him all the same.

"Was hoping I'd run into you guys this morning," Claire said with a wide smile. She gestured to two open seats beside her.

Ethan hesitated. He waited, hoping that Ashley would take the seat next to Claire. That way he wouldn't be guilty of doing so himself. Instead, Ashley sat in the other seat, studying Ethan's actions closely.

"Yeah, good running into a friendly face," Ethan said as he finally sat down.

Claire straightened her posture and looked to Ashley for a response. Ashley gave Claire a toothless smile, but her eyes were anything but smiling. Claire's own smile faded, but externally she remained perky and cheerful.

"I was sorry to see you didn't move on last night. *In Despair* was so much better than just another Robert Mitchelson novel. I mean they're all the same, it's getting a little old," Claire said to Ethan.

"Thanks. At first, I was really let down, but now it feels like that happened a week ago. I just want to enjoy the rest of the festival," Ethan said grabbing Ashley's hand. Ashley gripped him back, but it wasn't the same as it had been in the car.

Claire noticed their hands and her brow seemed to furrow a bit when she did. "Glad to hear you're taking it well. You really shouldn't let it get to you anyways. This whole thing is rigged if you ask me," Claire said, reaching for a pastry.

"How do you mean?" Ethan asked, "You moved on didn't you?"

Claire finished a small bite from the pastry. "Yes, I did. Exactly why I know it's rigged. My publisher made sure I schmoozed up the Book Club Members more than my opponent. They said it'd guarantee I moved on. They even gave me gift baskets to give them," Claire explained.

"Really?" Ethan asked squinting.

"Yup," Claire went on, "And with the amount of sales winning this competition can generate, I wouldn't be surprised if there's a lot more bribery than just gift baskets going on." Claire paused with a shrug. Then she grabbed her pastry again, but before she took a bite she said, "Real shame… I always thought this whole festival was about the quality of writing. Not just another popularity contest like the bestseller lists." With that, she took in a mouthful of pastry.

Ethan was about to respond, but Ashley interjected. "Are you trying to tell him that he didn't win because he didn't give out gift baskets?" She asked looking at Claire as if she were just an unpleasant odor drifting by.

Claire frowned at Ashley's aggressive tone. "Of course not. I'm only trying to -" Claire started. Ashley cut her off. "Whatever you're trying to do, you're being rude. Everything you just said means that your win is pretty much meaningless," she said.

Ethan's mind raced. He wanted to stand up for Claire. Ashley was overreacting over nothing.

On the other hand, he didn't want to risk going against Ashley. Things were going so well this morning, and she was just trying to stick up for him anyway.

Or is she just being jealous like the other day? Ethan realized. As he did, he noticed he was staring at Ashley with his jaw dropped. He hadn't even known he was doing it. He turned to Claire who gave pause for him to say something. When he hesitated she shook her head.

Claire picked up her plate and stood up. She looked right at Ethan, almost ignoring Ashley. "I don't need to listen to this. I only wanted to be friends with you guys, and I've been nothing but nice to you," she said, already walking away.

Ethan thought Ashley might say something else, but she remained silent as Claire left. He watched Claire as she walked away and briefly considered chasing after her to apologize. Instead, he faced his girlfriend. "Why did you lose it on her like that?" he asked, trying to sound as calm as he could.

Ashley's eyes widened and she directed her frown at Ethan. "Are you really going to defend her right now?" she asked in a hushed voice.

"Ash, it's not… I'm just trying to understand," Ethan managed.

"Trying to understand what? Why your girlfriend would stick up to an arrogant writer trying to rub your face in your loss? She's no better than Robert," Ashley scoffed. "You'd see that's what she was trying to do if you weren't so distracted by her looks," she finished.

Ethan sighed. "I'm not gonna be that guy that pretends she isn't attractive, but her looks have nothing to do with this. Babe, I could care less about some pretty girl when I've got you right here," Ethan elaborated.

"Sure," Ashley replied, "I saw Marcus practically fondling her with his eyes when we met her."

"How do Marcus' actions have any meaning here?" Ethan asked.

A stunned realization flashed on Ashley's face. "Well… I mean… You're both the same with that kind of thing. He's just so obvious, but I know you're better at hiding it," she explained as her cheeks reddened.

Ethan sighed. "Ash, I know you're upset, and I know Marcus and I are like brothers. But we're by no means twins, and when it comes to women we are nowhere near the same. I mean c'mon, he probably pictured Claire naked before he even learned her name. Is that what you think of me?" Ethan pleaded.

Ashley's face squinted like she'd just swallowed the world's most sour pastry. "I don't want to hear about the two of you picturing that attention whore naked! God dammit Ethan!" Ashley shouted, unintentionally making a scene. She stood up bringing her plate of pastries with her as she headed toward the nearest buffet table.

Ethan hurried after calling out to her, "That's not what I meant. I'm sorry, ok."

Ashley scoffed and turned toward him, stopping midway to the buffet table. "You're always sorry Ethan. But you know what? You're also always saying the wrong thing, and you're always making things worse. I think you need to ask yourself if you really care about this relationship. Because sometimes it almost seems like you're trying to sabotage it," she said.

Her words stabbed at him. The pain cut far deeper than Robert's insult the night before. He opened his mouth to reply but the words took a long moment to form. "Ashley. I'm… Can't we get out of here and just talk about this? I-" he started.

But Ashley cut him off as she turned away from him back toward the buffet table. "I'm going back to the cabin. I think it would be good if we had some space. Why don't you take a day to actually enjoy this trip. Focus on yourself a bit," she ordered as Ethan followed her up to the table.

Ethan was thrown off by her sudden outburst of anger and was unsure what to do. Maybe she's right. Maybe I just need to give her some space, he thought. His mind flashed to the poem he'd found in the cabin the night before. Maybe the answers lie in the heart of the forest, he reminded himself. It was then he decided that a day alone in town was the best solution, for more reasons than one.

"Maybe you're right," Ethan offered.

"Maybe," Ashley said bagging up her plate into takeaway containers laid out at the table. When she was done, she turned to face him. She looked like she wanted to say something, but instead, she turned to leave the breakfast area.

Ethan stood and watched as she left. As he did a loud voice cracked from the stage far behind him. "Good morning, everyone! Are you ready to kick off another fantastic day with some Poetry and Pastries!?" the voice asked booming from huge speakers.

Just kicking off another fantastic day, Ethan told himself shaking his head.

CHAPTER 12

The voice of a teenage girl, reading what sounded like her first-ever poem, slowly dissipated in the distance as Ethan made his way up Main Street and away from the banquet. He held his phone to his ear and listened to it ring. The call must have been one ring from going to voicemail when Marcus finally picked up.

"Hello?" Marcus asked with a groggy moan.

"Still sleeping?" Ethan asked in return, "Didn't mean to wake you."

Marcus managed a laugh entwined with a sigh. "It's a vacation, right?" he said.

Ethan smiled but said nothing for what felt like a long moment. Finally, he said, "Marcus, about last night. I'm sorry."

Marcus exhaled a long breath. "You've got nothing to be sorry about man. I totally overreacted. She's your girlfriend, and I know you were trying to save her just as much as I was. I shouldn't have snapped at you like that, but I was just scared. Y'know?" Marcus said in one of the most earnest tones Ethan had ever heard from him.

"I appreciate you saying that. But you were right. Thank God you were there because I wouldn't have reached her in time," Ethan admitted.

"None of that matters. Let's just be glad that nobody got hurt. I just hope you know that I'm sorry about how that went down. I just want us to be cool," Marcus said.

"We're cool," Ethan replied softly, "That's actually why I'm calling you."

"What do you mean?" Marcus asked.

The voice of the young girl stopped far behind Ethan, but it was followed by applause that echoed up the street.

"Ashley's on her way back to the cabin without me. We got in a stupid argument, and I'm going to hang out in town while she cools off. I was just hoping that you could do me a solid and make sure she actually cools off and doesn't stew over it," Ethan explained.

Marcus cleared his throat. "Oh man… I'd ask what happened but I'm sure I'll hear all about it soon… You've got it bud, I'll make sure she's cooled off for you. No fueling the fire from me."

"Thanks man," Ethan said, "You're a good friend."

Marcus paused and just said, "Sometimes."

"You are," Ethan insisted, "We're cool. I'll talk to you later, ok? Thanks again."

"Yeah, you got it. Later," Marcus said, and Ethan ended the call. Putting his phone into his pocket, Ethan spotted the Ustumah City Museum a little further down the street. He wasn't sure what he was looking for, but he felt that the Museum was the best place to start. Ethan took out the piece of paper he'd found in the gun and read the poem again.

"The heart of the woods,
fiction is reality,
there your answers lie."

A haiku on a small piece of parchment paper, Ethan thought. He realized earlier that it was no different than the poem by the Unknown Poet outside of the museum. Also a haiku, and also on a very similar small piece of parchment paper.

As Ethan reached the museum he looked at the poem on the wall again.

"All fear the lover,
Most dangerous beast of all.
Its greed knows no end."
-Unknown Poet

Looking at the poem with new eyes, Ethan felt different about it. He figured that this poem couldn't have anything to do with the one he was carrying. But after finding the cryptic poem everything the

Unknown Poet wrote seemed to carry so much more weight in his eyes. He felt a chill run up him and the hairs on the back of his neck shot up.

Ethan looked to the entrance of the museum where a large "Closed" sign hung. Defeated, Ethan considered coming back later. He was just about to turn away when he spotted a large man moving around inside the museum.

What have I got to lose? Ethan thought to himself as he moved toward the door. He knocked gently, yet loud enough to get the man's attention, who was now moving toward him. He opened the door and greeted Ethan.

"How can I help you?" the man asked in a heavy Jamaican accent.

"Yes, hi. Um, you see, I didn't realize the museum wasn't open yet and when I saw you inside, I was hoping you'd allow me to have an early look around," Ethan explained.

"And why would I let you do that?" the man asked frowning.

Ethan hesitated, but he figured there had to be some perks to being one of the sixteen writers attending the festival. "Well, um, I'm Ethan Garland. I'm one of the writers invited here for the festival. I was hoping that-" Ethan started, but the man interrupted.

"I know who you are," the man scoffed, crossing his arms. He stared at Ethan, looking him up and down. When he seemed satisfied he continued. "I guess I shouldn't upset the Book Club by denying you." He walked into the museum without another word, leaving the door open behind him.

Ethan followed and shut the door behind him. The museum was dimly lit, and though it was a foggy morning outside it took Ethan a moment for his eyes to adjust.

"Thank you," Ethan offered as he stepped further into the museum, "I really appreciate it.

Sorry, but I didn't get your name."

"Deaven," the man replied without even looking Ethan's way.

Ethan could take a hint and decided not to continue attempting small talk. Instead, he stopped and looked around. The museum was smaller than he had imagined. It was divided into three small sections. On the far side were exhibits that seemed related to the

Ustumah tribe, in the middle were exhibits that looked to be about the early settlers and the gold rush, and on the other side there was nothing but things related to the Unknown Poet. Ethan's first instinct was to check the section regarding the Unknown Poet. However, as he made his way over Deaven spoke up.

"No. The museum is best enjoyed chronologically," Deaven said glaring at Ethan. He pointed to the other end of the museum where the Ustumah tribe exhibits were located.

Afraid to offend Deaven any further, Ethan turned and walked to the other side of the museum. "Thank you," he said nodding at Deaven who didn't respond. Instead, the curator looked down at something at the desk he'd just moved to.

Ethan approached the first exhibits in the Ustumah tribe section of the museum. There was a wide range of handcrafted items from knives to bowls to simple paints. Ethan felt Deaven's eyes on him as he thoroughly read the descriptions of each item. His interest piqued at a large bowl. The bowl was excessively large, big enough to fit a meal that could easily feed twenty people. The inside of the bowl was covered by a mural. The mural depicted a tribe of people upon the outer edges of the bowl. The people all seemed to be either bowing before or offering gifts to a large figure in the center of the bowl. The figure was far more detailed than the simplistically drawn people of the tribe. At first, it appeared as a simple tree, but as Ethan looked at it longer, he began to make out that it was also a face. The face looked out at the people with stern eyes.

Ethan read the bowl's description outside its display case. This large bowl, known as a sharing bowl, played a very large part in Ustumah culture. Every full moon the tribe would cook a grand meal to fill the bowl. The tribe would then gather around the bowl and share the meal as tribal elders and other tribe members deemed worthy would share stories they had crafted since the last full moon. The Ustumah people believed that a powerful spirit lived deep within the forest. They believed that the spirit created the Ustumah for the sole purpose of regaling it with intriguing stories. They also believed that denying the spirit its right to stories, or telling stories it found unworthy, would incur the spirit's wrath.

Ethan thought back to the poem he had found. He almost pulled it out of his pocket but felt a strange intuition that he should not reveal it in front of Deaven. Instead, he turned to Deaven and asked, "This spirit of the forest that the Ustumah believed in, have you ever heard of it referred to as the heart of the forest?"

Deaven's eyes shot up, focusing on Ethan. As Ethan met his gaze, he noticed an uneasy similarity between the way Deaven was looking at him now and the way the wolves had been eyeing Ashley the night before.

"What makes you ask that?" Deaven demanded.

Ethan hadn't anticipated that reaction and didn't know what to say. "It's just that I'd heard that somewhere else recently. Just thought about it while I was reading about this bowl," Ethan explained. It wasn't exactly the truth, but it wasn't exactly a lie either.

Deaven narrowed his eyes at Ethan before looking back down at his desk. "Uh-huh. Well, you best continue with the rest of the exhibits. You will find your answer," he said shooing Ethan on.

Ethan continued toward the end of the Ustumah exhibits, passing by miniature models of living structures, examples of burial ceremonies, and more. The final exhibit displayed a drawing of what appeared to be an Ustumah Chief. Directly next to the drawing was a painting that depicted an army of men with rifles shooting down at the Ustumah tribe. In the painting, some of the Ustumah appeared to be fighting back, while most ran.

Ethan read the description:

Pictured to the left, the Ustumah Chief Maacam na Maawyk (or Chief Fifteen) was the last Chief of the Ustumah.

It was said that Chief Maacam na Maawyk gathered many of his people for a grand ceremony. As they all feasted the Chief regaled them with a tale about a people discovering a new land full of promise and new opportunity. Unfortunately, another less civilized people already held control of the land, and despite efforts to peacefully coexist a war eventually broke out. The proud people wiped out the savages and claimed the land for themselves.

After the story, the Chief revealed that this was his vision of the Ustumah people's future. The Chief had always wanted more for his people. He dreamed of leading them to further lands and taking them from what he deemed lesser tribes. Later when the new settlers arrived and an eventual conflict broke out between them and the Ustumah, many Ustumah blamed Chief Maacam na Maawyk' story.

They believed that the spirit in the forest was punishing the Ustumah people for their Chief's greed and had turned his story against him. They believed that the Ustumah were filling the role of the people whose land was now being taken from them. The conflict eventually ended in a slaughter of the Ustumah people by the settlers, pictured to the right. The Ustumah tribe's version of this history is preserved through distant relatives with loose interpretations or stories passed down from long-dead ancestors.

Most historians agree that the similarities between the Chief's story and the eventual fall of the Ustumah people was merely a sad coincidence.

When he was finished reading Ethan bowed his head. He wasn't sure why he'd done it, but he felt that he at least owed some respect to the tragedy of the Ustumah people.

After a moment he turned to Deaven and noticed that the tall man had been staring at him. Deaven made an effort to look away as if he had never been looking in the first place. Ethan ignored it and moved on to the next exhibits.

The next section focused on Ustumah City's history during the California Gold Rush. Ethan learned a lot about the city's history by browsing the exhibits. During the Gold Rush Ustumah City was still known as Doe Creek and was nothing but a small logging town. But after more than a few successful finds, Doe Creek went from being a quiet town full of loggers to the busiest gold mining town in Northern California almost overnight.

Many people had come to Doe Creek in search of gold, but none found any luck. One day a down on his luck man named Dallas Sutter set out into the forest in search of gold with provisions he purchased with the last of his savings. It was a last desperate attempt to change his life before he went broke. Dallas wasn't heard from for months, and many assumed he was dead. Eventually, he turned up back in Doe Creek. He told of a discovery of an enormous gold deposit in a cave deep in the forest. When his claims turned out to be true, Dallas became one of the richest men in Ustumah City's history. His discovery drew others to the area and Doe Creek grew into a large gold rush city.

With the sudden influx of people came a rise in crime as well as many other things. People began to talk of strange happening in the forest. At one point a local man was hanged after telling a story describing a brutal murderer who lurked in the forests late at night hunting young women. When a series of murders occurred that matched his stories with eerie detail, the town assumed that he had told the stories with the intention of eventually carrying out the crimes himself. The man pleaded his innocence, insisting that the forest itself had brought his stories to life. The man was of course thought to be insane and was hung nonetheless.

Later in life, Dallas Sutter went mad with his old age. He became obsessed with finding a place he referred to constantly as the Heart of the Forest. He claimed that it was a place of great magic that he had visited many years ago and that without it he would have never discovered the gold. Dallas' family had him placed in a facility where he could be treated when it became obvious his obsession with the so-called Heart of the Forest became unhealthy. He began to waste large amounts of his wealth hiring people to scour the forest for the magical place he described. Nobody ever found anything of the sort.

When Ethan read about Dallas Sutter's mention of the Heart of the Forest, he felt butterflies in his stomach. He turned to Deaven who was now openly staring.

"You find what you were looking for?" Deaven asked.

Ethan nodded. "I guess so," he admitted, "but I was mostly wondering if the Heart of the Forest was at all related to the Unknown Poet."

Deaven cocked his head to the side, inspecting Ethan curiously. "Not that I know of. But feel free to have a look," Deaven said motioning toward the last section of the museum.

"Thanks," Ethan said, noting the wolfish look in Deaven's eyes again. As he headed toward the Unknown Poet exhibits Ethan noticed from the corner of his eye that Deaven didn't look back down at his desk this time. Instead, his eyes were focused directly on

Ethan, watching his every move. Uncomfortable, Ethan shifted his gaze away from the man's staring.

Ethan read about the Unknown Poet, most of which he already knew. The only thing known was that they had lived in Ustumah City. Their actual identity was still a mystery. That mystery of identity certainly didn't stop, and possibly contributed to, the Unknown Poet's works being recognized as some of the most intriguing poetry to have ever been written.

Ethan browsed a few of the poems, but another in the haiku format stood out to him. The poem, Ethan thought, was a perfect example of why the Unknown Poet was so popular.

Warning to the fool,
Magic uncontrollable,
Best to leave it be.

It was cryptic enough to make the reader wonder what the poet had truly meant, but relatable enough that they could come away with their own interpretation. Ethan considered asking Deaven his opinion on the poem but decided against it. At first he'd felt that he had merely inconvenienced Deaven, but now he was starting to feel that the man's distaste for his presence was something more.

Ethan read on, viewing more and more examples of the poet's works. Mostly haiku, clearly the poet had a preference. One poem, however, stood out from the rest. Not just because it wasn't a haiku, but because it told a story. The other poems were vague statements, but this one had a beginning, middle, and end.

A writer with ambitions for the world,
Discovery of a power untouched,
Now temptation takes hold,
Curse self-inflicted by work rushed,
Innocents now pay the debt of this mistake,
To bring back balance the writer must atone,
To set things right, a choice they must make,
The price to be paid: to have never been known.

The final line made Ethan wonder if the poem was more autobiographical than it was fiction. Had they kept their work anonymous to punish themselves for something? He wasn't even sure if the Unknown Poet had kept their own identity secret, or if their works had been discovered after their death, and no one simply knew who they had been. There wasn't much information posted about how the poet's work had come to become public, and once again Ethan refrained from asking Deaven.

Not having found any mention of the heart of the forest in any of the poet's other works, Ethan continued searching. When he was done reading all the poems in the museum he still hadn't found anything. There was one other poem that grabbed his interest while browsing, so he decided to give it another look.

We all have stories that we'd like told,
But it's the world that decides which ones take hold, Though when
they come from the Heart we can still shape our fate,
We just have to do so before it's too late.

The poem had only initially grabbed Ethan's interest because it was the only other poem that mentioned a heart. On his reread though, he noticed one detail that made all the difference to him. The H in "Heart" was capitalized. A proper noun, Ethan realized. He knew that had to mean something, but it still didn't give him much to go on. He was going to have to shake his fear of an awkward conversation with Deaven and ask him for help.

Ethan started as he turned to address Deaven, "Does anyone know why the Unknown Poet chose to capitalize the H in-" As Ethan turned around, he stopped short. Deaven was towering over him.

"I think you've spent enough time browsing and asking questions. I still have a lot of work to finish before the museum officially opens," Deaven snapped, emphasizing the word 'officially.'

Ethan swallowed hard. "I didn't mean to offend you, it's just-" Ethan attempted an explanation.

Deaven interrupted, "I don't care for you writers. You come here thinking you're better than us. Now you're trying to stick your noses where they don't belong. You should know, I don't take kindly to outsiders who take too much of an interest in our history here. You best drop whatever it is you think you're doing. Understand?"

Ethan had a feeling that if he didn't agree, the huge man would crush him right there on the spot. So, he nodded. "You seem like a serious guy, so I'm gonna take that seriously. I'll just be leaving," Ethan said slowly sliding past Deaven who made little room for him to pass. Once he was around Deaven, he scurried toward the entrance.

As Ethan let himself out, Deaven called to him. "I hope this is the last time we discuss this, Ethan."

Ethan just nodded and shut the door behind him, letting out a deep sigh of relief.

CHAPTER 13

Ashley laid out on the bed. A light breeze blew in from the room's open window, cooling her naked body. She let out a relaxed sigh and brushed away a bead of sweat that crept down the side of her face. She rolled over and grabbed her phone from the nearby nightstand and checked the time. She'd been back at the cabin for about an hour. She wondered what Ethan had been up to on his own. Part of her wanted to call him and apologize. She felt that she'd been irrational at breakfast and the guilt was building up. In their relationship, guilt was not a new concept. Snapping at Ethan over something out of his control was far from the worst of her offenses.

As Ashley stared at her phone, the bathroom door to her room swung open behind her. *Here comes my worst offense now,* she thought to herself as she turned to face the bathroom.

Marcus walked out with a pep in his step, also completely naked. He smiled at her, hopped onto the bed beside her, and put his hand on her back. He let out a deep sigh. "That was nice. I hope you feel as good as I do. We need that," he said.

Ashley shrugged his hand off, rolled onto her side, and covered herself with a blanket. "I don't feel great Marcus," she said, frowning at him. "I just cheated on my boyfriend for the umpteenth time. I don't exactly feel like an amazing person right now."

The smile disappeared off Marcus' face, and he looked away from Ashley. "We've talked about this how many times now? We shouldn't be ruining what happy moments we get together by bringing the guilt into it. I don't love betraying my best friend like this, but I do love you. I'm sorry to admit it but that means so much more to me. You feel the same way, otherwise we wouldn't be here for the 'umpteenth' time," he explained.

Ashley scoffed. "Yeah, but you know what Marcus? Maybe you don't love me. Maybe I'm betraying a great guy that does, all because of a lie. Saying you love me is nothing but words." Ashley said quickly, raising her voice. "Your actions don't always show it."

"You're gonna bring Ethan's 'nothing but words comment' into this? Everything else aside, how does me charging into a pack of wolves not proof that I love you?" Marcus asked, frustration growing in his voice.

Ashley hesitated, but then she blurted, "If you love me, then why are you always looking at other girls? Like that poet Claire? You were practically already having sex with her in your head when we first met her."

Marcus stared blankly as her words washed over him. Then he leaned back and laughed, "Is that seriously what this is all about? You're having doubts about us because you're jealous of Claire? You thought Ethan had a thing for her. Now it's me?"

"I don't know! I just got so jealous when I saw you checking her out. And she's practically a match made in heaven for Ethan so that made me jealous too. Here I am struggling to keep our relationship afloat and dream girl walks up. I mean how fucked up is it that I'm sitting there insecure that my boyfriend likes this girl more than me, but at the same time I'm jealous that you are checking her out. You, my boyfriend's best friend that I've been sleeping with for over a year. I'm a fucked up person, I'm sorry!" Ashley shouted back at Marcus. When she was finished tears started streaming down her face and she started sobbing.

Marcus pulled himself up and grabbed Ashley. He pulled her head toward his shoulder and rubbed her back with his other hand. For a split second she resisted, but then she buried her face into his chest and let out even more tears. Marcus had so much he wanted to say, but at the same time he wasn't sure if there was even a right thing to say. So instead he kissed Ashley on her shoulder and fought back tears of his own.

When Marcus kissed her Ashley looked up at him, and still crying managed, "I'm sorry."

Marcus cupped her face in both hands and pulled her close. "I'm sorry too. I understand how you feel more than you know," he said.

Ashley held back her tears and placed a hand near Marcus' neck. "No, I know. I see it in you. I know this is as hard for you as it is for me. And I love you for it. And I'm a fucked person for it, but I do. I love you for it."

Marcus pulled Ashley closer until their foreheads were touching. "Then I'm fucked up too, because I love you too."

Then with neither sure who initiated it, they were kissing. They brought each back down to the bed, and one thing led to another. For those next moments the whole conversation and all of their worries flew away.

When their distraction faded, they found themselves lying next to each other on the bed. A taunting silence sat between them. The curtains at the other end of the room fluttered in the breeze, emphasizing the silence even more.

After what seemed like forever, Ashley broke the silence. "You know, I had a thing for you before I even started dating Ethan," she started.

Marcus nodded, "Same."

Ashley smiled weakly at Marcus and nodded back. He started to say more, but Ashley held up a hand to silence him.

"Let me finish this, ok," she said, continuing without giving him time to reply. "I only ever saw Ethan as a friend, but that never meant he didn't mean a lot to me. That night when he pulled me aside at the bar and told me how he felt, I don't know what changed but all of a sudden I knew I was supposed to be with him. I realized I loved him. I just couldn't see it before then." Ashley took a pause and swallowed before continuing.

"Then we started dating, and we were so happy. Happier than I ever thought I would be with someone. It was going great, until Ethan started to grow distant. I didn't know what it was, but things changed so quickly. I could hardly get him to spend time with me anymore. I was so lonely in the relationship. But you were there for me when I needed someone. And though I know neither of us planned it, we fell for each other. What happened, what's been happening, is wrong for more than one reason. But that doesn't change the fact that we have strong feelings for each other.

But our feelings don't change the fact that I've been trying to make things work with Ethan. All the while continuing to have this on the side with you. I think I've let this go on because I blamed Ethan for things going wrong in the first place. Maybe I've secretly thought that it didn't matter if we kept this up because there was no hope for me and him anyway."

Marcus cut in, "We've talked about this before Ash. If you don't think things with you two will ever work, then-"

Ashley put up another hand, cutting him off. "Sorry, but I still have more to say. Just hear me out," she said through sad eyes. "This whole idea that what we've been doing is somehow forgivable because Ethan's the problem, is all based on the idea that Ethan created the distance between me and him. But I'm realizing that isn't true. Like I said before, I had a thing for you before Ethan and I even started dating. When Ethan and I were together I was truly happy with him, but that didn't mean that my feelings for you just disappeared. I don't think I ever put those feelings away. And now, I think that I may have been the one to grow distant first. Somewhere deep down I knew I still had feelings for you, and I became unsure of my relationship with Ethan. How can I blame Ethan for being distant, if he was just reacting to a girlfriend who wasn't even sure she wanted to be with him anymore."

Ashley took another pause, taking a deep breath, almost trembling. "Marcus, as much as I want to say that this realization makes me want to leave Ethan and just be with you, that wouldn't be fair to me or him. This relationship deserves a chance. We were happy once, and I screwed it all up when I gave into my feelings for you. I need to put them aside and actually try to make things work with Ethan. I'm sorry, but I'm ending this," Ashley managed. Tears were streaming down her face, but she was much more composed than when she'd been crying earlier.

Marcus was silent for a long time, but finally he nodded. "Maybe you're right. I love Ethan like a brother, and it's worn at me knowing I indulged in my own happiness at the expense of his. Maybe we should have done this a long time ago," Marcus admitted. "But I will say one thing. I don't know if I can just decide to stop loving you, and I think you'll have the same problem. If you decide this is what you want to do, then the healthy thing for both of us is if I'm not around anymore. I should separate myself from you both."

Ashley shook her head. "You can't just abandon Ethan like that, you two are like family," Ashley blurted.

"Maybe once. But family doesn't betray each other like I have. Besides, you guys will be so much happier together if I'm not around. It's the right thing to do Ash," Marcus admitted.

Ashley hesitated. "Maybe you're right, but I don't think we need to decide on that now. Let's just go back to being friends and see if we can do it. At least until the end of the trip," she said grabbing Marcus' hand.

Marcus smiled weakly and nodded, "Yeah, until the end of the trip and we'll see. For me this whole trip was about trying to fix things between Ethan and me. Maybe I should start working more at that. Trying to put my feelings for you aside may be part of that same goal."

With that he released Ashley grip on his hand, got up off the bed and walked out of the room. As he was leaving he turned to Ashley and said, "I'm sorry Ashley. I love you." And then he was gone.

Ashley buried her face in her hands. Once again she was sobbing deeply, but this time there was no one there to comfort her.

CHAPTER 14

Ethan hurried down Main Street putting as much distance between himself and the museum as he could. Ethan had felt intimidated by Deaven the moment he met him, but at the end of their encounter at the museum his feeling had gone quickly from intimidated to threatened. He couldn't shake the feeling that Deaven knew a lot more about what was going on than Ethan could have initially thought. And for whatever reason, he really didn't want Ethan to know anymore than he already did.

When Ethan was a few blocks away, he slowed his pace, feeling more comfortable. The museum had revealed a lot about the "heart of the forest." It had been a huge comfort learning all that he had. Before he'd thought maybe he was going crazy seeing all of the examples of fiction playing out in reality. But now he knew that the area had a very long history of "stories coming to life." As reassuring as all the new information had been, Ethan had nothing new to go off of. This had all started with him wanting answers, and he wasn't satisfied that he'd found them. Ethan pulled the haiku out of his pocket and read it again.

"All fear the lover,
Most dangerous beast of all.
Its greed knows no end."

"There your answers lie," Ethan said aloud. Learning about the heart of the forest wasn't enough. He had to find it. He had to go there. Ethan looked down the street, past the park where the Poetry and Pastries event was still taking place, to the forest. The huge redwoods in the distance seemed to stretch on forever. Not gonna be an easy task, Ethan told himself. But then he had a sudden spark of inspiration. The "heart of" could easily mean "center." Even the large Ustumah ceremonial bowl had depicted the heart of the forest directly in the center.

Ethan felt a rush of excitement as he dug his phone out of his pocket, opening up his maps app. After messing with the settings for a few seconds, he was able to display a satellite image of the area. As he zoomed out, he got a bigger picture of the forest. It was immense, but it did have borders. Ustumah City was situated fairly deep within, but not so much the center. More toward the lower left "corner."

Ethan put a pin in the map at the dead center of the trees. Unfortunately, he noticed that there were no roads anywhere near that area. Starting to lose hope, he hesitated for a moment before another idea hit him in the face. He nodded to himself as he opened up the phone's web browser and searched for maps of local hiking trails. There were surprisingly more trails than Ethan had expected, and he was expecting there to be quite a few. Noticing that all of the local coffee places and restaurants were closed for the Poetry and Pastries event, Ethan took a seat up against a nearby wall. It took him a while, but eventually he had cross referenced all of the hiking trail maps with the map where he had pinned the center of the forest. He found that there was one trail that passed relatively close to the pin. Ethan wasn't much of a hiker, but he figured that he'd have to hike about two hours on the trail, and then anywhere from one to two more hours off the trail. The distance off trail was much shorter than on, but Ethan assumed that with no trail to follow he'd be slowed down significantly. At most, an eight-hour hike there and back, Ethan figured to himself. It was almost ten thirty at that point. He figured that by the time he had gone to the cabin, got ready, gone to the trail, gone on the hike, and back to the cabin, all in all it would be ten and a half to eleven hours. Doable today, Ethan realized. He didn't even bother calling Ashley or Marcus for a ride back. He didn't have the time to wait for them to drive into town first. Instead he opened up his favorite ride sharing app and requested a ride. When the car arrived Ethan took a moment to text Ashley and let her know he'd got a ride home to save her the trip.

Back at the cabin Ethan gave his driver a substantial tip. He'd noticed how annoyed they had been about having to take him so far into the forest, and up the dirt road. The driver smiled at the tip and thanked Ethan before taking off back down the dirt road. Ethan had butterflies in his stomach realizing that things with Ashley would probably still be tense. He stood at the door for a moment collecting himself, and then he entered.

It was colder inside the cabin than Ethan had expected, barely any warmer than it had been outside. A chilly breeze made its way through the cabin and Ethan shivered as he shut the door behind him. Ethan made his way towards he and Ashley's room, but stopped when he saw Marcus eating alone at the kitchen table. Marcus greeted him as he approached.

"Eating alone? I thought you were supposed to cool her down for me. You know I meant to make her less mad at me, not physically cool her down," Ethan whispered joking about the temperature of the cabin.

Marcus finished a bite of his pastry and put on a smile in response to the joke. He was smiling but Ethan could tell he seemed sad. "Don't look at me, she's the one who had a window open. And no guarantees but I think she may be cooled off," Marcus whispered back.

"You're the best, man," Ethan said starting toward his room. Marcus just nodded, breaking eye contact, "No problem bro."

Inside the bedroom, Ethan noticed Ashley on the bed. She was curled up wearing multiple layers of clothing and reading a book.

"Hey," Ethan said, testing the waters.

Ashley looked up at him and said, "Give me a second I'm at a good part."

Ethan obliged and headed straight for the open window, shutting it abruptly. At that, Ashley set the book down, which Ethan finally realized was his personal copy of *"In Despair."*

"You're reading that again?" Ethan asked, surprised.

Ashley grinned at him. "Again. With fresh eyes this time. Its a good reminder of how talented you are."

Ethan felt a wave of relief crash over him. Marcus or not, she was definitely cheered up. "Thanks babe. It actually feels really good to hear that," Ethan said moving to join her on the bed.

"By the way, I know it gets cold, but I like the fresh air," Ashley said, giving him puppy dog eyes.

Ethan laughed, hopped off the bed and threw the window back open. He opened one of the dressers and replaced his blazer with a sweatshirt. A clock on the nightstand caught Ethan's eye and reminded him that he was on a time crunch. Especially if he wanted to finish his search in the forest before it got too late. Instead of joining Ashley on the bed like he intended, he made his way over to his suitcase in the corner of the room.

Ethan turned to Ashley as he began digging through his suitcase. "I'm sorry about how everything went this morning," Ethan began.

"Don't be," Ashley interjected quickly. "It was all my fault. I should trust you more, and Claire didn't deserve that from me. I feel like a total bitch."

Ethan was surprised by her attitude, considering he'd half expected her not to even talk to him when he got home. "You don't have to apologize. You've been nothing but a supportive girlfriend this entire trip and I think you just finally snapped when I wasn't returning the favor," Ethan confided.

Ashley shook her head. "Don't put it all on yourself. We both have been really stressed. Things have been tough between us and we've been trying to make things better, but the pressure is just straining things even more," she said, stopping to get off the bed and walk over to Ethan. "Listen," she said, putting her hand on the back of his neck, "I don't think either of us have been our best selves lately. But I think we can be. We just need a fresh start. I want what happened this morning to be a turning point, not a boiling point. What do you say? Start over?" She finished.

Ethan looked into her eyes and smiled. He gave her a long kiss on the lips. When she kissed him back it felt great. Just like he'd felt in the car ride that morning, like everything between them was perfect. The only flaw in the moment was the quiet voice in the back of his head. It's all a lie. She could never truly love you. This kiss feels great to you, but she's straining to enjoy it. All because she feels bad for you. Pathetic. With that Ethan broke off the tender kiss.

"I love you. I wanted this trip to be special, and I want nothing more than to start over and give it that chance. I'm just lucky to have a girl like you. One that's willing to keep going at this," Ethan said.

"I know that we're worth it babe," Ashley said, pecking Ethan on the lips. "By the way what are you working on over here?" She asked, noticing Ethan pull a backpack, some shorts, and a workout shirt out of the suitcase.

"Oh yeah, earlier I decided I wanted to go on a hike," Ethan paused. "Honestly, I thought you may still be mad when I got back, so I made plans on my own. I hope that's ok?" Ethan admitted.

"Of course it's fine. Why don't I join you?" Ashley asked.

Ethan blinked. He hadn't expected Ashley to want to join, and he wasn't sure how he'd explain wanting to go on a trail so far from the cabin. He especially wondered what he would say when part way through the trail he decided to venture deep into the forest. He couldn't tell her the truth. Her and Marcus had both been extremely skeptical whenever he'd brought up his fears regarding fiction and reality.

"Well… Babe, the thing is, I was thinking this is something I should do alone. I'm glad we had this talk, and I'm glad things are good between us. You know I love hiking with you, but I thought this would be a good way to clear my head. Alone, you know?" Ethan explained.

Ashley silently processed Ethan's words, for longer than he would have liked. Finally, she perked up. "I get it. It's a good idea to get some space," she admitted. "But don't forget that there's someone in the other room you've been hoping to mend fences with," Ashley said, nodding toward Marcus in the kitchen.

Ethan was about to protest, but Ashley called out to Marcus, "Marcus, what do you think about joining Ethan on a hike while I go into town? I'll get something to cook all of us a nice dinner."

Ethan gritted his teeth. Ashley didn't know why he wanted to go alone, and he realized she was just trying to be helpful. After all he had told her that a big part of this trip had been for him to try to save his friendship with Marcus. But that didn't change the fact that it would be just as hard to explain the "finer details" of his hike to Marcus as it would have been to Ashley.

Marcus appeared in the doorway of the bedroom. "Sounds great to me. Been a while since we've gone on a hike together man," Marcus said gesturing to Ethan. "It'll be different, going on a hike out here in real 'nature.' Nothing like the hikes near the city."

Ethan considered making up an excuse to turn Marcus away, but he couldn't think of anything that wouldn't seem offensive. Things with Marcus were strained enough, and this was an opportunity to make things better. Instead Ethan happily agreed to let Marcus join. He knew explaining things to Marcus would be just as hard as they would be to explain to Ashley, but at least he'd have an easier time convincing Marcus to go along with it. If he told Ashley, she'd put a stop to it. Marcus was much more likely to begrudgingly go along with it. Ethan decided he would cross that bridge when he came to it.

Not an hour later Marcus and Ethan had packed their bags with water and snack bars, and were changed into more appropriate hiking attire. Ashley dropped them off at the trail on her way into town. Ashley's drive into town had been the perfect excuse to choose a trail, specifically that trail, so far from the cabin or town.

"Since you're going into town anyway, mind dropping us off at a particular trail. It's a ways away from the cabin, but it has excellent reviews," Ethan has said. Ashley had happily agreed, letting them know to call her for a pickup when they were finished.

When Ashley was gone, the two friends started off down the trail into the forest. Marcus quickly began happily rambling on. Ethan was only half paying attention, distracted by the future. What was he going to find when he reached the heart of the forest? How was Marcus going to take it when he learned the truth? The questions swirled around in his head as they moved deeper and deeper into the forest.

CHAPTER 15

A little over an hour into their hike, Ethan and Marcus were chatting about old times laughing and smiling. At first Ethan had been so distracted, but Marcus had a way of bringing out Ethan's more relaxed side. It had always been that way, and Ethan figured that's why they were such good friends. Ethan grounded Marcus, while Marcus opened Ethan up. Growing up they'd always been known as Marcus and Ethan. Not just Ethan, and not just Marcus. Brothers, not by blood, but by bond.

Along the way Marcus periodically stopped to appreciate the forest. It was an uncommon thing for Marcus to do, and Ethan normally would have appreciated it if it wasn't slowing them down. Every time Marcus would slow down or stop altogether, Ethan would nudge him along. Politely at first, but more urgently as it continued.

Eventually Marcus stopped at a large boulder and climbed atop it. "Good place to take a break, don't you think?" Marcus suggested through labored breaths.

Marcus was in much better shape than Ethan, and even he was starting to grow tired. Ethan was exhausted, but he couldn't stop if he wanted to make it back before it was too late. He knew Ashley was already going to be upset that they'd be getting back as late as they would.

Ethan stopped and looked up at Marcus, grabbing his sides and catching his breath. "Can't stop now," he managed through deep inhales and exhales. When Marcus made no sign of moving Ethan motioned onward, "Come on. The tough guy getting tired?"

Marcus narrowed his eyes at Ethan and sat down more comfortably. "You're way more tired than I am, I can see it. I mean shit man; you've been pushing me along the whole way. I've never seen you like this, normally you're the one enjoying the hike. What's the rush man?" Marcus questioned.

Ethan realized that Marcus wasn't going to listen unless he told him the truth. They weren't far from the point where they'd need to go off trail and head towards the center of the forest anyway. At that point Ethan knew he'd have to tell Marcus what was going on, so he figured it made little difference if he told him now or then. Ethan walked back and joined his friend on the boulder. Marcus waited silently for Ethan's reply, seeing the seriousness on his friend's face.

"This isn't just a fun hike to me. I originally planned on going alone, because there's something I have to do. I'm sorry I kept it from you, but I knew you wouldn't believe me or understand. I knew I'd have to tell you eventually, but I need you to promise you won't tell Ashley," Ethan explained.

Marcus shook his head. "C'mon man, don't make me get involved in some lie," he said.

"It's not like that," replied Ethan. "It's just that things between her and I look like they're finally going to get better. But I don't know how she's going to react if she thinks I'm going crazy."

Marcus widened his eyes at that. "So this is about your obsession with books coming to life? Dude, they're just coincidences," Marcus said plainly.

"At first, I couldn't admit they were just coincidences, but I realized you guys were probably right and I tried to let it go. But then, Ashley got attacked by those wolves just like a scene out of the *The Pack* and-" Ethan began.

Marcus interrupted, anger in his voice, "And you almost let her die because you ran in after that worthless gun. Why, because you read that's the way to save her in a book? C'mon man. That is exactly why obsessing over this is dangerous. Makes you make poor decisions."

Marcus had hit a soft spot, and Ethan felt his frustration growing. He didn't want to get into an argument with Marcus, so he tried to stay calm.

"Don't be an asshole. You know I feel horrible about that. That alone would have been enough to make me forget about it. But something else happened," Ethan explained.

Marcus said nothing and continued listening.

Ethan continued, "A piece of paper fell out of the gun when I checked to see if it was loaded. At first, I hardly even noticed it with everything that was going on. But afterwards when I was putting the gun back, I saw it lying on the ground and picked it up." Ethan fished the poem out of his pocket and handed it to Marcus who hastily took it and read it.

"It's a poem," Ethan said as Marcus read.

When Marcus was finished reading, he handed it back to Ethan and asked, "So what? This hike is all about finding the heart of the forest? All based on some poem?"

Ethan nodded confidently. "I know it sounds crazy, but I don't think it's a coincidence that I found this poem. That last line, 'There your answers lie,' really meant something to me. I don't expect you to understand, but I've been living with this feeling for over a year now. This feeling that there's something going on that I'm just con-stantly on the outskirts of figuring out. And I've just always felt that if I could figure it out, it would be the answer to all my problems. I know it sounds stupid, but when I found this poem it just made me all the more certain of it. If you don't want to be a part of this, fine. You can turn around whenever you want, I'll go alone. All I ask is that you don't tell Ashley," Ethan told Marcus.

Marcus swallowed and his pulse quickened. A tide of guilt was swelling inside his gut. His best friend was unknowingly describing Marcus' affair with Ashley, but didn't even know it. The guilt alone was enough to make Marcus understand Ethan's strange obsession with solving this mystery. He decided. He would support Ethan in this, no matter how ridiculous it seemed. But first, he needed more answers.

"I won't tell Ashley, and I'm not gonna let you just wander into the middle of the forest alone. I'm with you, but you gotta tell me why it is you're so sure about all this. It can't just be because of some poem you found. What else do you know?" Marcus asked.

Ethan was surprised by Marcus' receptive attitude, but more so he was thankful. Ethan told Marcus everything he knew. From the Ustumah tribe's worship of a magical forest deity to unexplainable happenings during the Gold Rush, and finally to his hunch that the

Unknown Poet was also somehow aware or linked to some magical power that resided in the area.

Marcus soaked it all in before responding. "Ok, I get it," he started. "I'm not saying I believe in magic or that any of what you are saying is real. But I can understand why you're so set on looking into it, I mean hell, you've piqued my interest."

"As stupid as it sounds, finding answers is more exciting to me then the prospect of proving the existence of some magical power," Ethan admitted.

The guilt was swirling in Marcus' stomach again. "No, I understand," he managed.

Without a word Ethan stood up and jumped down from the boulder onto the trail. Looking up at Marcus he said, "So I've got no idea what we're going to find out here. Or how long exactly it's going to take us to find it. Now, I don't know about you, but after that wolf attack I'm not looking to be out in this forest in the dead of night. That's why I've been in such a hurry. And no offense, but explaining this all to you just ate up even more time."

Marcus dismounted the boulder, joining Ethan on the trail. "Alright, alright. Let's go then," Marcus ordered, gesturing down the trail.

With that they continued down the trail, this time much quieter than before. As they walked in silence Ethan wondered if Marcus had really meant it when he'd said he understood Ethan's point of view. That or Marcus just hadn't wanted to tell Ethan he was being ridiculous.

Marcus, on the other hand, was weighed down by the growing realization of just how much his and Ashley's affair had affected Ethan. He wanted to apologize but knew he couldn't without admitting the affair in the first place. He knew that would only hurt Ethan more, so instead he chose silence.

Ethan and Marcus reached a certain point on the trail, and Ethan stopped looking down at his phone. "This is it for the trail. We make our own path from here," Ethan said stepping off the trail into some brush.

Marcus followed cautiously. "This ought to be fun," he joked.

The junction broke the tension between the two, and it wasn't long before they were chatting like old friends again. Ethan vented about the festival and his loss to Robert, while Marcus reminded him that the whole thing was rigged anyway. Both men lost their footing more than a few times, tripping on a loose root or stumbling over a bush. Marcus joked multiple times that the situation was a great reminder of why he hated nature.

A little over two hours passed this way, with the friends stopping a few times to rest, eat, and drink. Ethan was enjoying the day with his lifelong friend so much, he almost forgot his original purpose for heading into the forest. Today had been the first time in a long time that things between Marcus and him had felt pure and uncorrupted by the dark cloud that had loomed over them the past year.

The same held true for Marcus. For him it was great to spend time with Ethan without Ashley around. As much as he loved Ashley, she was a constant reminder that he'd betrayed his best friend, as well as that the love of his life was dating another man. Those two simple facts were the root of Marcus' deteriorating friendship with Ethan. The hike was a way for him to escape those things and appreciate Ethan for the friend and brother he had always been. It gave Marcus hope that their friendship could still be salvaged.

When Marcus finished a joke about how Ethan should spend the royalty money from '*In Despair*,' Ethan stopped and checked the map on his phone. "We're close. And I'm lucky to get any reception out here. I'd say maybe another half hour of walking and we'll be there," Ethan explained.

Marcus took the moment to scan their surroundings. The further they had strayed from the trail, the more the trees had blotted out the sun. Though now Marcus felt that the forest had suddenly taken a drastic change in lighting. It was not even dusk, though the forest had grown dark as night. "What exactly are we looking for when we get there anyway? A huge beating heart, a talking tree, or a wise old man?" Marcus asked.

"I have no idea, but I figure that we'll know it when we find it. Also, I can't tell if you're mocking me with those examples. Either way they're pretty creative. Maybe you should have been a writer," Ethan said smirking at Marcus.

Marcus scoffed, "Like I said, that writer crap just isn't for me. Any creativity I have is probably just from you talking my ear off about it all these years. I mean seriously man, if-" Marcus stopped suddenly. He'd seen something out beyond the trees in the darkest portion of the forest. It looked like a large looming figure, twice the size of any man. "Did you see that?" He asked Ethan.

Ethan looked over toward where Marcus had turned his attention but saw nothing. "What?" Ethan asked calmly. "It's the forest Marcus, there's plenty of animals out here."

"Are there?" Marcus asked morbidly. "Listen."

Ethan stopped and listened. He heard nothing. And it wasn't a comforting nothing that reassured him Marcus' sudden fear was unreasonable. Rather, it was a disturbing nothing. An absence of noise. Where moments ago there had been the sound of plants rustling and birds chirping, there was now nothing. The hair stood up on the back of Ethan's neck. He couldn't explain it, but he knew something horrible was nearby. Something much worse than a pack of hungry wolves.

"What did you see?" Ethan whispered to Marcus.

Marcus pointed into the darkness and Ethan saw a large shadowy figure moving in the distance. It was too far to make out in the dark. The sheer size of it led Ethan to believe it was a bear. In fact, he hoped it was a bear. Whatever it was it was moving toward them slowly.

Marcus kept his eyes trained on the figure and put himself between it and Ethan. Without looking away, he put his hand back and started pushing Ethan backward. "We need to leave, now. Quietly," Marcus instructed.

Ethan complied without even thinking. He slowly began backing away, keeping his eyes locked on the approaching danger. Marcus began doing the same, but remained about a dozen feet ahead of Ethan. Disturbingly, as the figure grew closer, rather than becoming clearer, it's true shape became more ambiguous. A quiet sound emanated from the figure, breaking the eerie silence of the forest. It was a constant but whispered breath as if something were quietly exhaling but never stopping to breath in. The sound sent a shiver through Ethan's entire body, and his eyes began to water. He realized that everything about the figure instilled him with fear. It wasn't so much that he was scared of the figure, though he was, but rather like raw fear was being torn from his depths. As far as Ethan was concerned he was being approached by something of pure evil. The realization made him even more fearful. Every fiber of his body was screaming at him to run and put as much distance between himself and the figure as possible.

Marcus, whose father had pushed him to be so, had always seen himself as the fearless, determined hero of his own story. It wasn't that he didn't get scared, but rather that he had learned to put fear aside as to not be affected by it. The quiet whisper of the figure grew slowly louder as it grew closer, and Marcus felt his legs trembling. It was taking every ounce of will he had to remind himself that they had not been spotted. To remind himself that the best course of action was to quietly put distance between it and themselves. All the while he was being bombarded with one thought.

Run.

The feeling of fear overtaking him was not something Marcus was used to, and it was distracting him. That was why he didn't hear Ethan lightly stumble over the large tree root behind them or hear Ethan's whispered warning. Marcus took another step back and his heel fully caught the root, causing him to stumble backwards. He landed hard and loud on a shrub behind him. In that instant the figure halted its approach and the sound of breath stopped, once again leaving the forest in disturbing silence.

As Marcus struggled to get up, Ethan watched the figure. It was silent for that one small moment, but then just as quickly as it had gone quiet, it started again. It remained a whispered sounding exhale, but now it was ear piercingly loud. It was almost as if the noise was coming from within Ethan's own head. At that same moment the figure began closing the distance between Ethan and Marcus at an unnatural speed. That was when Ethan finally saw it for what it was. It had the shape of a man, but was almost four times the size of any man Ethan had ever seen. It didn't seem to hold a solid form. Instead it was made of a shadowy gas loosely held together around its shape. It's eyes were what Ethan noticed most of all. Where it's eyes would have been there was nothing. Not a transparent nothing that he could see through. More like two black holes sitting in its head. They seemed to absorb more than just light. Even Ethan's hope drained as he looked into them. Its dark, evil eyes were all Ethan could take. He turned and ran, forgetting about Marcus, forgetting about the Heart of the Forest, only knowing fear.

Marcus struggled to get up as panic overcame all his other senses. When he reached his feet he saw Ethan sprinting far ahead of him. Marcus followed suit and threw himself into a full sprint. He turned to get a good look at his pursuer. It was slightly gaining on him, gliding just above the ground in some sort of otherworldly fashion. It was the closest thing to a ghost Marcus had ever seen, but it was made up of an intense shadow. It was such an unnatural being that Marcus almost didn't believe it was real, but that didn't stop him from running.

Ethan ran ahead with no regard to where he was heading. He hurdled past trees and through overgrown shrubbery, letting it slap him in the face as he charged through. All the while the ear-piercing whisper screamed from behind him. It went on that way for some time, but Ethan couldn't tell if it had been seconds or minutes. After falling through some thick shrubs and nearly avoiding slamming into a few large redwoods, Ethan realized he'd been turned around. He was lost, unsure which way he had originally been heading and where he had been running from. The whisper, however, was gone. And there was no sign of his shadowy pursuer or Marcus. Shit, Marcus, he thought worrying for his friend's well-being.

Marcus tried to quickly navigate through the forest, but his best efforts were having little effect. The ghost hovered through the forest paying no mind to any physical obstacles in its way. Marcus could not only hear it getting closer by the ever deafening sound of its breath, but he could feel it as well. The closer it got the more it sent both a shiver through his spine and a knot in his gut. Marcus fought back tears as they came, blurring his vision. He hadn't cried since he was a little kid, his dad had made sure of that. "If you cry, then you're not a real man. And if you're not a real man, then your life is pointless," his father had told him. An awful mantra that Marcus had lived most of his life by.

The thought of his father seeing him now, running for his life from a ghost with tears in his eyes, sickened Marcus. He could see the old man's disappointed face with contempt in his eyes. "Weak and fragile like a woman," he heard his father say.

Marcus responded without even thinking or meaning to. "Shut up! How can you judge me when you couldn't even stay loyal to mom!" Marcus yelled. It distracted Marcus just enough. He didn't see the terrain shift, and before he knew it he was tumbling to the ground once again. He looked up and saw the shadowed ghost only feet away preparing to envelop him. All he could hear was it's whispered breath. The sound drowned out everything including his thoughts. It grew closer and closer, and when it was less than seconds from reaching him, he turned away in absolute fear. He was allowed one last thought. This is how it ends, this is what I deserve, he told himself.

A long moment passed as Marcus cowered in terror, eyes sewn shut. Then he noticed that the whisper had stopped. So had the tingling in his body and the sickness in his stomach. He opened his eyes to a peaceful forest. The shadowy figure was gone. He expected to feel grateful. He had just been spared a terrible fate. Instead he felt the furthest thing from it. A jumble of emotions hit him all at once. Self-pity for everything he'd gone through with his father. Self-loathing for his affair with Ashley. Fear that he may lose them both. Ashley, the love of his life. And Ethan, the best friend he would ever have. The tears were still with him, but now they were pouring out. Marcus couldn't bring himself to stand up. Instead, he stayed on the ground defeated, letting out a lifetime's worth of tears.

Meanwhile, Ethan was desperately calling out to Marcus. No answer. When he realized that wasn't going to work, he pulled out his phone. He tried calling Marcus but the poor reception wouldn't allow the call to go through. He almost threw his phone to the ground in frustration, but he thought better of it. The reception was good enough that at least his GPS was still working. He checked the map and noticed he was less than fifteen minutes from the forest's center. He decided that his best course of action would be to continue on to the center and wait for Marcus there. Hopefully Marcus' GPS would work and he'd have the same thought. After all, it was where they'd initially been heading, and they were so close now.

When Ethan's GPS arrived at the center of the forest, he looked around. There was nothing special about the area. Just a bunch of redwood trees towering around him, while overgrowth struggled to keep up with them. Ethan felt a strange disappointment to have come across something so peaceful. He'd half expected something dangerous or overwhelming to be awaiting him. This isn't it. You failed again. You're nothing but a failure, Ethan's inner voice reminded him. He ignored it as usual, and held onto hope. He inspected every tree in the area. He got on all fours and crawled through the overgrowth hoping to find something. At one point he even shouted out to the forest.

"Well, I'm here. Where are my answers huh? Heart of the forest! Fiction is reality! There your answers lie! Where are my answers!" he yelled in desperation.

Nothing on the trees, nothing in the overgrowth, and nothing in response. If it was the heart of the forest, just coming there wasn't enough. Ethan doubted that though. Somehow, he knew that when he found 'the Heart' it would be obvious. And right then, it certainly wasn't.

Ethan sat down, his back against a redwood. He attempted to send Marcus a text, but it didn't go through. He wasn't even sure Marcus was still alive, but he didn't know what else to do. He decided to wait and hope that his friend was alive, and that he would find his way to the center.

Almost an hour passed, and Ethan was preparing himself to leave. Maybe his best hope was to head back to civilization and organize a search party for Marcus. The thought made him sick. It was fear of facing that reality that made him wait a little longer. To Ethan's delight, eventually Marcus walked up staring down at his phone which glowed in the ever-darkening forest. He didn't even see Ethan, who jumped out to greet him.

"Jesus!" Marcus yelled falling to the ground.

Ethan didn't even say anything. He just ran over, pulled his friend up, and hugged him. "What happened? Are you okay?" he finally asked.

"I'd rather not talk about it right now, but I'm okay. To be honest I'm not even sure what happened," Marcus confided. "I will say, there is definitely something fucked up going on with this forest. That thing that just chased us was nothing short of some kind of evil magic shit."

There was a long silence as the two appreciated the magnitude of what had just happened. "Well, I'm glad you're alright. I'm sorry I got you involved in this," Ethan finally said.

"Don't be sorry man. As terrible as this all was, I'm glad I know the truth. If you'd have experienced this alone and tried to tell me about it I would have thought you were crazy," Marcus admitted.

"But it was all for nothing," Ethan pointed out. "There's nothing here. I've been searching pretty much ever since we got split up." Ethan threw his hands in the air and started walking away as he continued speaking, "We should head back. Ashley is going to start wondering what's taking us so long."

As they followed Ethan's GPS back toward the hiking trail Marcus offered up an idea to Ethan. "Weren't you saying that the Ustumah Tribe worshiped some magic shit in the forest way back when before the settlers arrived?"

"Yeah," Ethan said inquisitively.

"Well, the area has got to have changed a whole lot since the settlers arrived. I mean wasn't this place just a huge logging town before they found gold?" Marcus offered.

"How do you know all that?" Ethan asked with genuine surprise.

"Dude we read it outside the museum. I'm not stupid, I know how to pay attention. I just generally don't care enough to find that kind of stuff out in the first place," Marcus replied a little offended.

"Either way," Ethan paused, "You're a genius. The center of the forest isn't where I originally thought, because the forest has been cut back since the early days. If we can find a map that shows the area when the first explorers and settlers arrived, then we can find the true center." Ethan was visibly excited.

Marcus on the other hand was skeptical. "Oh yeah, the first ever map made of this region. Shouldn't be hard to get our hands on that," he said sarcastically.

"Easier than you think," Ethan said with a grin. A spark of hope reignited in his eyes.

CHAPTER 16

"Sorry, but we're going to have to reheat dinner a bit. I didn't realize it was going to take you guys so long," Ashley confided on the drive home.

Marcus looked to Ethan, who shook his head. "Yeah, sorry about that. We were just having fun. Lost track of time and followed the trail a little too far," Marcus lied.

Back at the cabin the three enjoyed a quiet dinner. Trying to break the silence Ashley suggested that tomorrow the three of them should all go into town and enjoy the festival. Ethan eagerly agreed, and Marcus nodded in an agreement of his own. After dinner while Ashley was in the shower, Marcus and Ethan discussed their plan.

They both agreed that it was best not to tell Ashley about what had happened in the forest.

First, because they agreed that it served no purpose other than to needlessly stress her out. And second, because they knew she would never believe them.

"Now that we've agreed on that. I have a plan," Ethan said.

Marcus listened as Ethan outlined the plan. The next day at the festival, Ethan would stick with Ashley and distract her while Marcus went off on his own to the city courthouse. Ethan explained that he thought it was best if he stayed with Ashley since they were trying to fix things between them. He knew it would look suspicious if he tried to go off on his own. Ethan also explained that the courthouse was the best place to look when trying to find old maps like the ones they were looking for.

"Yeah but are they really going to let some random tourist just look at some historical maps?" Marcus asked.

"They're not ancient artifacts. As far as I know all of that stuff is open to the public. There's no reason they shouldn't let you look at them," Ethan assured him.

There was some debate over that, but ultimately Ethan won out and Marcus agreed.

Afterwards Ashley finished her shower and the two ended the conversation. The three spent the rest of the night talking and joking like they had done back in the day. It was a good night with no grieving mothers, blood thirsty wolves, or shadowy ghosts.

The next morning they slept in. They'd stayed up late enjoying each other's company the night before. It was day four of the festival and there was not much going on in town that they would miss out on by arriving late. That night was the announcement of the winners of round two of the festival contest. Ashley expressed that all she really cared about was making sure they got to see Mitchelson's *The Pack* lose the competition, stating that she'd had enough of wolves.

Once they arrived in town they made their way to Main Street. There they could see all of the contestants' stands, and see who had been paired against each other earlier that morning. As they approached the stands of the contestants still in the running, Ethan noticed the stands of the other eliminated contestants in the distance. Too late he noticed his own stand for *"In Despair,"* where a furious looking Sarah was marching toward him.

Ashley noticed too and warned Ethan. "Here comes Sarah, and she looks pissed."

Marcus looked to Ethan and gave a quick nod. "Well, I think that is my sign to get out of here. I'm gonna go have a look around on my own. I'll meet up with you guys when the big bad publisher is gone. Sound good?"

Ashley smiled and gave Marcus a nod, as did Ethan. In Ethan's eyes Marcus saw a look of approval. He had been wondering how he was going to separate himself from Ashley and Ethan without it seeming strange, and Sarah had just given him the perfect opportunity.

Marcus set off in search of a festival volunteer, hoping they could point him in the direction of the courthouse. He figured it had to be on Main Street, but wasn't sure. As he distanced himself from his friends, he looked over his shoulder at them. Sarah was giving Ethan the scolding of a lifetime. Ethan looked more scared in that moment than he had the evening before. Apparently, Sarah was even scarier than an otherworldly being. Ashley had wrapped herself around Ethan's arm for support but was avoiding any eye contact with Sarah. Marcus realized he was even more glad to be avoiding Sarah than he was to be on his way to inquire about the maps.

Research. Marcus couldn't help but feel that this was task more suited for Ethan than it was for him. Even the word didn't sit right with Marcus. But he couldn't really argue when Ethan said that he needed to spend more time with Ashley. She was his girlfriend after all.

Marcus had always been perfectly fine when Ashley and Ethan would spend time alone. They were dating so it only made sense. Not to mention, as messed up as it was, Marcus knew he and Ashley would usually have their own alone time later. However, their recent conversation had given him doubts. Now he realized that he was jealous that Ethan and Ashley were together without him.

It was for the best Marcus knew, but that didn't make it any easier. Ashley had become a pillar in his life, and he wasn't sure what he was going to do without her. But it was what was right, and he would have to deal with the consequences alone. Marcus had always been exceptionally good at putting emotions like that aside, burying them, and never dealing with them again. But with Ashley it was different. On top of that, after his encounter with the ghostly shadow, Marcus was finding himself feeling more emotional, and having a harder time dealing with those emotions.

Maybe that ghost didn't spare me after all, Marcus thought to himself.

It didn't take long for him to find one of the volunteers in their bright yellow jacket. Marcus politely asked if they could point him in the direction of the courthouse. It was located near the bottom of Main Street.

It took Marcus quite a while to make his way through the crowds of people filling the street. Once he got inside, the courthouse was dead silent; a complete contrast with the hectic noise that filled the street just outside. The receptionist looked up at him from behind a desk near the entrance.

"Can I help you?" She asked inquisitively.

She was an older woman. You could see the years on her face, and they had not been kind. Marcus could hear the hint of frustration in her voice and knew she wasn't going to make this easy for him.

"Yeah, hi," Marcus said, stumbling over his words. "I was, um, hoping to look at some maps."

"Maps?" the woman asked annoyed.

Marcus paused. He wasn't sure how to respond. "Yes, maps. I am looking for original maps of this area. Like, the ones the original explorers made when they first came through," he managed.

The woman eyed Marcus and began impatiently tapping a pen on her desk. "Like, the original maps, or the original maps?" She asked, emphasizing 'like' and 'the'.

What a bitch, Marcus thought. He bit his tongue and responded.

"Sorry. The original maps please," he said passive aggressively.

The woman picked up on his attitude and the room went awkwardly silent with the sudden absence of tapping from her pen. The woman stared at Marcus without saying anything for a lot longer than he was comfortable with. Finally she said, "Sorry, those maps are not available for public viewing. If you'd like to submit a request with your reason for needing to view the maps, we can review it and will get back to you in a few weeks." She stared at Marcus with great attention, eagerly awaiting his response.

Internally Marcus knew that the woman had to be saying that just to spite him. Ethan had been so sure the maps would be available to view, and he knew that kind of thing. Marcus had to think of something quick. "A few weeks is way too long. My boss and I will be out of town by then, and he needs the maps for research on a new novel he is working on," Marcus lied.

"And just who is your boss?" The woman asked curiously.

"Ethan Garland, author of '*In Despair*,'" Marcus said, straightening his posture, proud of his quick lie. "I'd hate for you to somehow get in trouble when my boss throws a fit. I'm sure your boss would hear about it from the Ustumah City Book Club."

The woman raised an eyebrow at that, but then she called his bluff. "Well, I'd certainly not like that. But I worry that I'd be in even more trouble if something happened to such historic maps. I can't just let anyone look at them," the woman said giving her pen a couple quick taps on the desk.

There was a long silence as the two analyzed each other, and Marcus felt like he saw the woman even flash a cocky grin at him. This isn't going anywhere, Marcus realized. He had never been good at convincing people. In fact, this time he had even managed to make the person less inclined to help him. Time for my go-to method, Marcus admitted to himself. He turned around, pulled out his wallet, and looked inside. He had Four-hundred forty dollars in twenties plus some change. He'd brought a lot of cash with him because he'd figured that at festivals like this, you never know. Marcus pulled out three-hundred dollars in twenties and turned around to show them to the woman behind the desk.

"Listen, this is three-hundred dollars. I really need to see those maps. I just need to look at them for at most twenty minutes. I won't even touch them," Marcus pleaded holding out the money. "How much are those maps really worth to you?"

The woman showed a toothy smile. "About three-hundred dollars," she said as she reached up and grabbed the money out of Marcus' hand. Then she stood up and motioned for Marcus to follow as she made her way up some nearby stairs. "Right this way," she said in a cheerful tone.

Ethan might be the well-spoken one, but I've never had a problem a couple hundred didn't solve, Marcus told himself.

The woman led Marcus to a far back corner on the second floor. She spent a few minutes sifting through a large set of keys. She stopped a few times and tried a few different keys in a large cabinet before her. Her fourth attempt worked, and the cabinet swung open. A distinct smell rushed out of the cabin signifying that it had not been opened in some time. The woman carefully removed a large rolled up paper, and unfolded it on a table behind her, placing the corners in plastic notches to hold it in place and stop it from rolling back up. She then grabbed an average sized piece of paper out of the cabinet and placed it in front of Marcus, also handing him the pen she had been tapping on her desk earlier.

"You'll need to sign this. It's just a record of who viewed the maps and when," the woman told Marcus.

Marcus obliged and hunched over while he signed his name and the date on the paper. There was also a place for the "stated reason" for his access to the maps. Marcus just wrote "research," and figured that would be sufficient. As Marcus was about to hand the paper and pen back to the woman, he noticed something. All of the previous signatures were dated at least thirty years before Marcus, except one. The most recent signature had been only eight years ago. It was signed by a Deaven Palmer, with the stated reason as "historical interest." Marcus noted the name. Maybe this Deaven Palmer knew something historical that could help Ethan and him.

Once Marcus handed the paper back to the woman, she placed it in the cabinet and began to walk away. "When you're finished, don't try to put the map away yourself. Come downstairs and let me know," she ordered.

Marcus nodded and she left him. He moved around the table to get a better view of the map. The map had not aged well. Marcus realized he had been spoiled by technology as he struggled to read the map, wishing it was just a satellite image like the ones he could pull up on his phone. Then Marcus did just that, pulling up a current map on his phone. He used the similar geographical features he could find between his phone and the old map to try and get an idea for where Ustumah City would be on the old map. A nearby mountain range proved the most useful, and after a few minutes Marcus had figured out what was where between the current day and historical maps. Next Marcus took some mental measurements of the huge forest in the historical map, and used those measurements to eyeball it's center. After triple checking, Marcus was confident that was the closest he would get to the center of the sprawling forest. He then cross referenced that midpoint with the map on his phone, placed a pin where it would be, and just like that he'd found Ethan's and his new destination.

The pin was actually not far from Ustumah City, though there were no trails that passed near it and it was a relatively deep hike into the forest. Marcus' mind flashed terrible images as he imagined what terror they might witness on their next hike. He shook it off though and prepared to meet back up with Ethan and Ashley, proud to share his successful discovery with Ethan. He texted Ethan and Ashley in a group message asking where he could meet them and headed downstairs. He told the woman at the desk that he was done with the map. She gave him permission to go.

On his way out the woman called out to Marcus, "Pleasure doing business with you."

CHAPTER 17

Ethan had completely forgotten about Sarah once he'd been eliminated from the contest. Clearly though, she had not forgotten about him. She always seemed frustrated with Ethan, but this time Sarah looked furious. He held his breath as she approached, watching as Marcus quickly disappeared into the crowd, and envied him.

Ashley sensed Ethan's unease and wrapped herself around his arm. She saw Ethan watching Marcus, but when she turned to look, he had already disappeared into the crowd.

Sarah was on them seconds later. "Ethan, Ethan, Ethan," she said, shaking her head trying to mask her anger. "Where have you been? I've been sending you constant emails. What made you think you could just ignore me because you fell out of the contest? There's still a lot going on at this festival you know."

Ethan was honestly surprised. "Stupid mistake," he admitted, "I really thought you and your bosses wouldn't anything to do with me after losing. And I haven't been checking my emails... Why didn't you call me?"

Sarah half shouted her response, "Why didn't I call you?" She put her fingers to the bridge of her nose. "I am not your secretary, I'm in charge of you. You should be calling me, not the other way around. There's still money to be made off your book just by being here. Don't be such a sore loser," said Sarah.

Ashley interjected, "Hey Sarah, that's not fair. You don't know what it's like to lose something you're so excited about."

Sarah looked to Ashley as if she was just now noticing she were there. "Neither do you honey. And I hate to break it to you, but your boyfriend here isn't exactly the image of emotional stability."

The words stung Ethan hard. A little because he felt she was right, but mostly because the normally calm and robotic Sarah was now tearing him apart in public. Right in front of his girlfriend too.

Ashley was about to say something, and Ethan knew it wasn't going to be good so he stepped in. "Listen, I get you're mad Sarah. But can we not make this so personal? You're the one always talking about professionalism." Ethan said.

Sarah thought about that for a moment. "You're right. I'm over-reacting. Though in my defense it is a little upsetting when you are making it so hard for me to do my job," she admitted. "Clearly you have no interest in partaking in the rest of the festival as an author, and that's your choice. I'll take care of everything else for the next four days, and you can do whatever it is you've been doing. Just don't expect to do any more business with Cardinal's Nest Publishing. I wouldn't work with you again, even if you wrote the next American masterpiece." With that Sarah spun on her heels and charged off toward where she had come from.

Ashley called after her, but Ethan stopped her. "It's fine," Ethan said. He had deserved that he thought. He had ignored her and his obligations. He couldn't really expect anything else.

Ashley knew some of what Sarah had said was true, but Ethan hadn't deserved to be treated like that. It made her feel sick to her stomach. But Sarah was gone, and all she could do now was try to make sure the rest of Ethan's day went well.

Ashley suggested they go look more in depth at some of the po-ets. She pointed out that they had not been able to enjoy the Poetry and Pastries breakfast banquet, and it would be nice to look at some of the poetry at the festival. Ethan agreed and they made their way over to the poetry stands. Ashley was embarrassed at the thought of running into Claire, but she'd needed a way to distract Ethan. She would have taken him to the writing section instead, but it was too close to the *In Despair* stand and Sarah. Also she worried that Ethan would compare himself to the competition rather than enjoy him-self. With the poetry he couldn't do that.

When they made it to the section of Main Street that had been divided up for poetry they stood eyeing their options. For a moment they both waited for the other to make a move toward a particular stand. Ashley realized it had been her idea so it should be her. She looked at the nearest stand, didn't see Claire, and decided it was good enough. She hardly took a step forward before a voice called out from the crowd behind them.

"Ethan Garland?" asked the rough voice.

A fan of Ethan's, Ashley hoped. An enthusiastic fan picking him out of the crowd might be just the thing to make the day.

Ethan and Ashley turned to face the voice. Emerging from the crowd toward them was a rugged looking man wearing a sheriff's uniform. Ethan recognized him as Officer Riley, the same officer he'd had a confrontation with earlier in the week.

"Officer Riley?" Ethan asked, "How can I help you?"

Ashley looked surprised to see that Ethan was familiar with the officer. Riley gave a slight nod to the couple, but his face remained stoic.

"I was hoping I'd run into you today. I have some questions I would like to ask you back at the station. If you'd come with me," Riley motioned in what must have been the direction of the police station.

Though he was surprised, Ethan saw no reason not to cooperate. He nodded, but before he could say anything Ashley took a small step toward Riley and asked, "What kind of questions? What is this all about?"

Riley seemed surprised by Ashley's defiance, but a look that seemed a lot like respect briefly flashed across his face. "Nothing serious, I can assure you, Ms…?" Riley said, asking for her name.

"Ashley Hollins. I'm Ethan's girlfriend," she said confidently, still standing her ground to Riley. Even though he was acting politely, her intuition was telling her that the officer didn't have good intentions.

Riley smiled. "Good to meet you Ms. Hollins. I only want to ask your boyfriend some questions about a conversation we had earlier this week," Riley said gesturing to Ethan.

Ethan stepped up to Ashley and placed a hand on her shoulder, "It's ok. I'll be fine. It's about my book."

Ashley looked puzzled, "What about your book could warrant questioning at the police station?

Riley showed his first sign of frustration. "Mr. Garland is more than welcome to share the details with you after I ask him my questions," he said with anger appearing in his tone.

Remembering the officer's temper, Ethan attempted to diffuse the situation. "Ash, I'll be fine. Come with me, and we'll talk as soon as he asks what he needs to ask. To be honest, I'm not quite sure what could be so important either. But it must be important enough for him to come looking for me in this crowd," Ethan explained reassuringly.

Ashley still looked hesitant, but she agreed.

Officer Riley led the way through the crowd while Ashley and Ethan followed. As they walked, Ethan noticed Claire at her poetry stand. She watched them follow Officer Riley with curiosity, giving Ethan a shy and worried wave. Ethan started raising his hand to wave back and let her know everything was alright. Ashley noticed the movement, and he decided against it. The way this day was going, the last thing he wanted was to start another fight with Ashley. So instead, Ethan lowered his hand back down and looked away from Claire. From the corner of his eye, Ethan saw Claire shaking her head disappointedly.

At the police station, Ashley was asked to wait in the lobby while Ethan followed Riley to a questioning room. The room was plain with nothing but a camera, poor lighting, two chairs, and table between them. Ethan had never been in a questioning room before, but it didn't feel all that different than they seemed in the movies. Ethan sat down and looked around uncomfortably, adjusting to the new setting.

As Riley sat across from him, he spoke, "Don't be intimidated by the room. If you watch too many movies it seems like only suspects are brought in here. I assure you, it's just standard procedure." He pointed to the camera, "This way we get everything on tape in case it's important."

Ethan relaxed a bit at that and nodded. "Alright. So, what can I help you with officer? I hope we're all good. I didn't mean to upset you the other day, I'm really sorry," Ethan said earnestly.

Riley waited to reply longer than Ethan would have liked. He seemed to be sizing Ethan up. "We're good. I shouldn't have lost my cool like that. This missing person's case is really getting to me, and this festival has always driven me nuts. Nothing personal, just really bad timing."

Ethan let out a deep breath. It was nice to know that Riley wasn't holding to any animosity. Or at least, so he said. There was still a sort of fire behind the officer's eyes whenever he looked at Ethan. The look was worrying, but he just chalked it up to his own insecurities.

Riley continued, "As for how you can help me. The other day you mentioned that there were some similarities between my conversation with my partner, and a scene from your book. Well, I did some reading and that isn't only similarity between your book and this case. Some are disturbingly on point. I just wonder what you might be able to tell me about that?

Ethan shifted uncomfortably in his seat. He knew what was about to come, but he wasn't sure how to handle it. Riley waited for Ethan, but when he didn't say anything, the officer spoke up.

"Well writer boy? You were very insistent about me reading your book, and now I've done it. Seems to me like you have a theory about what's going on here, and that's why you got so excited the other day. Care to share?" Riley asked with mounting frustration. The understanding and forgiving face Riley had been wearing was melting away. Now, Ethan was starting to see the same officer who had become physical with him a few days before.

Even though Ethan knew the question about the link between his book and real events had been coming, it still hit him like a ton of bricks when heard Officer Riley ask about it.

Ethan wished he could tell the officer the truth. That a magical power dwelling in the forest was making stories come to life, and unfortunately for some poor family, that magical power had chosen 'In Despair.' But Ethan knew that Riley took this case to heart, and he'd already shown that he could act irrationally, just like the lead investigator in his book. That character also had a bad temper and would act violently, without thinking.

Despite his fear, Ethan still wanted to help. So, he made up a lie. A lie that wouldn't make him seem crazy, but one that would put Riley on track to solving the case.

"Ok, yeah, I do have a theory," Ethan said, "but it just sounds ridiculous to say it out loud."

"Let's hear it," Riley demanded impatiently.

Ethan straightened his posture and pulled his chair closer to the table. "Ok, so *In Despair* came out a long time ago relative to the festival. It's only just now blowing up because of the festival. What I'm thinking is that someone who lives in the area read my book some time ago. Now I don't know why someone would want to do this, but it could well be that they are trying to recreate the details of the case in the real world," Ethan explained.

With everything that was going on, Ethan hadn't given the missing girl much thought. But knowing the pain of the characters in his novel, it saddened him to think of what these real people were going through. So much of the pain in *"In Despair"* was because no one ever found out what happened to the missing girl. Not until years later when her body was discovered in a small underground cave. She had been playing in the forest and got lost. Somewhere along the way she accidentally fell into the hidden entrance of the cave, hit her head, and died on the spot. Part of Ethan knew that the real missing girl, Ella Schaeffer, was lying dead in some cave in the forest. Perhaps that was his fault for having wrote the book in the first place. Or perhaps it was the fault of some malicious magical power residing in the forest. The more Ethan thought about the "Heart of the Forest," the more he grew to hate it.

Either way, Ethan felt that if he could convince Officer Riley that his case was a recreation of Ethan's book, then he could set him on the right path. Riley would focus the investigation on searching for underground caves in the forest, and he'd find the body. The news of the girl's death would hurt, but it would spare them all the years of pain caused by never knowing.

"Maybe this whole thing could be solved if the investigation were based off of the details of my book," Ethan explained.

Riley looked Ethan over for a long time. "I skimmed your book, but I didn't actually read it. Now you want me to base my investigation off of it. Where does your self-centered ass draw the line?!" Riley asked, slamming a hand on the table.

Ethan withdrew backward as Riley's hand hit the table. "I'm sorry, I'm just trying to help," he managed.

Riley relaxed slightly, but he was still clearly very upset. Then he laughed as if he'd just come to some realization. "Can you imagine. Then you'd really be a best-seller… 'The novel that inspired the real-life case…'" Riley said regarding Ethan with contempt.

Ethan tried to respond, but Riley cut him off, "When exactly did you arrive in Ustumah City, Mr. Garland?"

Ethan knew where this was going, and he didn't like it. He thought of asking for a lawyer, but Riley was becoming unhinged, and he thought it would be better to calmly cooperate. "3 days ago. I got here early on the first day of the festival," Ethan said.

"And this is your first time in Ustumah City?" Riley asked with a sense of buildup in his voice.

"Yes," Ethan replied confidently.

"And is there anyone who can vouch that you didn't take any long trips in the last month?" asked Riley.

Ethan, "Yes. Both my girlfriend, Ashley, and my best friend Marcus." Riley laughed at that. "Anyone who wouldn't lie for you?"

The question caught Ethan off guard. He was thinking of a way to answer when the interrogation room door swung open.

Ethan turned to see Riley's partner Officer DeMarco standing with Sarah. "What the hell is this, Demarco?!" Riley asked furiously.

Demarco just put his hands in the air. "Nothing I could do," the Officer replied.

Sarah marched into the room, grabbed Ethan by the shoulder, and picked him out of the chair.

"Who the hell are you?" Riley asked.

Sarah glared at Riley. "His lawyer. And next time you want to interrogate him I'll have my whole firm sit in on it. I'm not sure what this is all about, or what you are trying to pull, but trust me when I say that we eat small town cops like you for breakfast," she said calmly, but with a certain attitude only Sarah could bring. "Come on Ethan, we are leaving." And she ushered Ethan out of the room.

Riley and DeMarco said nothing, and just stood back and watched as they left. In the waiting room, Marcus was sitting with

Ashley. They got up and followed Sarah and Ethan out of the station.

"Something seemed off, I didn't know who else to call," Ashley said to Ethan.

Ethan assured Ashley that he wasn't upset. In fact, he was thankful. That had not been going well, and Sarah pulled him out at the perfect moment.

"I didn't know you were a lawyer," Ethan asked Sarah as they continued away from the station.

"I'm not. But those Podunk sheriffs don't know that," she said.

Ethan let that soak in before asking another question, "I thought you were done with me? Why help me?"

Sarah blew out a short laugh. "I have a job to do. Whatever legal issues you are getting yourself involved in can wait until the festival is over. The last thing I want is a writer getting arrested on my watch. Doesn't reflect well on me," she explained. "Now please, stay out of trouble. I really am over cleaning up your messes." And then before anyone could say anything Sarah walked off.

"What were they asking you about anyways," Marcus asked. Ashley seconded the question. Ethan explained how his previous conversation with Officer Riley had led him to believe

Ethan could help with the investigation, but that it had turned into Riley beginning to accuse him of some involvement in the girl's disappearance.

Ashley gave a quick "I-told-you-so" lecture about when she had first warned Ethan of telling everyone about his magic theories. "You've got a great imagination. Just put it in check sometimes. I don't want you to get yourself into trouble," she finished.

Ethan agreed and put an arm around his concerned girlfriend as they walked into town. He glanced over at Marcus who was trailing slightly behind them, cell phone in hand. Marcus held up the phone and zoomed in on his map, angling his screen toward Ethan. A pin sat in the forest, not far from Ustumah City. Marcus gave a big thumbs up, and Ethan nodded.

CHAPTER 18

Marcus walked to Ashley's side, opposite Ethan, and threw his arm around her. "So Ash, Ethan and I were thinking of going on another hike today. This time a little earlier so we don't lose out on sunlight. What do you say?" Marcus suggested.

Ashley looked from Marcus to Ethan, "You guys want to ditch me again? I was glad to give you some boy time yesterday, but you kept me waiting forever. Festival or not, this town, and especially the cabin, are not the most exciting places to hang out alone." She was upset by the idea and didn't care about showing it.

Ethan wanted to hide the magic from Ashley, mostly to protect her from its dangers. He didn't want to risk upsetting her, by leaving her alone while he went off searching with Marcus. But he also couldn't risk taking her with them either. The search would just have to wait. He and Marcus could leave early the next morning while she was still sleeping.

"No, of course not. We talked about going on another hike today, but honestly, I'd rather just enjoy some of the festival with you. We can figure out a better time to go on a hike," Ethan said, widening his eyes at Marcus while he mentioned finding a better time.

Marcus took the hint and nodded. He took his arm off of Ashley and threw his hands in the air, "My bad, you're right. Yesterday was just a lot of fun. Been a while since we've done something like that together."

The thought of Ethan and Marcus mending their friendship made Ashley concede slightly. "Maybe you can have some bro time tomorrow? I'm sure I can find a book to read," Ashley joked pointing out all of the nearby stands. "But let's just spend the day together. Tonight we get to watch David Kowalski take Robert Mitchelson out of this competition."

"I can't argue against that," Ethan smiled. "I was hoping we could check out some of the other author's stands today too. I haven't had a chance to read some of the other authors' books. The fellow writer in me is dying with curiosity."

Ashley and Marcus agreed. "This is your trip, whatever you want to do," Ashley said, grabbing Ethan's hand. Ethan led the way toward some of the stands, making sure to avoid the poetry section. More importantly, to avoid Claire.

It was true that Ethan was curious about the other writers' works. He appreciated a good novel, and he also wanted to compare himself. Though it was true, it wasn't why Ethan had suggested it. He needed to prepare himself and Marcus for whatever would happen next time they went searching for the 'Heart of the Forest.' His story wasn't the only one coming to life, and he needed to do his research. Maybe I can even find a way to manipulate what happens. What scenes come true, Ethan thought to himself. He had no idea how the reality altering power worked, but he knew that there had to be some reason to it. Even magic has rules, he thought.

The first booth they visited was for "The Broken Peoples", by Art Petty. Ethan read up on the book. It was about a group of people who had been chosen as the first to settle the planet Mars. It was a story about nothing going according to plan, and the worst-case scenario always prevailing. While Ashley was distracted by something else, Marcus approached Ethan.

"You think some of the stuff in these books might come true?" Marcus asked.

"I know it," Ethan replied. Ethan was surprised Marcus had come to the same conclusion. "I just don't know what will come true, or when." I at least want to focus on things that could pose a threat to us. Skim through the books and ignore anything that couldn't threaten us. We have no idea what we are dealing with. Safety should be our first concern."

Marcus agreed, and the two split off.

Next, they made their way over to the booth for *The Winds of Change,* by Patrick Smith. Ethan had heard talk of a Netflix adaptation of the book, but he knew little about its plot. Ethan picked up a copy and read the summary on the back.

"Five years ago, a deadly virus swept across the globe, killing a majority of the human population. Mysteriously, the airborne virus only affects people who inhale during the wind. A slight breeze will set off some nasty side effects, but a person can recover. Heavier winds can lead to death within moments. Even more mysteriously, strong winds seem to have taken on a mind of their own, moving around like entities on the hunt."

"Jack Marsh has been struggling in the post-apocalyptic world caused by these events. It didn't take long for other people to become just as dangerous as the wind. Jack has had to make immense sacrifices and do things he never would have thought to survive. Often, he feels he has nothing left to live for, wondering why he even bothers. This is the story about a man who tries to find hope in a world that offers none."

A likely candidate, Ethan thought. It was both life threatening, and supernatural. Two themes Ethan had seen in his earlier run-ins with danger caused by the forest. He grabbed a copy and purchased it.

Ashley followed Ethan, but Marcus was already at the next large, tent-like stand. It was the stand for David Kowalski's book, "Temptation Ablaze."

Marcus noticed them heading over and set down a copy of Temptation Ablaze that he had been nose deep in.

"I didn't know you were a sucker for romance novels?" Ashley asked.

Marcus laughed awkwardly. "I'm not. I just wanted to see if there was anything interesting in the book. There isn't," Marcus said nodding at Ethan.

Ethan took the hint. He figured there wouldn't be anything useful to them. It was a book about two lovers and their story of will they or won't they. Despite that, Ethan's years of knowing Marcus told him that something wasn't quite right. He was suspicious, but chalked it up to Marcus being embarrassed at having been caught holding something from that genre. Besides, Ethan was quickly ambushed before he could put more thought into it.

"Ethan Garland! Great to see you," a familiar voice called out from within the tent. Ethan turned to see David Kowalski making his way over to the group.

Ethan greeted David warmly and introduced Marcus and Ashley.

"I was very sorry to see that you didn't progress last round. I hope you didn't take it too hard. The Book Club Members and Mitchelson have always had a mutually 'profitable' relationship," David confided. "I'd read anything you write far before Mitchelson's cheap thrills."

"Thank you so much for that. There's no higher praise than hearing you prefer my writing to that of another famous author," Ethan replied.

David smiled at that, then looked around at the festival attendees gawking. He put a hand on Ethan's shoulder. "The important thing to remember is that now, you are a famous writer," David said, emphasizing the "you" in the statement. "Now, I just wanted to say that, because I figured you needed to hear it. But I should get back to the fans. Tonight, I'll take Mitchelson out of the festival. Not just for myself, but as a little revenge for you too."

"Please. Nothing would make our night more," Ashley said.

With that, David nodded and returned to mingling with his fans. Afterwards, a small group of onlookers approached Ethan. Marcus and Ashley waited patiently as he signed a few books and answered a few questions. After that, the three of them went to find somewhere to eat lunch.

After lunch they spent the rest of the day wandering around the festival, not doing much but enjoying each other's company. It was a good day, and both Ethan and Ashley felt like their relationship was returning to how it had been in the beginning. Happy.

Later that evening they made their way to the stage at the bottom of Main Street, along with most of the festival attendees. The winner's ceremony was hardly any different than it had been the second night. The only key differences were that there were half the contestants. Ethan was actually able to enjoy himself a bit now that he didn't have a stake in the game. Other than seeing Robert lose of course.

Claire won again. This time with a nearly unanimous vote. Even Ashley clapped.

She may win this thing, Ethan realized. He was happy for her. She seemed like a good person that he could have been great friends with. *In another life maybe,* he told himself. In this life she was a danger to a relationship that was far more important to him, so he'd pushed her away. She didn't deserve to be treated so rudely, and Ethan felt guilty. But his decision had been the right one. He was never going to put anything before him and Ashley ever again.

Except for your obsession with this magic living in the forest. You're pathetic. Even a fairy tale distracts you from your relationship, whispered the doubt in his head. Just when things were going good again, that voice resurfaced. A bigger enemy than anything else Ethan was dealing with, magic or not. He ignored it.

The winners' announcements continued until there was only one pair left to announce. David Kowalski and Robert Mitchelson. Both Authors were superstars that had been to the festival many times over. They were given the lengthiest introductions, and the crowd cheered the loudest for both of them. Ethan realized that this moment was the climax of the festival.

Whoever won tonight was likely to win the Novel portion of the festival. It's all downhill from here, excitement wise, Ethan told himself.

"And the winner tonight, between these two titans of fiction, is…" The announcer said. The crowd fell silent, and you could almost hear the heartbeats of everyone in the audience.

"… Robert Mitchelson and '*The Pack*!'" the announcer finished with an excited shout. The crowd exploded into a massive blend of cheering and clapping. Everyone but Ethan, Ashley and Marcus.

The look of disappointment on David's face was clearly visible, even from far away. He shook hands with Robert and congratulated him all the same, before giving one last wave to the audience and making his way off stage.

"Thank you, thank you," Robert started as the announcer handed him the microphone. "I wish I could say I was surprised, but honestly I'm not. And when I say that I mean no offense to Mr. Kowalski. Clearly, he is a great writer, but this," Robert said as he held a copy of *"The Pack"* into the air, "This is my greatest work yet. If there's one thing my career in writing has taught me, it is how to recognize the winners. And this book is a winner!"

The crowd cheered, reacting surprisingly well to Robert's narcissism. He continued, "If you haven't read it yet, you are missing out. For your own good, please go out and get a copy. You'll be able to say that you read *The Pack* before it was crowned first place at this year's Known Poets and Authors Writing Festival."

The crowd cheered again, as Robert finished his speech. Ethan, Ashley, and Marcus all looked at each other in disbelief. Ethan looked out at the surrounding crowd and was hard pressed to find a single person not clapping or cheering for the egotistical Robert Mitchelson. Until one individual caught Ethan's eye. It was Deaven from the museum. He was among the crowd, but he was paying no attention to Robert. Instead, his stare was fixed on Ethan. He was watching him like a hawk, and made no attempt to shift his gaze when Ethan noticed.

Uncomfortable, Ethan looked away, but he could still feel Deaven's gaze burning into his back just like it had at the museum.

As the ceremony wrapped up, everyone made their way out of the park. Ashley led the way back to the car, and Ethan noticed Deaven staring at him again as they walked off.

"Guys, have you noticed that guy staring at us all night?" Ethan asked quietly, nudging his head in Deaven's direction.

With no tact at all, the two of them turned around to look toward Ethan's nudge. Clear as day they saw Deaven staring, and they quickly turned away.

"Don't look!" Ethan pleaded too late.

"How else are we supposed to see who you're talking about," Marcus pointed out.

"Didn't notice him tonight, but I saw him plenty of times throughout the day," Ashley stated. "I chalked it up to my imagination, but there was a bit where I thought he might be following us. Should we let the police know?"

Ethan looked at her, wondering if she was serious. "I don't think it's at that point. Yet, at least… And even if it were, I don't think we'd get much help from the police right about now," he said.

Ashley looked dissatisfied with his answer, but she knew it was true. "What the hell is this all about? Do you know that guy?" she asked.

"Yeah, his name is Deaven. He's the curator at the museum, and he doesn't like me very much," Ethan admitted.

Marcus chimed in, "Why not?"

"Well, when I visited the museum yesterday morning, he got upset with me. Told me I was sticking my nose where it didn't belong. He doesn't seem to like out-of-towners taking too much of an interest in the local history," Ethan explained. It was a half-truth. Ashley didn't need to know about Ethan's particular interest in the 'Heart of the Forest.'

Marcus realized the connection and stayed silent.

"Well, I don't care if the cops are out to get you or not. If some mysterious stranger continues to stalk us, I'm getting them involved," Ashley stated. At that moment they arrived at the car, and piled in. Looking around, none of them could spot Deaven. Satisfied that he'd gone, they headed back to the Chekhov Cabin.

Back at the cabin Marcus pulled Ethan aside when Ashley was distracted. "When I was looking up those old maps, they made me sign a paper that keeps track of who's looked at the maps. Besides me, the only person in relatively recent history to look at those maps was someone named Deaven Palmer. And I'm guessing the Deaven you mentioned, our stalker, was pissed at you because of the purpose of your research. The Heart of the Forest," Marcus explained.

"That was the feeling I got, yeah," Ethan said.

Marcus nodded his head repeatedly and had a concerned look on his face. "Do these sound like coincidences to you?" he asked.

Ethan conceded with an ominous tone, "No they do not…"

CHAPTER 19

Ethan woke to his phone vibrating beneath his pillow. He quickly moved to turn off the alarm.

Ashley stirred, but didn't wake. The night before, he and Ashley had stayed up late enjoying each other's company, in more ways than one. Strangely, Marcus had turned in early, leaving the couple with some much-needed alone time. Before Marcus had gone to bed, he and Ethan agreed to wake early and head for their newly discovered center of the forest. Ethan wanted to keep Ashley out of it. Even though she had mentioned being alright with Marcus and Ethan going together, Ethan felt the only way to guarantee she didn't come was to leave before she woke up.

It was the day of Fiction and Festivities in town. A carnival style event that celebrated fiction. The event started early, but was best enjoyed later in the day. Ashley hadn't set an alarm, and Ethan figured that if he and Marcus were quick, they could be back before she even woke up.

Ethan crept out of the bedroom, across the hall, and into Marcus' room. "Marcus," Ethan said, nudging his friend.

Marcus rolled over and looked at Ethan with disgust. "No," he said defiantly.

After some coercing, Marcus started to wake up and finally agreed. The two got changed into some warm hiking clothes and met in the kitchen. On the kitchen table Ethan put out multiple water bottles and washcloths. Afterwards Ethan flipped to a particular page in his copy of "The Winds of Change" and ripped it out.

"What are you doing?" Marcus asked.

Ethan turned to him and held up the page. "I'm taking this with us. I know this sounds crazy, but I feel like this magic has a mind of its own. It's shown before that it tends to put us in dangerous situations. Well, I found a dangerous situation I think it won't be able to resist," Ethan explained.

Marcus looked confused, "So what? We get to pick how we die?"

"No," Ethan shook his head, "I chose this page on purpose. The two characters get pretty close to death, but they survive. As long as we follow the details, we'll survive too. Then the magic will have wasted it's best shot."

Marcus looked doubtful. "It's magic, can't it just keep trying. And it feels weird to think about it like some person out to get us. I think it's just magic," he pointed out.

"Maybe it can keep trying. But from what I've seen, it doesn't work that way. And for all we know, it is a person out to get us," Ethan said.

Marcus nodded, "Deaven."

Ethan shrugged. "Maybe. We have no idea how it works, I'm just making my best guess based on what I've seen. It's not just that though. I know this sounds crazy, but I have this gut feeling, like I know I'm right. If we take this page out there, this will happen," Ethan finished.

"I hope so," Marcus conceded. He moved to start packing the items into a backpack, but Ethan stopped him.

"Wait," Ethan said, wiggling the page, "Let me read it to you. That way you'll understand what those are even for. We need to make sure that when the magic starts, we're ready to follow these details to the dot."

Marcus put the backpack down and pulled up a chair. Ethan began to read the page.

"Jack led the way through the woods, and Luke followed close behind.

'How much further,' Luke moaned.

They were only a few hours out from the bunker, or at least where the map said the bunker was.

'All the distance behind us, and you choose now to bitch about it?' Jack said looking back, 'We'll get there when we get there, just shut up and follow.'

Luke said nothing, and Jack liked it better that way. Luke had saved him twice now, but he'd saved Luke just as many times too. It was a partnership of convenience, not a friendship. Jack had lost more than a few friends, and he wasn't looking to lose anymore.

They continued on for a little over an hour, and Luke spoke up again, 'Shit, I'm tired. At least tell me how close we are. If we got a way to go, I need to take a break.'

Jack pointed to the ground and kept on walking. 'Take a seat then, but I'm not waiting and neither is the wind,' Jack snapped.

Luke stopped and threw his water bottle at Jack's back. 'Fuck you, this is bullshit,' he shouted.

Jack furious, turned around, picked up the water bottle, and started marching toward Luke. 'I don't have time for this pussy shit. It doesn't matter if we're minutes or days from the bunker.

We slow down, we die. Keep up, or we part ways,' Jack explained shouting. He tossed the water bottle violently back at Luke.

The leaves near their feet rustled quietly.

Luke fumbled, but caught the bottle. There was a moment of hesitation before Luke spoke again, 'Look man, you're right. But I'm asking as your friend, just one break.'

Jack's eyes narrowed. 'You and I are not friends. You keep up or find your own way,' he said shrugging.

Again the leaves snuck around beneath them. Above, the tree line swayed discreetly.

Luke sighed, "I get the whole 'we're not friends thing,' but…" Luke's sentence was interrupted by a quick cough. He moved to speak again, but this time he was met with an even more violent cough. Blood flew from his mouth and onto his hand as he moved it to cover the cough. Luke looked from his hand to Jack with panicked eyes.

It was too late to take another gasp of air, they'd have to work with what they had. Quickly they both knelt down and threw their backpacks off. As they did a light gust blew past them, kicking up the nearby leaves. A quiet whistle passed through the trees. The two men dug through their backpacks each grabbing a washcloth that they had stored inside. They doused the cloths with water and slapped them to their faces.

The tree line began to sway with incredible force, dancing back and forth menacingly. The single hushed whistle turned to a chorus. The leaves took full flight, and began swirling around and above them.

Jack did his best to close his mind. He could feel that he wasn't working with much breath. This would take all his concentration. Luke was knelt across from him and staring intently into his eyes.

The wind picked up even more, and Jack could feel it rushing around them. He struggled to keep his balance against the powerful gusts. With the roaring winds and the fluttering of the leaves, the sound was deafening. It went on for what felt like a lifetime. His lungs burned as he desperately tried to clear his mind, but the noise of the wind was all too distracting. It wasn't dying down, and Jack pressed the wet cloth to his face as tightly as he could.

He was writhing in agony. One breath and it was over. He had to hold on.

Another lifetime passed and his vision began to blur. The cloth held firmly to his face became his only reminder that he wasn't to breathe. It wasn't just his lungs that craved the oxygen now, but his brain too. He began swaying in the wind, like the trees above. He could barely make out Luke's face just a few feet in front of him.

Still no sign of the wind stopping. Things were going black. All he could see was the silhouette of Luke's head shaking back and forth in front of him. Then, just black.

There was no noise, no vision, no feeling. Nothing. Just one thought screaming in the back of his head. 'Breathe!'

Jack loosened his grip on the cloth and prepared to taste the sweet nectar of oxygen around him.

'No!' another voice shouted. Another wet cloth slapped his face held by someone else's hand.

Jack fought to breathe, but he was half conscious and weakened. The other hand was stronger, and he suffocated under its weight. He fought to breathe through the pressure, but he couldn't.

He felt himself leaving. This was death. It was easier than fighting, so he stopped. This was the end.

For a third lifetime, he sat in that place. The place between life and death. He was just about to leave and never return. But then he felt the pressure that had been so forcefully held to his face removed.

Desperately he began sucking in air, gasping violently. Then his senses began to return. No more wind blasting against him. No more howling throughout the forest. No more leaves in the air. Just Luke, gasping next to him in awe.

When they'd both caught their breath Jack walked over to a nearby tree and rested against it. Luke followed and did the same.

Jack looked at him and nodded. 'Thanks. I wasn't going to make it,' he admitted.

'You'd have done the same. That's why we're together. Not because we are friends,' Luke said calmly.

Jack fought back a smile. 'What do you say we take a break? There's only about an hour left, but I think we could use one,' he said."

The heavy scene hung in the air of the kitchen, and Ethan had to remind himself to breathe.

Marcus took a deep breath. "Sounds fun," Marcus joked solemnly. "But why the washcloths?"

"Earlier in the book they explain," Ethan started, "They use them as a last line of defense if they can't hold their breath. Instead they'll end up trying to breathe through the wet cloth and won't be able to."

"That scene is a lot heavier than something I would have picked to have happen to us. Why did it have to be that scene in particular?" Marcus asked.

Ethan grabbed a few washcloths and water bottles and stuffed them into his backpack. "It's the only scene where two guys are walking around in the forest. It's pretty similar to what we'll be doing, so it should be predictable," he explained. "Besides, every other 'dangerous' scene in the book ends with someone dead or injured."

Marcus thought about that, "Well why don't you just write something? You are a writer."

"One, I'm not sure it works that way. Two, I don't have time," Ethan said as he watched the sun rising through the kitchen window. "Now c'mon, pack up your stuff. We gotta get going, I want to be back before Ashley misses us."

Mention of Ashley seemed to shut Marcus up. He just nodded and started filling the backpack.

Ethan drove while Marcus gave directions.

"There aren't any hiking trails near this point. We're going to have to pull over on the main road and trail blaze," Marcus explained.

They did just that. Found the spot on the road closest to the point, pulled over, got out and started walking into the forest. Near the road the forest wasn't very dense with shrubs or rough terrain, and it was an easy walk into the forest. The two men started off relatively silent. They were in nervous anticipation of what was to come. Death bearing winds, or something even worse.

Marcus was the first to speak. "So, you and Ash are doing alright now huh?" he asked.

Ethan smiled at that. If Marcus was noticing, then there had to be some truth to it. Maybe he and Ashley had a chance after all. "Yeah, I think so. I'd been letting my insecurities get the best of me, and I think that is what started the downward spiral. I'm really trying to move past that now," Ethan confided.

Marcus, "I'm glad to hear that. What insecurities are you talking about though? You're a great guy."

Ethan sighed. "I don't know. Growing up, you always got the girl. Most girls only talked to me, because they wanted to get closer to you. Made it hard to believe a girl would ever be into me. Especially a girl like Ashley."

Marcus frowned. He knew it was true, but it upset him all the same. "You shouldn't let that make you feel less desirable dude. It just reflects shitty on the girls that did that. Not on you," Marcus offered.

"I know you're right. But it's one thing to know it, and another thing to feel it," Ethan said with a pause. "Hell, the whole reason our friendship started to get weird was my fault. I was jealous of you. There was always a part of me that believed Ashley would rather be with you than me. And because of that I started treating you both like crap and ran away to my writing."

Marcus looked down. He couldn't face Ethan after hearing that and said nothing.

Ethan started again, "I'm sorry man. You've always been like a brother to me, I shouldn't have been so childish. I'm so close to being able to figure myself out and move past that dumb shit. But even though I can admit the role my insecurities played, I still can't shake that gnawing feeling that there's something more going on. That's why we need to find the Heart of the Forest. That's where I'll get my answers."

Marcus didn't know what to say. He was riddled with guilt. Still, he felt a duty to his friend to at least acknowledge what he was saying. He walked up to Ethan and hugged him. Ethan resisted slightly at first, but eventually embraced his friend. It was a long hug, and both of them felt it release tons of weight off of their shoulders. They always said it to each other, but in that moment, they realized that they truly were brothers.

As they broke off the hug, Marcus looked at Ethan and muttered, "Don't get weird on me, ok."

Ethan laughed, "Yeah, ok."

They changed the subject to something more light, and continued on their hike. Along the way, there were a few scares when the wind would pick up. It was a strange feeling to live in fear of the slightest breeze. Not only that, but the two hadn't fully put their encounter with the wolves, or the shadow behind them. The darker parts of the forest put them on edge, and the briefest sound of wild-life made them jump. But that was all it was turning out to be. Fear.

A couple hours into the hike Marcus pulled out his phone to check the map, something he'd been doing periodically. "Damn, I gotta see how close we are, because I'm starting to need a break," Marcus said catching his breath.

Ethan felt the same way and was about to agree. But then he realized. "No don't!" Ethan shouted.

Marcus looked at him confused. "What? I'm just looking at my phone," Marcus explained.

Ethan realized it was too late. In trying to prevent it, even he'd played his part. He hurriedly took his backpack off and opened it. "Marcus, this is how it starts,' Ethan blurted.

Marcus understood and began removing his own backpack. He looked out into the forest, and as if on cue a light breeze shuddered toward them from beyond the trees.

As fast as he could, Ethan took a deep breath. But as he did, he also let out a slight cough, and with it a small spat of blood.

Ethan uncapped one of the water bottles and doused the wash-cloth before applying it to his nose and mouth. He moved toward Marcus and knelt before him. His mind was racing. On the page, Luke was the one to complain about taking a break, and Jack had been the one who nearly passed out and died. Here, Marcus had broached the subject of a break, and that meant Ethan was the one who would face death's door. He began to panic.

Marcus had caught up, and was kneeling next to his friend, a damp cloth of his own held firmly to his face. A second breeze passed, followed by huge and violent gusts of wind. Marcus held his breath and remained locked on eye contact with Ethan.

Ethan was struggling to hold his breath already. The bloody cough had not been alone. He wasn't just trying to hold his breath; he was fighting back a coughing fit.

It was getting harder to hold their breath with every moment. Marcus tried to concentrate on clearing his mind, but couldn't. The situation was too real. It wasn't just some page in a book anymore. He could die, and all he could think about were his regrets. To his own dismay, Marcus realized that his biggest regret was not betraying his friend's trust, like he'd expected. His regret was not giving himself and Ashley a chance. He couldn't explain it, but he knew that Ashley was the love of his life. They were meant to be together. He had wanted to give his friend a chance at happiness. So he had ignored his feelings, and instead had let them become nothing but a stupid affair. The worst of both worlds. As selfish as it was, more than anything Marcus regretted ignoring his own feelings for the benefit of his friend's.

At that point, they could hardly stand their ground against the strong winds as they howled and moaned throughout the forest around them. Still, Marcus was more distracted by his regrets than his surroundings.

Ethan on the other hand, had discovered that the cough had been a blessing in disguise. He realized that telling yourself to hold back a cough was easier than telling yourself not to breath. Luckily, in this case they were one in the same. He desperately fought back the urge to cough, and he could feel his chest starting to ache for air. He knew it wouldn't be long before he could no longer hold his breath, and he could only hope that Marcus would save him, just as Luke had saved Jack.

Moment after moment passed, and Ethan began to feel dizzy. His chest was on fire, but his head was beginning to feel a strange combination of light and heavy. The temptation to breathe grew exponentially with every second. In response, Ethan pressed the wet cloth to his face with more and more strength. He knew that soon he would start to pass out, just as Jack had. But he had to hold on until that moment. All the while, Ethan kept his eyes locked on Marcus.

Marcus did not seem to be doing as well as Ethan would have expected. Marcus was blinking a lot. Every so often he would shut his eyes for what seemed like a long moment, before lazily opening them again. C'mon, Marcus, hang in there. I need you to save me, Ethan thought to himself. The wind howled menacingly around them. To Ethan it sounded almost like a mocking laugh.

Long moments passed, and Marcus only looked worse. Ethan felt himself waning as well. Things were going dark, and he wasn't sure how much longer he could hold on. Soon, he had reached his limit. He could only hope that Marcus would stop him, because he could no longer stop himself. The temptation to breathe had won. Ethan loosened his grip on the cloth covering his mouth and prepared to taste the air around him.

In that same moment, Ethan saw Marcus close his eyes, begin to stumble over, and remove the cloth from his face. Ethan didn't think, he just acted.

Ethan called out, "No!" without any intention of doing so. He tore the cloth from his mouth and nose, quickly moving to Marcus and applying it to his face. Marcus struggled against him. It was unnatural to feel someone suffocating under his own hand, while knowing that doing so was saving their life. Ethan had to put the uncomfortable feeling aside.

Ethan no longer even realized he was holding his own breath. His concentration was elsewhere. Ethan held and held, and Marcus struggled and struggled. Eventually Ethan felt Marcus begin to weaken. Panic kicked it as Ethan realized he was about to suffocate his friend to the end.

If Marcus was going to die, he didn't want it to be by his hand. He made a split-second decision to take his hand away. As he did, the winds stopped. No gusts. No breezes. Nothing but a silent forest around them.

As soon as Ethan removed his hand and the cloth, Marcus began choking for air. Ethan followed suit and gasped in the air around him. They had survived, just as the page said they would. Between the page and reality, there were some differences. But in the end, they had survived.

A few minutes later, they had both caught their breath. "I couldn't do it. You saved my life man," Marcus said softly.

"You would have done the same," Ethan said. Internally he laughed at that response. It had been what he wanted to say, but he knew it was no coincidence.

Marcus seemed to feel the same way, because he let out a light laugh and said, "So, about that break?"

CHAPTER 20

After a short break to rest and appreciate being alive, Ethan and Marcus continued toward the midpoint Marcus had marked on his phone.

"As terrifying as that was, it confirmed a few of my theories about how this magic works," Ethan told Marcus. "I still don't understand it, but my guess is that the magic is more likely to work on stories in closer proximity to the forest. Maybe even in closer proximity to the Heart." Ethan pointed to the pin on Marcus' phone.

"Totally worth almost dying for," Marcus said in a dry sarcastic tone. He didn't say it with his typical humorous attitude. He seemed upset.

Ethan picked up on Marcus' attitude but went on anyway. "Maybe not. But we also confirmed that regardless of how much we can try to make similarities, the magic will still alter the events," Ethan explained.

Marcus looked at Ethan with concern. "And what are we going to do with that information? I understand why it means a lot that you find this 'Heart of the Forest,' and I mean, my curiosity is definitely piqued. But this is getting seriously dangerous. If this…" Marcus said pointing to the pin on his map, "If this isn't the right place, then I think we need to drop this. I don't want to go on fighting some magic power."

"This is it. We'll be done after this," Ethan said with a fiery confidence.

Marcus did not look convinced. The run in with the wind had drained him. "I hope so man, I hope so," he said.

A little over a half hour later they arrived at the point marked on Marcus' phone. Just as they did, they came across a clearing. For miles around giant redwoods dominated the land, but in this spot no tree stood. Instead, there was a lonely log cabin. No roads, no paths, no fences.

Just a lonely cabin in the middle of the forest.

Marcus was shocked, "No maps I've looked at said anything about a cabin."

"Considering there isn't even a trail leading here, I think this place is supposed to be a secret," Ethan said, "This is it Marcus. This is the Heart of the Forest." A satisfied smile spread across his face.

The pair cautiously approached the front of the cabin. As they got closer they could make out the cabin much clearer, and even see through its windows. The cabin was well taken care of, and appeared lived in.

Ethan approached the front door with some hesitation, and Marcus followed closely behind. Ethan brought his knuckles to the door and knocked three times, hard and loud. No answer after a few moments of waiting. Ethan knocked again and called out, "Hello? Is anyone home? We just have a few questions." Still no answer.

Ethan hesitated once more, before he grabbed the doorknob and turned it. The door was unlocked and opened with ease.

"Are you sure we should just barge into somebody's house?" Marcus asked.

Ethan looked at Marcus, "We've come this far facing a shadowy figure and apocalyptic winds. I'm not going to let an unlocked door and common courtesy get in the way now." Marcus sighed, but said no more, and followed Ethan inside.

The inside of the cabin was surprisingly cozy. It was still chilly outside, but the cabin held a warmth. Though they were all turned off, Ethan noticed the cabin had lights as well as a couple stand up heaters. He figured there must be a generator hooked up somewhere nearby.

The various lamps and heaters were not the only thing Ethan noticed. The cabin was modestly large, but only consisted of one large room. There was a kitchen area to one side, a small dining table next to that, a lounging area littered with books, a bed with a nightstand, a wardrobe, and a desk covered in papers. An expensive looking typewriter sat upon the desk.

The most attention-grabbing thing inside the cabin was the wall behind the desk. Nearly the entire wall was covered with various types of pages. Ethan approached the desk first, if only to get a better look at the wall. He picked a random page and read it.

"I am wanting. I am waiting. I am worthy. I am wanting. I am waiting. I am worthy. I am here at the Heart. Please. Lend me your gift. Please."

Ethan picked another page.

"Perhaps the heart is not in the center, Perhaps the fool has been led astray. Please show me the way, please give me a sign. I will wait."

Another page.

"A writer with ambitions like no other, the power he awaits is coming, He makes home in the Heart, He waits, he does not rush."

The writing reminded him of the poems he had read from the Unknown Poet. But something was off. Ethan couldn't quite explain it, but the writer in him said that these had not been written by the same person whose poetry he had read at the museum.

Ethan looked to yet another random page.

"The day finally came. An agent arrived in Ustumah City looking for the next great talent. This was an agent that did not see with greed. Instead, they saw with hope. They did not have to look far to discover the humble local. His works filled the agent with awe. 'You will be the next household name,' the agent told the local. And so it became. The local became a household name. And all the writers of the festival who thought themselves so mighty had to accept the truth. They were not worthy. Not like the local was. He was the writer whose words would shape the world."

As Ethan read more and more pages, he saw a lot of the same. They either spoke of someone awaiting the power of the Heart of the Forest, or foretold events that had not yet transpired. At least not to Ethan's knowledge.

While Ethan had been reading the wall, Marcus had been sifting through the papers on the desk. He grabbed a particular paper and handed it to Ethan.

"Check this out," Marcus suggested.

Ethan grabbed the paper and read.

"Dear Mr. Deaven Palmer,

Again, thank you for your submission. You truly have a unique writing style, and I am glad that writing as a hobby has allowed you to experiment with this uniqueness. Your most recent submission showcases this unique style even more so than your past submissions. It was quite a read.

However, as I have said before in past letters, this style is just not what we are looking for here at Lion's Roar Publishing. Also, as I have asked before, please do not submit any more work to me. Especially if the work is of the same nature as your past submissions. This is the last time I will reply to a submission from you.

I hope that writing as your hobby will always bring you joy, but I must be honest and tell you that your pursuit to become a paid writer is not realistic. Your time will be better spent elsewhere. I hope I do not offend; I only wish to offer my professional opinion. Best of luck in your future endeavors.

Best,

Arnold Mueller"

Ethan looked to Marcus, "So this is Deaven's home?"

"Looks like it," Marcus nodded, "There's a lot of similar letters from different publishing companies."

"Damn," Ethan said, "I've received my fair share of rejection letters, but nothing that harsh. It's hard enough to hear 'no,' let alone 'stop writing.'"

Marcus picked up a stack of papers that included newspaper clippings. "There are these too," he said as he handed the stack to Ethan.

Ethan quickly flipped through the stack, gleaning what information he could. All of the papers and clippings appeared to be about a dangerous Jamaican gang with ties all around the United States. Ethan put the stack back where Marcus had found it.

"Deaven may be more dangerous than I initially thought," Ethan admitted.

Marcus shook his head. "Well then we definitely shouldn't be sneaking around in his house," Marcus pleaded.

Ethan sighed, "Unfortunately, you're right. I don't even think this is the Heart of the Forest."

"What makes you say that?" Marcus asked.

Ethan pointed to the wall. "We're not the only ones trying to find the Heart. Deaven seems obsessed with it. It explains why he also checked out those maps. He must have thought this was it. But judging by all his writings, I don't think it is," Ethan explained.

Marcus looked disappointed, but he was still moving to leave. "C'mon let's get out of here," he urged.

Ethan followed, and on his way out he glanced at the books piled in the lounge area. Strangely, Ethan noticed most of the books were cookbooks. He'd expected to see a lot of poetry or fiction books, perhaps even books from the current and past years of the festival. The only non-cookbooks Ethan noticed had titles he'd never heard of.

As the two friends approached the front door, Ethan looked across the cabin to a back door that he hadn't paid much attention to coming in. "Real quick. Let's see what's out back," Ethan suggested as he moved toward the back door.

Marcus hesitated and looked concerned. Despite his doubts, he said nothing and followed.

At the door they slowly pulled it open and peeked out. There was nothing except a path of stepping stones that descended down a slope into the forest.

"We have to," Ethan said, looking at Marcus.

Marcus sighed again, but after a moment shook his head and followed Ethan down the path.

As they descended the stepping stones they began to hear music. They couldn't quite make it out, but it sounded like some sort of jazz or classic rock. They continued down cautiously. They couldn't see past the thickness of the forest, but they also used that to their advantage. They couldn't see much, but they'd be hard to spot themselves.

As they reached the bottom of the path Ethan could make out the song that was playing. It was "You Making Loving Fun," by Fleetwood Mac. Ethan could make out a figure in the distance that seemed to be dancing along. He approached slowly and hid behind a tree to get a better view. Marcus followed stealthily behind.

With a better look, Ethan could clearly see that the figure was Deaven. Deaven swayed side to side to the beat of the music. He was standing in a sort of makeshift outdoor kitchen. There was a pan sizzling over a fire to one side, and a large cooler with a small radio on the other. In front of him was a stone counter top that had been placed atop the stump of a redwood.

With a large knife in hand, Deaven was grabbing fish from the cooler and filleting them on the counter. He sliced away happily and sang aloud to the music.

"I never did belie-e-e-eve in the ways of magic, but I'm beginning to wonder why," Deaven sang out as his knife cut through the fish's flesh. Deaven sang the song surprisingly well, despite his strong accent. It seemed to Ethan that this was far from his first time singing along.

Marcus, awkwardly behind Ethan, tried to move past him to get a better look for himself. As he moved a small branch snapped underneath his foot, and he froze. Ethan looked wide eyed at Deaven.

The tall man perked up at the sound and half looked in their direction, but didn't stop what he was doing. After a few moments he turned his head back toward the counter. "Don't, don't break the spell. It would be different, and you know it will," he sang as he continued along with the lyrics on the radio.

Marcus looked to Ethan and whispered, "Let's go. He's got a knife and seems a little crazy." Ethan thought for a second. At this point he was relatively convinced that this was not the Heart of the Forest. But a part of him felt that there was still something to learn about whatever it was Deaven was doing out there. He weighed that against Marcus' worries that Deaven was dangerous. Ultimately, he decided Marcus was right, mostly because of the papers they'd found about a dangerous Jamaican gang. Ethan nodded and began to slowly back away. Marcus did the same, and they started to make their way up the path.

They were hardly a few feet back when Deaven stopped singing and spoke out. "I already saw you. Don't think you can just sneak off," he said turning around, knife still in hand.

Ethan and Marcus looked to each other unblinking, and then to Deaven. "Hey Deaven," Ethan managed softly. Marcus, who looked ready for action, awkwardly waved.

"So, are you going to tell me what you're doing here?" Deaven asked.

Marcus looked to Ethan who stumbled over an answer, "Well, the thing is. We were looking for, well I guess kind of searching for…"

Deaven broke in, "Searching for the Heart of the Forest."

Ethan couldn't do anything but nod silently. To Deaven he must've looked like a sad puppy dog that had made a mistake.

Deaven twirled the knife in his hand. "You know, back at the museum I thought I told you to stop sticking your nose where it doesn't belong. And you seemed like you were going to listen," he said with a tinge of frustration in his voice.

Marcus spoke up, "Would you mind putting the knife down? It's making me a little uncomfortable."

Deaven laughed, "You're the ones who just snuck up on someone in the middle of the forest," He set the knife down on the counter behind him. "Maybe I should feel uncomfortable."

Ethan ignored their exchange and responded to Deaven's previous statement. "You did tell me, and when you did I had a feeling you knew more than you were letting on. I don't mean to upset you, but I couldn't just let this go," Ethan explained. "Whatever is going on has put me, my friend, and more importantly my girlfriend, in serious danger. I wasn't about to let that go just because you told me to." Ethan stood confidently as he spoke, even taking a step toward Deaven.

A wide grin spread across Deaven's face. "I believe that's half true. But we both know the real reason you keep looking into this. You want something. And however you figured it out, you realized that the Heart could give it to you," he stated boldly. "You're in way over your head, and you really need to let this go."

Ethan felt like Deaven was toying with him. At the least he was treating him like a child. He wasn't going to take it. He'd come this far. "And what if I don't let it go?" Ethan asked defiantly, "You like to make a lot of vague threats."

"Ethan," Marcus said, placing a hand on Ethan's shoulder. Ethan shrugged him off and remained locked on Deaven.

Deaven's grin disappeared. Instead, he regarded Ethan with a more serious tone. "I'm not threatening you. I'm telling you that an entitled writer like yourself is no friend of mine. I don't like you, and I don't like you taking an interest in this," Deaven said laying it all out. "But... I also don't want something bad to happen to you. You're right that the Heart is dangerous. If you don't know what you're doing you could end up dead."

Marcus stepped forward to stand next to Ethan, "Is that another threat?"

Deaven grinned again, looking at Marcus like he was a dumb child. "It's a warning. But if you want to think of it as a threat, then who am I to stop you," he said with a casual coldness.

"Is this the Heart of the Forest? How does its power work? What are you doing out here in an unmapped cabin off the grid?" Ethan blurted out.

Deaven leaned back against the stone counter top, relaxing. "You're not getting any answers from me. Now leave before I call the sheriff. This cabin may be off the grid, but this is still my property," he explained, waving them up the path.

The three men stood there staring at each other in silence. After a few seconds Marcus relaxed and grabbed Ethan. "Come on, let's go," he said.

Ethan wasn't happy about it, but he followed Marcus back up the trail. As they made their way up, they could hear Deaven happily singing to another song playing from the radio. They kept on, to the top of the path, around the cabin, and back into the forest they'd come through.

"That's definitely not the place," Ethan said to Marcus. How do you know?" Marcus asked.

"I guess I don't. I already suspected it wasn't, based on the writings on the wall. But now I'm even more sure. I don't know what is going on, but I get that feeling that Deaven wouldn't have reacted so casually if we were truly at the Heart," Ethan explained.

Marcus didn't respond for a while. When he did, he just said, "I think it's time to drop this. Deaven even said we could end up dead. Warning or threat, I don't think that is something worth getting involved in. We had our little witch hunt. Let's just forget any of this ever happened and move on."

"It's not that easy," Ethan replied without even thinking.

Marcus scowled at Ethan and raised his voice. "Yes, it is that easy. Coming here you were hoping to fix things with Ashley, and you're doing that. Why mess that up? Is this really that important to you?" Marcus shouted.

Ethan thought about that. Marcus had a good point. But even still, Ethan could not shake the feeling at the back of his head that nothing would ever truly be right until he found the Heart of the Forest.

Ethan said nothing, but nodded at Marcus, which calmed his friend down. Then they continued through the forest silently until they got to Ashley's car.

CHAPTER 21

Ashley was just finishing a late breakfast when Ethan and Marcus arrived back at the cabin. Ethan came straight to the kitchen to greet her, but Marcus went straight to his room without a word. Ashley watched him go as Ethan spoke to her, his words flying over her head.

"You there, babe?" Ethan asked, squinting at her. Ashley looked at him. "Yeah sorry, what did you say?"

"I was just saying, sorry. I hope you weren't waiting up long. We tried to be quick," Ethan said.

Ashley saw the look in his eyes. Ethan was worried she was upset and needed assurance.

Comfort even. She walked up to him, gave him a hug, and could feel him relax as she did. "I slept in for a while. Barely noticed you guys were gone. Did you have a good time? Marcus seemed quiet," she pointed out.

Ethan nodded. "Great time," he said, but it was an obvious lie. "He's just tired. We were really marching. I'm beat too, you just don't notice because I'm so excited to see you." He winked at her and kissed her forehead.

Ashley blushed. If there was one thing Ethan knew how to do, it was flatter her. He'd never made her feel like he didn't love her. However, he had a bad habit of making her feel second to his current interests. With Marcus she felt like the only girl in the world. Of course, until there was another girl and her jealousy kicked in. Ashley shook the thoughts away. Ethan was her boyfriend. It was time to put Marcus behind her. It was the right thing to do.

Ashley pushed Ethan away playfully. "You just want me to make you something to eat," she joked.

Ethan smirked, "As nice as that sounds, I was thinking Marcus and I will just grab something at the festival? We'll just shower, get changed, and head over ASAP. No need to make you wait any longer, I know today's fair is what you've really been looking forward to."

It was true. Ashley was a sucker for fairs and she'd been looking forward to day five of the festival since Ethan had told her about it. The whole idea of a writing festival had never really excited her, but she knew that the fair would at least be some fun. "You're not wrong. If you guys wanna eat there, it works for me," she said.

Ethan smiled, "Good. Today's going to be a good day."

Ashley smiled back, but then smacked Ethan in the rear. "Well, what are you waiting for, get in the shower. You too Marcus, I don't hear any water running!" she shouted.

With that, Ethan moved into the bedroom. No response from Marcus, but a few minutes later both showers were running. Ashley had some getting ready to do herself, and she worked on it while they showered.

It wasn't long until they were all ready to go, and in the car on their way into town. Ashley was driving with Ethan in shotgun, while Marcus sat silently in the back. Ashley and Ethan attempted to plan out what kind of activities they wanted to check out, but Marcus' silence dominated the energy in the car. Ashley looked back at him through the rear-view window a few times. Once she caught him reading but trying to hide the fact that he was. Ashley peaked and saw he had a copy of "Temptations Ablaze." She almost called him out, but then thought better of it.

In town, things were crazier than they'd ever been. The entirety of Main Street had been turned into a fairground, ending at the park at the bottom. The street was lined with more stands than any other day. The first section of the street was clearly for food. There was a stand selling pretzels, a stand for hot dogs, one for caramel apples, one for ice cream, one for this and one for that. Each stand had a cute name to go with the theme of fiction. "Hyperbole's Hot Dogs! For when you're so hungry you could eat a horse!" and "Plot Pretzels! Finally, a plot with a real twist!"

It was all so outrageous, but that was what Ashley loved about fairs. For a moment she was so distracted by it, that she didn't notice Marcus and Ethan fall behind. When she turned around, she saw them talking. Ethan looked concerned, but Marcus patted him, smiled, and said something that appeared to ease Ethan's mind. Then Marcus looked to Ashley and waved weakly. She waved back, confused. He then turned and walked over to a hot dog stand. He seemed so sad, and Ashley felt her heart aching with his.

Ethan rushed over, and she immediately questioned him. "What's going on with Marcus?"

Ethan thought for a moment and sighed. "He's just in a weird mood today. There was a weird moment between us on the hike, but I didn't think it was that big of a deal. He told me he just wants some time to himself and wants us to enjoy the fair as a couple," Ethan explained.

"We've never minded him third wheeling before. Why would he think we would now?" Ashley asked.

Ethan shrugged. "I don't know. Like I said, he's in a weird mood today. Let's just enjoy the fair, you and me. We can worry about Marcus later; I just want to be with you."

Ashley knew he was right. It was the perfect day for them to just enjoy as a couple. Ethan wanted a pretzel and they walked to get one. Ashley looked back at Marcus once more. He was staring at them, and when he saw her look over, he looked away.

Ashley wondered if it was related to what her and Marcus had spoken about. Is this him stepping out of the picture, she thought. It was supposed to be the right thing to do, but it didn't feel like it. Her head was a mess with emotions. She decided to push the thoughts of Marcus aside. Today was going to be about her and Ethan.

Once Ethan had his pretzel, the couple continued further down the street and into the fair.

There was a kids' section with a ball pit set up, and multiple arts and crafts stands. They walked by most of them, but stopped for a moment to admire a particularly interesting stand. Multiple children sat scribbling away on pieces of paper while excited parents looked on and murmured to each other. The sign above read, "-Children's Short Story Sprint Contest- Will Your Child be the Next Future

Bestselling Writer?!" Ashley and Ethan didn't stay to hear the stories, but it was fun to watch the kids rapidly write down their thoughts.

"I had the craziest story ideas when I was that young," Ethan admitted. "I'd be so embarrassed if I'd had to share them in front of a crowd like that. Good for those kids."

Ashley laughed and grabbed Ethan's hand, caressing it. "I can only imagine the kind of stories a young Ethan would think up. The thought of it is as cute as it is scary."

They moved on from the children's section until they reached an area clearly meant for the more writing minded individuals of the festival. There were tons of stands belonging to small time authors Ashley, and even Ethan, had never heard of. The authors were handing out free copies of their work. Sadly, there weren't many takers. Most people in the area were flocking to other stands trying to sell people on writing workshops. Or the Short Story Sprint Contest stand, an adult version of the children's stand they had passed earlier. Ashley quickly tried to convince Ethan to join.

"That would be in bad taste I think," Ethan said. "Not that I think I'm an amazing writer, but as a contestant I'd look arrogant entering a contest with a bunch of randoms."

"Afraid you'll lose?" Ashley teased.

Ethan caught on and threw the ball back in her court, "Why don't you enter? I'd love to see if any of my talent rubbed off on you last night."

The thought of entering the contest horrified Ashley, and the conversation quickly ended after that. They moved on. Once they were out of the writing area they found themselves surrounded by carnival games. Ashley was in heaven. The carnival games were the thing she loved most about fairs. She wasn't sure why she loved them so much, perhaps it was nostalgia. Her parents had taken her to plenty of fairs when she was younger. Either way it didn't matter to her. She just knew she loved them.

"Wanna play some?" Ashley asked.

Ethan smiled, "You kidding? We're playing them all. This is totally your thing!"

Ashley blushed again. She realized that sometimes she took Ethan for granted. He wasn't the perfect boyfriend, but he loved her and he knew her. He didn't just know things about her, he cared enough to learn the nuances. He truly wanted to make her happy. Shouldn't that be enough, she thought. It wasn't like she'd been a perfect girlfriend.

The couple walked over to the closest game. It was a spin on the classic ring toss. Rather than toss the rings at a bunch of random bottles there were only 5 bottles set up in a triangle shape with the point of the triangle furthest from the player. The left two bottles of the triangle were slightly closer than the right two. The bottles were labeled from left to right: "Exposition - 1 Point, Rising Action - 3 Points, Climax - 5 Points, Falling Action - 4 Points, and Resolution - 2 Points."

The game was seven dollars to play, and you were given seven rings to toss. A score of twenty-six won you a huge stuffed animal of your choosing. A score of twenty-one won you a toy that looked like it came out of a fifty-cent machine.

Ethan loved the writing theme of the game and was eager to play. He picked up the 7 rings and started tossing. His first throw was toward the closer, two point, "resolution" bottle on the far right. The ring landed far from its mark. He threw another, this time toward the even closer "rising action" bottle. The ring hit the bottle and bounced off. Frustrated, Ethan threw the next ring toward the furthest and center "climax" bottle. The ring glided easily onto the bottle.

"Five points! Maybe we're reaching the climax!" the game runner shouted with cartoonish enthusiasm.

Ethan, looking proud of himself, picked up the four remaining rings and tossed them one by one at the center bottle. One more managed to land on the bottle. The other three, Ethan's aim was slightly off and he accidentally landed on the "rising action" bottle.

"Looks like we might be more in the rising action! Three rings for four points and two for five, that's twenty-two points! Congratulations sir, here is your prize," The game runner said as he handed Ethan a quarter sized prize. It was a miniature book titled "Bestseller," and Ethan realized it was a pencil topper.

Ashley giggled. "Nice job bestseller. Let me show you how it's done," she said.

Ethan rolled his eyes and paid the man another seven dollars. "I bet you can't beat twenty-two," he challenged.

The man handed Ashley seven rings and she began to toss. With expert-like precision she landed her first four rings on the middle "climax" bottle, one after the other.

The game runner shouted excitedly after each toss. "Now here's a woman who knows how to get to the good part of a story!" he said after her fourth toss.

Ashley stuck her tongue out at Ethan, enjoying watching him squirm. "I'll play it a little safer for these last few. Gotta make sure I win that giant rabbit," she continued teasing, pointing to a huge stuffed animal rabbit hanging above the bottles.

Her next three tosses were just as finely aimed as the first four. Each ring landed skillfully around the four point "rising action" bottle.

The game runner, clearly impressed, said nothing. He just clapped loudly before announcing her score, "Thirty-two points. Highest score of the day. Somebody's played the ring toss before." Then he grabbed the giant rabbit, handing it to Ashley.

Ashley thanked him and turned to Ethan. "Hold this for me," she said as she shoved the awkwardly large stuffed animal into his arms.

"Alright, you're the best. I know that's what you want to hear," Ethan said muffled through the giant rabbit covering his face.

"Oh, nice try. You've still got a lot of games to lose before you concede," she said spreading her arms to the dozens of game stands surrounding them.

Ethan sighed as they moved to the next game, but Ashley could tell it was all a show. He loved it when she showed off. He'd told her on multiple occasions. And she had to admit, she liked it too.

Game after game, Ashley won and Ethan's hands grew more and more full. At one point they had to make a trip back to the car just to stow some of her winnings. Hours later they'd played every game there, some more than once. The game runners politely asked her to stop when they realized that she'd all their prizes if they let her keep playing. When they were done with the games they continued on down Main Street to see the rest of the fair.

As they made their way down the street, they noticed a small crowd forming around a hysterical woman. "Have you seen her? Have you seen her anywhere? Do you people even care?!" the woman shouted angrily at the crowd.

Ethan frowned and became suddenly silent. "What's wrong?" Ashley asked.

"That's the mother of the missing girl. The one I ran into the other night. Her name is Elisa. Her daughter's name is Ella," Ethan said almost robotically.

The woman screamed on. "What is wrong with you people?! My daughter is missing and you're all out here partying?! Don't you care?! Don't you care?! Don't you..." Then she started to cry uncontrollably.

Ethan started to walk toward her and turned toward Ashley. "We should do something. She is hurting, and those people are just staring," he said.

Ashley nodded and started to follow. But as they walked over, Officer Riley appeared from the crowd and put his arms around the woman trying to comfort her. It only made her cry even harder. Riley began waving the crowd away. "Ok everyone, get out of here. Enjoy your day and give this woman some space please."

Ethan stopped at the sight of Riley. As the crowd dispersed, Riley escorted Elisa away. At one point Riley noticed Ethan and the two locked eyes. Riley glared at Ethan until he was out of sight.

Ashley could see the guilt on Ethan's face. "Babe, I told you, it's terrible, but you can't blame yourself just because your book has some similarities. Don't let it ruin a good day. You're too hard on yourself. Not everything is your fault."

Ethan nodded. "You're right. We're having a good day. And not everything is my fault, but sometimes things are more complicated than they seem," he said.

Ashley wasn't sure what to make of that, but she felt that part of what she'd said had gotten through to him. He seemed to cheer up a little.

The last section before the park hosted some slightly bigger attractions. There was a rock-climbing wall known as the "Fourth Wall." Also, an apple bobbing station called the Alliteration Apple

Area. Both looked like fun. But before they could decide to take an interest in either, a nearby woman began calling to them.

"Lucky us folks! It's one of the festival's fiction contestants, Ethan Garland. Come on over here sir, don't be shy," she shouted waving them over.

Startled, Ethan and Ashley hesitated before eventually making their way over. The woman was standing next to a large dunking booth where a man in a swimsuit was waiting on the collapsing seat. The man appeared relatively dry. The target that activated the collapsing seat was rather small, and Ashley figured that not many had hit it.

"Hello there Mr. Garland. A pleasure, a pleasure. Thank you for joining us," the woman said vaguely.

Ethan looked at the woman and the small family of three standing around her. "Of course, thanks for having me. Um, this is my girlfriend, Ashley." he said, his voice shaking slightly.

Ashley almost felt bad for him. But she figured it was good for him to get some recognition, even if it made him a little nervous. "Hi, nice to meet you," Ashley said.

The woman waved excitedly at them both. "My name is Michelle and that is my partner Joseph," she said, pointing at the man on the collapsing seat. Joseph waved down to Ethan and Ashley. "We work for the World of Writing Foundation. We're a global non-profit charity that focuses on teaching writing to those not fortunate enough to learn on their own."

Ashley nodded, "Oh yeah, I've heard of you guys. You make a real difference in the communities you touch."

Michelle smiled at that. "I like to think we do. Thank you for saying that," she said pausing for a moment.

"Now I'm going to cut to the chase. This dunking booth was supposed to be a way to bring in some money for the charity, but it's seeming that nobody cares about dunking a no name like Joseph over there. Except for this fine group of people here of course," Michelle said pointing to the small group of three that had been there when they arrived.

"I saw you passing by, and I know this a lot to ask, but I was hoping we could get you up there above the tank. A big-name writer like yourself will surely draw some attention. Again, sorry for being so abrupt but I had to ask," Michelle said. Now she'd become the one who was nervous.

Ashley looked to Ethan expectantly, but his reaction hardly surprised her. "Of course! I'm not sure I'd consider myself a big-name writer, but I'd love to help a good cause like this," Ethan said. He eagerly dug his wallet and phone out of his pockets, handing them to Ashley.

As she put them in her purse she gave him a kiss, whispering a quick, "I love you," in his ear. Ethan just winked and moved toward the tank where he switched places with Joseph.

Michelle thanked Ethan again before grabbing a megaphone from the stand. Then she began calling out to the masses. "Who's ready to dunk a man for a good cause?! Today we have Ethan Garland, author of *'In Despair,'* awaiting you folks lucky enough to hit the target and send him into the tank! Only five dollars a try, and the money goes to helping spread the art of writing around the world! What is there to lose?!"

Michelle repeated the message over and over. Each time she did, more and more people arrived at the stand. Her and Joseph quickly began taking payments and handing people balls. It wasn't long before people we're chucking balls at the target. The first two people missed, but the third connected. Ethan's eyes went wide as the seat collapsed beneath him and he fell into the water. The crowd that had gathered cheered, attracting even more people.

Ethan whose clothes were now soaked, climbed back onto the seat and awaited his inevitable fate again. People paid and threw their ball over and over like clockwork. About one out of three people hit the target, and Ashley was getting a kick out of watching Ethan fall in again and again. Some people shouted things at Ethan as they took their shot. "Loved your book," "Can't wait for your next story," "Haven't read it yet, but I will now," and even "You should have won!"

Ethan was up there for a good hour, and really seemed to be enjoying himself. But toward the end he started shivering. Being constantly soaked was catching up to him. The next time he got dunked, Michelle broke in.

"Alright everyone. It looks like Mr. Garland has been dunked more than enough times. We don't want to get him sick, even if it is for a good cause," Michelle said motioning for Ethan to come down. "Stick around though, you can all get a chance to dunk my partner here, Joseph."

Ethan didn't budge, instead he motioned Michelle over and whispered in her ear. She returned and waved Ashley over, handing her a ball. "Alright, our favorite author had one request. He wants to give his girlfriend Ashley one chance to dunk him. If she hits the target, Mr. Garland will donate five hundred dollars to the World of Writing Foundation."

The crowd clapped excitedly for both Ashley and Ethan. Ashley just looked at Ethan and laughed. All he did was smile and wink back, his signature move of the day.

Ashley got into position, and carefully aimed. She threw the ball. The target made a satisfying ding as the ball made contact, and Ethan plunged downward into the tank one last time.

"A big round of applause for the most modest writer at this festival," Michelle yelled to the crowd as she clapped. The crowd cheered and clapped along with her.

Ashley helped pull Ethan out of the tank and kissed him on his way out. "Who cares about the contest, I think this is the biggest win of the festival," she said.

Ethan smiled. "Definitely. But mostly because it's been a great day with you," he said looking into her eyes.

Ashley blushed, and Ethan went over to settle things with Michelle and a large group of fans waiting to talk to him. As she waited, she reflected on the day so far. It had been a great day, and she'd been glad they spent it together. However, her mind wandered, and she found herself thinking of Marcus. She hoped he was having a good day, and she wished he'd been with them. It hurt to realize that even happy thoughts of Ethan led her to sad ones of Marcus. She cared about Ethan, she loved him. But a part of her knew that she didn't love Ethan the way she loved Marcus. It was different. All she could hope was that someday that would change. Maybe Marcus was right when he said that the best thing for all of them was if he separated himself.

But it just made Ashley sad to think of Ethan and Marcus losing their brotherhood. And even sadder to think of her and Marcus losing their bond. She shook the thoughts away. Today, she just wanted to enjoy being with Ethan.

Ethan dried off the best he could, signed a check to the World of Writing Foundation, and chatted with his fans. After, he and Ashley made their way to the park where a band was playing on the stage. On the way over a kid stopped them. He couldn't have been older than eighteen.

"Excuse me, Ethan Garland?" he half asked.

"Yeah that's me," Ethan answered.

"Listen, I'm sure you get this all the time, and I'm really sorry, but I'm a huge fan," the kid said.

Ethan grinned. "Always good to meet a fan. Don't worry; you're not bothering me at all. What's your name?" Ethan asked, stretching out his hand for a shake.

The kid eagerly took his hand and shook it. "I'm Lance. Lance O'Day."

"Nice to meet you, Lance. This is my girlfriend Ashley," Ethan said, motioning to Ashley.

She took Lance's hand and shook it too. "Nice to meet you," she said.

"Oh man, I'm so nervous," Lance admitted. "Your book changed my life. I've always wanted to be a writer, but *In Despair* showed me what is really possible with writing. The emotions it can help people understand. One day I hope I'm half the writer you are."

Ethan laughed nervously. "I'm glad you liked the book; it's always nice to hear. But don't compare yourself to me. With passion like that, I'm sure you'll be a great writer one day. Much more than half the writer I am."

Lance's eyes lit up. "Thank you so much for saying that Ethan. I mean, Mr. Garland!"

"Ethan is fine," Ethan said, trying to calm Lance.

There was a moment of silence, and then Lance reached into his back pocket and unfolded a large stack of paper. "This is a manuscript for something I've been working on. I'm sorry if it's asking a lot, but I was hoping you would read it and tell me what you think."

Ethan was stunned and didn't respond for a moment. Ashley could see Lance's nerves building. "Never mind! I'm asking too much!" Lance blurted out.

Ethan stopped him. "No, not at all. I was just surprised. Nobody has ever asked me that. I'd be honored, Lance."

"Wait, really? It would mean the world to me. Thank you so much!" Lance said.

Ethan took the manuscript and exchanged phone numbers with Lance so that he could contact him after reading it. Lance thanked Ethan about ten more times before he started to leave.

"Thanks again, Mr. Garland. I'll let you get back to enjoying the fair. Thank you so much," Lance said as he ran off into the crowd.

Ethan handed the manuscript to Ashley, and she put it in her purse. "Are you actually going to read it?" Ashley asked.

"Of course," Ethan answered quickly. "I love that he looks up to me enough to want my opinion so badly. And he reminds me a lot of myself when I was younger. That might be a really good story in your purse, and if it's not, maybe I can help him make it one. I wasn't kidding when I said with passion like that he could be an amazing writer."

Ashley knew Ethan was one of the few writers at the festival that would actually read a fan's manuscript. He was a good guy, and she was glad to be with him. She grabbed his hand, and they continued on their way to the park where the band was playing.

In the park there were also stands selling beer. Ashley, a sucker for a craft beer, made sure she and Ethan had more than a few. They drank their beers and danced to the music with the rest of the crowd. The band on stage was from a local town, and Ashley had never heard of them. They played a lot of original songs, but Ashley liked it.

Slowly getting drunk and enjoying the music, Ashley and Ethan danced together for what felt like hours. It reminded Ashley of when they'd first met back in college. Drinking, partying, and dancing was a part of their daily routine. The memories were warm, and she lived halfway in them and halfway in the present. It was the perfect way to end a great day. Or it was until Ethan took a trip to the bathroom. When he came back, everything seemed different.

CHAPTER 22

Ethan realized he was pretty drunk as he danced to the music with Ashley. The local band was pretty good, but their music was nowhere near as mesmerizing as watching Ashley's body move to the rhythm. Ever since he'd met her, every time he saw her dance, he wondered how every man in the room wasn't fighting for a closer view. She'd always been the most beautiful woman he'd ever seen, and he knew she always would be. Dancing with her brought back so many memories. Memories of a time when they were just friends. A time before he worked up the courage to tell her how he felt and make the move to something more.

He never regretted telling her. Being with her had been the best thing that had ever happened to him. But sometimes he missed the days when they were just friends. Things were simpler then. He had been so much less afraid that he would lose her. He was happy now, but a part of him envied the past. As he danced with her, he felt himself living partway in that past, and it was an amazing feeling. An honest reminder of just how lucky he was.

The band sang out in calm country voices, "All we needed was a day for each other. We wished it would last forever. I knew I was the luckiest man. I hope I showed you that I am. That day you finished the game. And I had to face my fame. Together we're better. No matter the weather. I was soaked by the end. But you were still there, my friend." Lyrics from their own original songs. "Now all I want to do. Is dance with you. I'm here in the now. But I'm remembering how. Let's just stay until we can. I want to be your man."

Ethan was definitely drunk, but as he listened more closely to the song, something about the lyrics made him feel slightly uncomfortable. He realized he needed to go to the restroom, and he let

Ashley know as he made his way out of the crowd. On the way to the restrooms he thought about the lyrics.

A day for each other. Finished the game. Face my fame. I was soaked by the end. I'm here in the now, but I'm remembering how, Ethan thought to himself. He replayed those lyrics over and over. They were the ones that stood out to him. His drunken mind struggled, but finally he realized. The song was a retelling of his day up until that point. It had been a great day. But now he wondered if it was even real. If the forest brought the lyrics to life, had any of it been free will?

No matter how hard he tried, Ethan couldn't escape the reach of the Heart of the Forest. He had been obsessed with finding it. Even after Marcus had pointed out that it wasn't worth it, he still couldn't shake his curiosity and need to find the answers it offered. But he had tried. He'd known Marcus was right, and he'd spent the day with Ashley trying to forget the forest. But it constantly reminded him of its presence. Taunting him. First with the distraught mother, Elisa, and now with a lesson that no part of his life, good or bad, was free of its influence. It was all Ethan could think about now. He wondered just how much of his time at the festival was being dictated by words written on a page.

That was when, almost as if it were fate, he stepped on the flier. It made a crumpling sound under his foot and he looked down at it. It was a flier about the festival. It was advertising the two runners-up for the best poem of the year — Claire's "The Human Journey" and her competition. Ethan reread Claire's poem.

The Human Journey
Nothing so familiar as the concepts of ourselves.
No mystery greater than that of me. A threat if left unchecked,
overwhelms.
The path to the solution, now plain to see. To begin to understand
we look to the past.
From there we face demons with those we call friend. Perhaps our
answers lie in a place things were stashed. Yet there will always be
others who cannot comprehend.
When the winds of change come, we must be ready.

Next, we stumble upon the crimson beast we know not about.
Now finally we realize we've had the answers already.
The next place we go will fill us with doubt.
Seeking help from another we visit a corpse approved. Finally, we
venture to a place, expectation removed.

Written by Claire Donaghue

Ethan shook his head and laughed in frustration as he read the poem. He couldn't have known the first time he'd read it, but it was still upsetting to know that the answers had been right in front of him the entire time. Just like the song, if Ethan took the time to think about it, the lines of the poem outlined the events of the past few days.

It was the line about the winds of change that allowed him to make the connection. The title of the book was right there, clear as day. It could only be referring to his encounter with the wind earlier that day. From there he worked his way backward through the poem.

There will always be others who cannot comprehend, Ethan thought to himself. At first the line made no sense, so he went to the next one. Our answers lie in a place where things were stashed. He had to think about it, but he figured it was talking about Marcus' trip to the courthouse and the old maps. He told himself that it made sense. After all, it was where he had thought the key to finding the Heart of the Forest was. Right after their encounter with the shade in the forest.

Ethan nodded to himself and read the next line, We face demons with those we call friend. That terrifying spirit was the closest thing to a demon he'd ever seen.

With the context of the other lines, he had an idea what the line about "others not comprehending" meant. He assumed it was his "interview" with Riley. He'd wanted so badly to tell Riley the truth, but had known he wouldn't understand or believe him.

Ethan went on working backwards to the next line. To begin to understand we look to the past. Everything was clicking for Ethan now. He'd found himself on that first hike with Marcus because of what he'd found at the museum, looking to the past. Next line,

Ethan thought, the path to the solution, now plain to see. The haiku that had set him on his entire search in the first place. The poem mentioning the Heart of the Forest.

The first three lines of Claire's poem were vague enough to mean a lot of things that he could relate to the past few days. Ethan didn't bother himself with trying to figure out exactly what, he just knew that they did. Instead, he moved on past the line about the winds of change, working forward through the poem. The crimson beast we know not about, he said to himself. He thought, but couldn't link it to anything in particular that had happened since that morning. He toyed with the idea of it referring to the cabin or Deaven, but couldn't make a connection.

Maybe it hasn't happened yet, he realized.

Ethan moved on to the next line anyway. Now finally we realize we've had the answers already. The line gave Ethan an uneasy feeling as he realized. It was him, right then, right there, reading the poem. He couldn't help but once again feel the forest was taunting him. The more he thought about it, the angrier he got. Magical entity or not, he was done being its plaything. If the current line was what was happening now, then the remaining three lines of the poem were still going to happen. But he wasn't going to wait around for that. He'd skip right to the end by interpreting the final line. He'd cheat at the forest's own game.

Finally, we venture to a place, expectation removed.

Ethan thought about it. But nothing came to him. It was easy to connect the lines with things that had already happened. But it was much more difficult to use them to predict the future. He kept thinking about it as he made his way to the restroom. He finished up there and made his way back to Ashley.

She was still happily dancing away and pulled him closer when he arrived. She danced with him, pressing her body close to his. He moved with her, but his heart was no longer in it. Not like it had been just minutes ago. Now all he could think about was the line from the poem, and where it would lead him.

Finally, we venture to a place, expectation removed.

Ashley noticed Ethan's sudden change and was pulled out of the happy trance they had been sharing. "What's wrong babe?" she asked.

There was a real concern in her voice that Ethan knew he should address. The problem was that he didn't know-how. If he tried to tell her the truth, he doubted she would even believe him. Even if Marcus backed up his story, it was something someone needed to see to believe. On top of that Ethan felt that even if she believed him, it would be of no benefit to her. So he lied.

"Nothing. Well, I mean, not nothing. Just…" Ethan hesitated, "I'm not feeling so good. Maybe that pretzel I ate, being soaked earlier, or the beers. I'm just feeling a little sick."

Ashley stared at him. They'd been together long enough that not only did she know when he was lying but he knew when she knew. Right then she knew. Even still she just said, "Oh babe, I'm sorry. Do you want to head back to the cabin? It's been a long day for you, and we've had our fun."

Ethan nodded. "Yeah, I think that'd be best. Sorry to ruin the end of the day."

Ashley shook her head. "No, it was a great day. You're not ruining anything. Let's go find Marcus," she said digging her phone out of her purse.

Ethan agreed and followed her up Main Street as she called Marcus to meet up. Ethan couldn't wait to get back to the cabin. He needed some time to himself to focus and think. He had to interpret the poem's ending so he could finish the mystery that had been swallowing his life. Nothing else mattered to him.

Finally, we venture to a place, expectation removed, he thought again. *Where would that be?*

Once Ashley had Marcus on the phone, it didn't take long for them to meet up. When they did, Marcus seemed to be in a much better mood. Or at least he was doing a better job of pretending he was. On the other hand, Marcus noticed Ethan's attitude and knew something was up. He didn't say anything though and just acted normal. The three friends picked up an early dinner, went back to Ashley's car, and they were back at the cabin in a little over an hour.

At the cabin, Ethan was eager to change out of his still slightly damp clothes and get into the shower. In the shower, he relaxed and let his mind wander. It truly was the best place to think.

Where is a place that people go without any expectations? he asked himself. The more he thought about it, the more he came to the same conclusion. Everything people did, and everywhere people went, they had expectations. Lack of expectation is situational, he thought. He began to lose hope that he would be able' to find an answer he could use.

When Ethan was done with his shower he spent some time with Ashley and Marcus. Ashley and Ethan caught Marcus up on the events of their day, and Marcus did the same to them.

Marcus claimed to have spent a large part of the day enjoying different parts of the fair. The details didn't add up though, and Ethan was suspicious that Marcus had left the fair shortly after splitting up with him and Ashley. He wasn't sure what he thought Marcus had done with his day instead, but he was fairly certain it wasn't spent at the fair.

Once they'd all caught up, Ethan said he was going to turn in early because he wasn't feeling well. Ashley decided to join him, but went to take a shower first. While she was in the shower Marcus approached him.

"What's going on? I know that look. Something else about the Heart of the Forest?" Marcus asked.

Ethan almost told him the truth, but he remembered what Marcus had said in the forest earlier that morning. About giving up on the search for the Heart and instead focusing on his relationship with Ashley. Something in Marcus had changed, and Ethan didn't feel like he was on his side anymore. If he told Marcus what he'd learned, Marcus would just argue with him to let it go. Ethan couldn't do that. So he lied, knowing full well that Marcus would know it but not say anything. That was all Ethan really needed. He felt he could finish on his own now.

"Really, it's nothing. I actually do feel kind of sick. Not just that, but I realized you were right. I'm feeling a little down on myself for putting that whole thing before Ashley. Stupid of me," Ethan said.

Marcus looked at him knowingly, but it also seemed like a part of him wanted to believe Ethan's lie. "It's in the past. You can move forward now, don't be hard on yourself. If you need anything let me know," Marcus offered.

Ethan thanked him, and they both went to their separate rooms. Ethan got comfortable in bed, and when Ashley finished her shower she joined him. They talked briefly about their day and reminisced on their friendship before they'd started dating. They both commented on how the music and the dancing had brought those memories back. The conversation quickly turned into them kissing. And that led to more. It was a romantic night that Ethan had been wanting for years, but he was hardly present. Thoughts on his interpretation of the poem were gnawing at him.

Later in the night when Ashley was asleep, Ethan was wide awake. He lay there staring at the ceiling and thinking. He felt that he'd been onto something when he realized that lack of expectation was situational. Maybe the poem wasn't referring to going somewhere that lacked expectation, but going anywhere without expectations. He decided that was the best bet he had. Tomorrow he would go somewhere in the forest. Anywhere in the forest. And he would just see what happened. No expectations, he thought. He'd finish the poem and be done with the forest's games.

CHAPTER 23

Ethan was exhausted the next morning. He'd fallen asleep late, and Ashley had woken him up much earlier than he would've liked. He, Marcus, and Ashley had a simple breakfast with what little food remained in the cabin. The breakfast had been awkwardly quiet with a strange tension that Ethan felt went beyond his situation. He understood why both Ashley and Marcus wouldn't have had much to say to him. They both separately knew that he had lied to them the day before. What was strange, Ethan thought, was that Ashley and Marcus seemed to be avoiding speaking to each other. There was a tension between them that Ethan felt had nothing to do with him. He'd have been more interested if he hadn't had more important things to worry about. For example, how he was going to get a chance to separate from both of them long enough to venture into the forest.

Ethan realized that there was little chance he would be able to leave on his own. Ashley would want to go with him, and Marcus would suspect he was going off in search of the Heart. So instead, he devised a plan. When breakfast was finished, he took his phone from his pocket and tossed it underneath his bed. Then he, Ashley, and Marcus got ready to head into town.

It was day six of the festival. Tonight they would find out who won the contest. Would it be Claire and her poem *The Human Journey* or her opponent whom Ethan hadn't even paid much attention to. And would it be Robert's *The Pack* or 'The Broken Peoples' by Art Petty. If Ethan was honest, he didn't even care anymore. But the rest of festival goers would. Day six was typically the most popular and energetic day of the festival.

In the car they all discussed the remaining contestants and their works. The consensus between the three was that Claire's poem was a sure winner, and that they would be happy to have seen any other author win over Mitchelson. They didn't talk about much else. It seemed like they all had little to say to each other. Being in the quiet car made Ethan sad as he realized how little had changed since their first day arriving. It felt like they'd been in Ustumah for a lifetime and so much had happened. Yet nothing had really changed. He'd felt that things between Marcus and him were getting better. But now they could hardly speak to each other.

Something had changed. Yesterday had been a great day for him and Ashley, but it hadn't mattered in the end. None of it mattered until Ethan could find the Heart of the Forest and get the answers he needed. Then he could put it all behind him, leave the forest behind, and know that his fate was in his own hands.

Ashley parked the car and the three began walking into town to see what the day would hold. They didn't get far before Ethan stopped.

"Whatsup?" Marcus asked.

Ethan began frantically patting his pockets. "I think I left my phone in the car," he said.

Ashley sighed and started walking back to the car, and Ethan and Marcus followed. "Do you really need it?" Ashley asked.

"I'd really like it. If I get caught up with fans or something like that, it'd make it a lot easier to meet back up with you guys," Ethan explained.

Back at the car, Ashley unlocked it and the three of them did a quick search. The phone, waiting underneath the bed at the cabin, was nowhere to be found. "Shit. I really don't want to be without my phone all day. I must've left it back at the cabin. I'll just go get it real quick, I'm sorry," Ethan said.

Ashley and Marcus looked at each other and both tried to speak, but Marcus was first. "I'll come with you," he said.

"No, no. It's my mistake. You guys enjoy yourselves and I'll be right back," Ethan insisted.

He held out his hand for Ashley to turn over the car keys.

Ashley and Marcus both looked uncomfortable about the idea, but the awkwardness of the situation didn't leave them much room to argue. So reluctantly, Ashley handed Ethan the keys.

"Hurry back babe," Ashley said.

Ethan nodded, apologized again, and hopped into the car. He quickly drove off without even looking back. Ashley and Marcus silently walked back toward Main Street, wondering what to say to each other.

Ethan was back at the cabin in under an hour. He quickly grabbed his phone, also taking a moment to pack a few snacks into his backpack. Then he was back in the car and on the road again. He drove until he found a safe place to pull over, got out of the car, put on the backpack, and made his way into the forest.

Going nowhere in particular, Ethan marched deeper and deeper into the forest. He was surprisingly relaxed and comfortable all things considered. The forest had been a dangerous place for him those past few days, but he was becoming familiar with it. The large redwoods towering overhead were starting to feel like old acquaintances. Not the intimidating onlookers they had been before. It was the first time since he had discovered the note in Chekhov's gun, that Ethan felt he had the upper hand over the forest. He knew about the poem and was going to use that knowledge to end all of this once and for all.

As he went on, his mind wandered to Ashley. He'd been so happy with her the day before. Realizing the lyrics of the local band's song had been the narrative of their day had shattered that happiness. He wanted to believe that it had been real, but he couldn't. He was dead set that it had all been an illusion conjured up by the forest. It was that realization that drove the motivation he held so strongly. His primary goal was to fix things with Ashley and Marcus. But he felt that he couldn't do that while the forest controlled his life. Dealing with that had to be his first priority. At least, that was what he told himself. There was no more room for doubt in his mind.

He continued on into the forest with some difficulty, doing his best to make a trail as he went.

He spent two uneventful hours like that. At one point Ashley called him, but he had let it go to voicemail. He had no idea what he was going to say to her. All he knew was that it would have to wait until he was finished. Not long after her second attempt at reaching him had gone to voicemail, Marcus tried calling as well. After that Ethan switched his phone off. He couldn't afford the distraction.

After a while Ethan had to stop. He was exhausted. He just laid down in the middle of the forest and gazed up at the canopy formed by the trees above. He hadn't known what he'd expected to happen, but he'd expected something. Anything other than nothing. So much for no expectations, he realized. The thought was disheartening, but Ethan wasn't ready to give up yet. So he waited.

Another couple hours passed. Ethan ate the food he had packed and drank most of the water. While he sat there waiting for whatever would happen, he reflected on the past. He thought back on his relationship with Ashley and it's slow descent into the wreck it had become. It had all started with his own insecurities. First the thought that he wasn't good enough for her. Then a jealousy of Marcus. At times he had felt that Ashley truly wanted to be with Marcus. He was more charming than Ethan and had an objectively better body. He'd wanted to say something to either of them, if just to put his mind at ease. But he never had. He had been scared of how insecure it would make him look. Instead he had grown distant from them both. The distance from those he cared about began to feed a deep depression. Like a snowball rolling downhill, the depression only made things worse. He distanced himself more and more, until all he could feel were the most negative emotions available. Much like how a person who loses their sight explains that it seems to enhance their other senses, Ethan's loss of positive emotions enhanced the feelings of the negative ones. He experienced them all on a level he never thought possible. They were his life back then. Envy. Doubt. Jealousy. Frustration. Shame. Fear. Grief. Guilt. Despair.

It was how Ethan had come to start writing *In Despair*, his first successful novel. The silver lining of hitting rock bottom was the inspiration it gave him. He'd wanted to share those emotions, for better or worse, through his writing. Give people an insight into the human condition when it seems like all is lost. He'd realized how pathetic his own situation would seem. From the outside he'd seem dramatic. But inside he knew his emotions were as real as they could be, and no person possessed the strength to combat them. Instead of his own situation, he chose to write about a woman who had lost her daughter. Something everyone would be able to agree was worthy of such a fall into negative emotions. Writing the book, while an amazing outlet for his feelings, had been a double-edged sword. He had never been so distant as he'd been while writing *"In Despair."*

When Ethan finished the novel he'd felt hope for the first time in a long time. He finally saw a future where he could be happy again. He'd tried to start mending things with Ashley and Marcus. But things were different, and it seemed like it may be too late.

"In Despair" had quickly become a best seller and Ethan was notified not long after its release that he had been invited to the Known Poets and Authors Writing Festival. Ashley and Marcus had been so excited for him, and it seemed like the festival was going to be the spark he needed to fix everything.

So far that had not been the case. That was a hard truth for Ethan to face. Even harder was the acknowledgment that it had been all his fault. He'd been blaming the forest this whole time. While he still held it partly responsible, he was now facing the realization that his search for the Heart of the Forest was just his new *"In Despair."* The deeper he delved into trying to solve the mystery, the more he distanced himself from Ashley and Marcus. He had spent half the trip rebuilding those relationships, but he'd spent the other half undoing his own efforts. It was a pointless realization Ethan told himself. It didn't change anything. He still needed to find the Heart of the Forest. He still needed to get answers. Without them he would never truly be able to move on.

As he continued to wait, he realized that nothing was going to happen. He doubted himself. He doubted that coming out into the forest had been the right thing. He doubted he would ever be free of the feeling that something beyond his control was causing his pain. He doubted that he could outsmart Claire's poem.

He recalled the line that was supposed to happen next.

The next place we go will fill us with doubt.

It had come true despite his efforts. He couldn't control it. It could only control him.

Ethan stood and looked around the forest. He wanted to say something to it, but he didn't know what. He wanted to yell, perhaps even scream at it, but he didn't know what to say.

Instead he began to walk back toward the car. As he walked, he thought. Maybe he couldn't control it because it was already controlling him. What he needed was another opinion.

Someone who it wasn't controlling. Someone who could interpret the poem better than anyone else. The person who wrote it.

It was the last thing Ethan could think to try. He'd go to Claire and he'd ask her to interpret the lines. The interpretation of the poet herself would have to mean something. It was the only idea he could think of. He'd ask for her help and go wherever he needed. He'd thought the idea would give him hope, but instead it just filled him with more doubt as he recalled the next line of the poem.

Seeking help from another we visit a corpse approved.

CHAPTER 24

It took another couple hours for Ethan to make his way back to the car, and by the time he made it he was exhausted. He'd spent a good chunk of the day in the forest, and he could only imagine what Ashley and Marcus were thinking. He'd expected that he would be done by now, and have his answers. He'd expected that he'd know what to say to them when he saw them next. None of those expectations had been met, and now he was beginning to panic. He realized he just couldn't afford to worry about Ashley and Marcus right then. Instead his focus had to be on finding Claire and getting her interpretation of the final lines of the poem.

Once in the car, Ethan sped into town. He decided to park on the outskirts of Ustumah City and walk the rest of the way. As he got into town he kept a wary eye out for Marcus and Ashley. If they spotted him, he wasn't sure what he'd do. Luckily it was one of the busiest days in Ustumah. Ethan kept his head down and blended in with the huge crowds. It would've been a miracle if anyone picked him out of that sea of people.

Ethan took a moment to figure out where he was going. Half of Main Street had been dedicated to the two remaining Poets, while the other half had been dedicated to the two remaining fiction authors. Unfortunately, Claire's section of Main Street was all the way on the other side of town. Ethan had no choice but to slowly make his way down the street, diving in and out of large groups of people. The amount of care he put into avoiding detection made Ethan feel like he was in a spy thriller.

As he made his way down the street he was constantly looking around for Ashley and Marcus. Eventually he spotted them. They were sitting closely together outside of a cafe with half eaten meals.

Ashley looked as distraught as Ethan had ever seen her, and a tinge of guilt wallowed up inside of his chest. Her makeup was smeared from tears and she was listening to Marcus speak. She looked like she was holding back even more tears.

Ethan slowly moved on, but he continued to watch them. Marcus looked angry. Not at Ashley though, Ethan knew it was at him. Marcus was waving his hands around like he tended to do when he was so upset. But then suddenly his entire demeanor changed. He relaxed and leaned in toward Ashley, talking calmly to her. She was looking down as he spoke, but for a moment she looked up at him and whispered a few words. Then they gazed into each other's eyes, and for a long moment nothing was said.

Ethan felt a sick knot in his stomach. If two people were ever about to kiss, it was in that moment. But it never happened. Instead Marcus placed one hand on the back of her head and pulled her into him so that their foreheads were touching. She made no move to resist. He held her like that for a long moment and then softly spoke. She said something short back to him before they broke their embrace. Then, they said nothing for a few moments, before starting another conversation that seemed like business as usual.

Part of Ethan was furious to see his best friend and girlfriend embracing each other so passionately. His initial instinct was to rush over there and ask what the hell they thought they were doing. But then his logical mind kicked in. Clearly they were both angry and worried about him.

Can I really be upset at them for comforting each other? he asked himself. Of course you can, a familiar voice replied. His voice of doubt. His voice of insecurity. Why wouldn't you be upset? They've probably been doing this kind of thing and more behind your back for years. Probably since you started dating, or even before.

Ethan ignored the thoughts. He was tired of letting his insecurity control him. There had always been a part of him afraid of losing Ashley to Marcus. But he'd always known they wouldn't betray him like that. He couldn't let this situation shatter that trust. He was the one in the wrong today, and he'd have to deal with that later. He wouldn't let himself place the blame on them. So Ethan looked away and continued on down the street toward where he hoped to find Claire.

Sure enough, Ethan made it to a section of the street where a large tent was set up with the words "Claire Donaghue and The Human Journey" were printed on top. Ethan quickly slipped into the crowded tent. The tent was filled with shelves and shelves of all the poems Claire had written, as well as the poetry books she had been featured in. The same imagery that had been on Claire's stand at the Meet the Writers Event filled the inside of the tent. Pictures of a towering mountain, blending into a wild forest, continuing on to the skyline of a great city, making its way into a great cosmic collage, before blending back into the towering mountain. All being traversed by a small and insignificant person with a walking stick.

Ethan navigated his way through the tent until his eyes found Claire. She was sitting at a table with stacks of poetry around her. An eager fan was chatting her ear off, while a long line of other fans waited just behind. Ethan knew how that could go, and realized she must've been doing it for hours. Nevertheless, Claire wore a soft smile and responded to the fans every moment she could. Ethan walked past the line and waited for an opportunity to grab Claire's attention.

The fan she was speaking to thanked her for her time and left. Claire looked out toward the line as the next fan walked up. As she looked over Ethan waved at her. She spotted him and locked eyes on him. She frowned for a split second and looked away. She smiled at the new fan and began chatting with them as she signed a poem to give to them.

Ethan was surprised that she was so unhappy to see him. He had not anticipated that. But as he recalled his last few experiences with her, he wasn't sure how he could have expected anything else. Getting Claire's help wasn't going to be as easy as he'd initially thought. He moved closer toward her table.

When Claire and the next fan were done with their conversation, Ethan cut in front of the next person. He turned to them and apologized. "I'm sorry, this will only take a moment," he said. The fan looked astonished, and Ethan turned toward Claire before they could even respond. "Claire, I'm so sorry to ambush you like this, but I really need your help."

Claire looked at him with surprise. "It's nice to see you Ethan, but I'm a little busy," she said with an innocent laugh as she pointed down the line.

"Trust me I know," Ethan said, "But this is really important. I wouldn't do this if it wasn't."

Claire studied him, narrowing her eyes. She was upset with him, he could tell. But he could also see that she seemed to feel sorry for him. She hesitated for a moment before she responded. "Listen, I'll be glad to help you out, but you have to wait in line like everyone else. I can't give you special treatment over my fans," she said shrugging at him.

Ethan didn't know Claire well, but he knew her well enough to understand. She wasn't so upset as to not help him. But that didn't mean she didn't want to punish him a little. "C'mon Claire, I'm sorry. That line could take hours," he pleaded.

The fan behind him butted in. "You're Ethan Garland. I didn't realize at first. You wrote that book '*In Despair.*' Great read! Go ahead and cut in front of me, I don't mind," the fan said earnestly.

Ethan thanked the fan and turned back to Claire who shook her head. "I know Mr. Garland and he understands that fans are important. He wouldn't give me preferential treatment over his fans. A guy like him would be happy to wait in line. He knows it's the right thing," Claire said smiling at Ethan like he was an old friend.

She'd backed him into a corner. If he refused he'd look like an asshole. And Claire would certainly ignore him. His only choice was to accept the punishment and go to the back of the line. "Of course, you're right. I'll wait," Ethan conceded. He made his way to the back of the line and began waiting.

At one point the person ahead of Ethan turned around and began asking him all about *In Despair*. Normally he would've been glad to talk to a fan. But right then he was too stressed and slightly upset. It was a grueling conversation that seemed to make waiting in line take that much longer.

Ethan spent almost two hours in line, looking over his shoulder hoping that Ashley and Marcus would not turn up. Luckily, Ashley's distaste for Claire likely kept them away. And finally, it was Ethan's turn to talk to Claire.

Claire smiled at him as he sat across from her, looking pleased with herself. "Wow, you actually waited. You couldn't take a second to acknowledge me the past few days, but now you can wait in line for two hours?"

"Yeah, about that. That was wrong," Ethan admitted. "It was Ashley, she…"

Claire held up a hand. "Listen, I'm sorry that I created some rift between you and your girlfriend. I didn't mean to do whatever it is I did. But don't blame her for how you've been. You were the closest thing I had to a friend at this god forsaken festival. I couldn't trust the intentions of most other people. And as a fan of yours I was eager for us to talk about writing. You snubbed me because it was easier for you. Don't blame it on Ashley. You didn't want to have the argument with her, and it was just easier to ignore me. I understand that, but don't expect me to feel sorry for you."

Ethan absorbed what she said. He hadn't thought about it like that, but Claire was right. He could see why she was so upset with him. He'd been avoiding responsibility for the problems he'd been creating for so long. He didn't necessarily blame others, but he always made it seem like he didn't have a choice. But he did. He couldn't promise himself that he would start making the right choice, but he promised himself right then and there that he wouldn't act like it had been his only choice. He needed to start taking responsibility and he knew it.

"You're right," was all Ethan could say. He couldn't even look in her eyes after that.

Claire shifted uncomfortably in her seat and frowned. "Hey, maybe in another life we could have been great friends. You're not a bad person, we just had a rough start."

Ethan managed to face her. "Maybe. I am sorry."

"Let's just move on. You said you came here for my help. What is it that you need? I am a little indisposed tonight. Kind of a lot going on," Claire said motioning to everything around them.

Ethan straightened up. He could feel sorry for himself later. Right then he needed her help. "Yeah of course. Good luck tonight by the way. You can help me from right where you're sitting," he explained.

"Thanks. I'm gonna need all the luck I can get. So what is that you need?" Claire asked a second time.

Ethan pondered how exactly he would explain his situation, realized there was no easy way to put it, and just asked. "This is going to sound really weird, and I'm going to need you to just give me the benefit of the doubt that I'm asking for a good reason."

Claire smiled coyly. "Ok, you got it. Just tell me," she said with a growing impatience.

Ethan nodded and grabbed a copy of "The Human Journey" from the table and flipped it around for Claire. "Your poem. The last two lines," Ethan said pointing at them. "What is your literal interpretation of them? Like, if someone was going to live out a story based on these lines, what would happen?"

Claire looked at Ethan like he'd gone mad. "That does sound really weird, you're right." She sighed and thought for a moment. "It's written figuratively because it's about people and their journey to find themselves. I've never thought of interpreting it literally," Claire explained.

Ethan gave another quick nod. "I understand. I figured that, but I need your help. If you were to interpret it literally, what would those two lines mean?"

Claire sighed again and looked back down at the poem as if she were reading it for the first time. She was silent for a long time. The people in line behind them couldn't hear their conversation, but they caught onto the lack of one. They began to get restless and impatient. Ethan could feel their eyes falling on his back.

Finally, Claire spoke up, "Seeking help from another we visit a corpse approved. That's still metaphorical even when I think of it literally. It'd be someone asking for help. But they wouldn't just get the help they wanted. They'd get the help they needed. Like, a part of them would die. But it would be good, it would be a part of them that was weighing them down."

Ethan thought about that and it confirmed his suspicions. Coming to see Claire was just him acting out the second to last line of the poem. He'd suspected it coming there, but now he knew. Claire had shown him that he wasn't taking responsibility, and he'd just minutes ago sworn to end that.

"Ok, that's really helpful. But even more important is that last line. Where is that place Claire?" Ethan asked with an anxious hunger in his voice.

Claire looked back down at the poem and was silent for another couple of minutes. She shook her head when she looked back up. "I always thought of it as the final step in our journey. Realizing that expectation is the enemy of our own happiness. You know, learning to live without it and finally be truly happy. It's hard for me to think of it literally."

Ethan was desperate. "Please Claire, you've got to have some thoughts on it. If it were a literal place where would it be?"

She shook her head again. "If I had to make a guess… It would be the last place the person would think of. They'd have no expectation from that place, because they wouldn't even think of it," she said with a shrug. "I don't know Ethan, I'm sorry but that's the best I've got."

It was a vague answer, but it was something Ethan could use. He was ecstatic. "No that's perfect. Thank you so much Claire, you have no idea how much you've helped me. I gotta go now, though. Thanks again," Ethan said as he hurried up. "Oh, and honestly, good luck tonight. You deserve to win."

Claire looked at him again like he was crazy, but the look of pity appeared again as well. "Thanks Ethan. Good luck to you too. In whatever it is you're doing. I hope everything turns out ok."

Ethan smiled at her, waved, and was off. He made his way out of the tent, once again with a sense of purpose.

CHAPTER 25

A few hours earlier that day, Marcus and Ashley walked out to the parking lot where they had last seen Ethan. They'd hoped that Ethan, or at least Ashley's car would be there somewhere. They weren't. Marcus tried Ethan's cell for an eighth time. Straight to voicemail. He let the call go on past Ethan's voice instructing him to leave a message after the beep. He hung up fifteen seconds into a silent voice mail. Marcus was so frustrated he wanted to throw his phone. Instead he just gripped it a little tighter and cursed at Ethan in his head.

Ashley looked to Marcus expectantly. "Did he answer?"

"No, straight to voicemail again," Marcus responded.

Ashley looked like she might start crying at any moment. "Marcus, I'm really worried about him. We had a great day yesterday, but all of a sudden he started acting really weird. He's been so stressed lately, I mean, what if he hurt himself?" she asked shakily.

Marcus shook his head. "He wouldn't do that. I've known him all my life."

Ashley continued pleading with him, "But what if he found out about us? That would explain why he was acting so weird all of a sudden. That would break him. How can you be sure?"

Seeing Ashley so concerned about Ethan was making Marcus more and more angry. He was worried about Ethan too, but not for the same reason Ashley was. He knew that whatever was keeping Ethan, it had to do with his obsession to find the Heart of the Forest.

Marcus worried that something terrible had happened, and it just made him more frustrated. Ethan could have asked Marcus for help, but he'd likely been too prideful to admit that he couldn't give up his search. So now, Marcus was left worrying about him. Even worse, Ashley had no idea what was going on and was losing her mind over it. Seeing the pain Ethan was causing her pissed Marcus off more than anything.

Marcus wanted to tell her the truth, but he wasn't sure if it would make things better. Or that she would even believe him. "Ash, he didn't find out about us. I'm sure he's fine, we just need to stay calm."

That was when Ashley's tears started. "No, he did. He did find out about us," she sobbed. "I couldn't stop thinking about you yesterday. I realized I was going to lose you, and I couldn't stop thinking about it. He must have sensed that. It's all my fault." Tears were streaming down her face.

Marcus grabbed her and held her close. "It's alright, that's not it. Please Ash, let's stay calm."

Ashley violently pushed him off her. "Don't touch me," she said, glaring at him. She was still crying but she was angry too. "Our affair has done enough damage. I'm not gonna stand her hugging you while Ethan is out there. He could be dead. I'm not going to be calm about that," she yelled. As she did a few people walking nearby looked over at them concerned.

"I understand, but-" Marcus started.

Ashley interrupted, "But nothing! We need to call the cops."

Marcus shook his head. "That's not a good idea. The cops around here don't really seem to care about Ethan's wellbeing anyways," Marcus offered.

Ashley pushed Marcus and yelled at him. "Why don't you care? Why don't you want to help him?" she demanded.

Marcus broke. "Because he doesn't want our help! He's only thinking of himself right now! I'm worried about him, but there's nothing we can do!" he yelled back.

Ashley looked confused. "What do you mean? What are you talking about?" she asked, calming down slightly.

Marcus hung his head. He had to tell her the truth. It had been a mistake to keep it from her in the first place. "There's something you need to know. It's going to sound crazy when I tell you, but you have to believe me. I hope you know I wouldn't lie to you about something like this," he said.

"What?!" Ashley demanded, her frustration boiling up again.

Marcus struggled to find the words. "It's about Ethan's thing. The thing where he was saying the story from his book was coming to life," Marcus managed.

All the anger drained from Ashley's face and was replaced with concern. "He's having some kind of mental break. You knew more? Could we have helped him?" she asked.

"No, that's not it," Marcus answered quickly. "I know this sounds crazy, but he was right. It's true. His story was coming to life. Well, not just his story, it's complicated."

Ashley's face went blank. She stared at Marcus with a look that he couldn't even begin to decipher. She didn't say anything, she just kept staring at him.

"Well say something," Marcus demanded.

"What do you want me to say," Ashley replied. "You expect me to believe that?"

Marcus sighed. "Yes. I know it sounds crazy, but that's why I asked you to trust me. I wouldn't lie about this. It sounds crazy because it is. But it's true. I've seen things that can't be explained by anything but magic."

Ashley studied Marcus for another long moment. Then she grabbed the bridge of her nose and sighed. "Ok. So let's say I believe you. What does that have to do with Ethan?" she asked.

Marcus let out a long deep breath. "That's a long story," he said.

Ashley motioned around them. "We've got time. Tell me what the fuck is going on," she demanded. She had calmed down a lot. The idea that Marcus knew something she didn't seemed to help. She was no longer assuming the worst.

Marcus agreed to tell her everything but offered that standing in a parking lot wasn't the best place to do it. They agreed to head back into town and grab food at a local cafe. On the way Marcus started explaining. He told her everything Ethan had told him about the Heart of the Forest. He told her about their first hike together into the forest. At the cafe he waited to mention the terrifying shade creature that had haunted them until they were seated far from the earshot of anyone who might overhear.

He went on, telling her about his trip to the courthouse for the maps. He told her about their "research" into the different books at the festival. He told her about their near death experience with the wind. He told her about Deaven and his cabin in the forest. And he told her about how he had urged Ethan to leave it alone. How he'd thought that it just wasn't worth it anymore.

At times Ashley looked at Marcus like he had lost his mind. Other times she was wide eyed with concern. For the most part she listened quietly, asking the occasional question. She seemed mesmerized by the story, stuck in a limbo between disbelief and captivation. When Marcus was finished she didn't hesitate to take her turn.

"So you're saying that Ethan is out there somewhere trying again?" she asked.

Marcus nodded in agreement, "That's exactly what I'm saying. He can't let it go. Don't get me wrong, I'm interested too. It's not often that someone encounters magic in the real world. But at some point you have to cut your losses. You have to understand when you're in way over your head and just stop. Ethan can't do that."

A tear fell from Ashley's eye. "Everything you said makes this power in the forest sound really dangerous. I mean, Ethan could be in real danger," she said.

"Yeah, he might be. And I'm worried about him. I just don't even know where to start when it comes to helping him. Even if he's alright, he will keep pursuing this until something terrible does happen," explained Marcus.

Ashley buried her face in her palms. "We can't do nothing. If we care about him, we should help him," she blurted to Marcus.

"What do you want to do Ash? The cops won't believe us, and there's an entire forest out there," Marcus said pointing down Main Street to the sea of redwoods beyond.

"I just don't understand. Why would he do this? Doesn't he know we'd be worried sick with nothing to do about it?" Ashley asked.

Marcus' anger flared back up. "He doesn't think about that stuff Ash. He's selfish. He keeps saying that he needs to find the Heart of the Forest because he thinks it will help him fix things with you. Yesterday morning I tried to tell him that he was already doing that.

Things between you two were getting better. This wild goose chase of his was only going to get in the way of that," Marcus said. "He obviously didn't care about that. It's easier for him to face a magic entity than it is for him to face the truth."

Ashley looked up at Marcus and asked, "What truth?"

Marcus hesitated. He'd been wanting to say it for over a year, but he never could. Now was the perfect chance, but he still struggled. "The truth… The truth is that it is going to take a lot of effort to fix things between you two. You guys aren't meant to be together. It was great in the beginning but that's gone now. Look at you two. Why are you trying so hard to make this work."

Ashley didn't say anything at first, but her eyes said that she saw some truth in what Marcus was saying. "Because we love each other and we owe it to each other to give it a chance," she said finally.

"At what point do you give up on that? At a certain point, is it even worth it to try? You're both miserable trying to make it work," Marcus said.

"I love him, Marcus. I don't know what else to say," Ashley said.

Marcus looked her in the eyes. "And how do you feel about me?" he asked, "Because I'm in love with you."

Ashley didn't say anything, instead she just stared at Marcus through sad eyes. Looking into her eyes, Marcus could almost feel her mix of emotions. He'd felt it before, and he knew she loved him. But there was a part of her that loved Ethan too. He'd seen that as well. She didn't know how to handle those two feelings together, and he didn't blame her.

"I know we talked about ending things between us. And I know I said that the best thing to do was leave both of your lives after this festival. But…" Marcus began, not able to continue.

Marcus looked into the cafe and stood up. He walked inside and grabbed a book from a table that featured all of the works from the festival's contestants. He handed the cashier some cash for the book, and told her to keep the change. As he sat back down with Ashley, he smacked the book down on the table to draw Ashley's attention to it. It wasn't just any book, it was *Temptation Ablaze*.

"Like I was just saying, the Heart of the Forest brings stories to life. Do you know what this story is about?" Marcus asked.

Ashley just shook her head. "I know it's the third in a series. Some love story," she explained.

"Some love story," Marcus said softly. "It's not just any love story. It's one of the saddest stories I've ever read."

Ashley just listened, letting Marcus continue.

"I've only read this book. But I looked up a summary of the rest of the series. Basically it's about two people who meet and realize right away that they've found true love." Marcus began, "Of course it's not that easy and there's always something keeping them from each other. At the end of the first book, they end up with each other despite a lot of things pushing them apart. In the second book, it all kind of catches up with them. Even though they love each other, the world just seems to be pushing them apart. They're still together at the end of the second book, and happily in love. But in every other way, their lives are so much worse off than they ever were."

When Marcus paused, Ashley prodded him to continue. "What happens in the third book?" she asked.

Marcus continued, "In the beginning of the third book they hit rock bottom. They desperately try to rebuild their lives, but they aren't able to do it until they leave each other. The rest of the book is them trying to move on. They meet other people and try to start new lives. A lot of the plot is them trying to live without each other. When they can't, they start having an affair. The affair goes bad and their lives start to go under again. Finally, at the end they decide the only way to have any kind of life is to end things between them once and for all. So they do. They each go on to live their own life, and things finally start going well for them."

"Ok," Ashley said confused, "So what does that have to do with anything? Are you saying that this story is coming to life with me and you? That makes it sound like we were right for deciding to end things."

Marcus shook his head. "That's not the end. The book ends with both of them separately realizing that they aren't happy. They realize that despite how hard it was for them to be together, and despite the world's best efforts to keep them apart, that together was the only way they were ever happy. They both look at each other's new 'happy' lives and assume that the other couldn't possibly feel the same way. So they go on with their lives and they never see each other again. And they're miserable. The book ends with them both getting old and reflecting on the regret they have for choosing the easy path over the path of true love. Then it's over. It was the most depressing thing I've ever read."

"Marcus," Ashley started, but he held up a hand.

"Just let me finish," he asked. "It was so depressing, because I realized that, yes, this story is coming to life with you and me. I realized that it was going to be my life now. Even harder to accept, was that it was going to be your life too."

Another tear rolled down Ashley's face. Marcus only hoped that she felt the same he did about it.

"But you know what? I said fuck that," Marcus said waving his hands in the air. "I don't care about some magic fucking forest. I love you, and if you feel the same way, I want to be with you. I don't care about anything else. Not even some bullshit magic is going to keep me from you. And I'm a terrible friend for saying this, but neither is Ethan. He doesn't deserve you."

Ashley looked down. She couldn't meet his eyes after he'd said that. He worried that he was wrong. Maybe she didn't feel the same way after all. Maybe he was just some asshole trying to steal his best friend's girl.

Marcus let out a deep breath and calmed down. He leaned in close to Ashley and continued. "Just tell me Ashley. What do you really want? Do you feel the same way I do? If you don't I'll respect that and we can move on, but I need to know."

There was a pause, but then Ashley looked up at Marcus. Their faces were only inches apart. "I wanna be with you," she admitted.

Then the two looked into each other's eyes. While they did, so much was said without words. They could see it in each other's eyes. Marcus could feel the tension between them, and wanted to kiss her. But it wasn't right. Not out in the open like that. They at least owed Ethan that, and knew Ashley felt the same way, because she didn't kiss him either.

Instead, Marcus grabbed the back of Ashley's head and pulled her forehead to his. He held her tightly and whispered, "Everything is going to be ok. We're going to figure this out. Ethan is going to be ok too. When we find him, we'll try one last time to help him. Then we'll tell him everything and go from there."

"He deserves the truth, and so do we," Ashley said. With that, Marcus let go of her and they sat back in their chairs.

Nothing was said for a while, but then Ashley spoke up again. "Ethan's fine. I can feel it. But we need to find him before something bad does happen to him," she said.

Marcus agreed. "But where do we start?" he asked.

"Somewhere," Ashley said with a cold tone. "We may be choosing each other, but I still care about him. I know you do too. I'm glad we had this talk, but we can't sit here doing nothing anymore. Ethan needs us."

CHAPTER 26

Ethan rushed back up Main Street through the crowds of people. It had been hours since he had seen Ashley and Marcus at the cafe. Still, he glanced at it as he passed by. No sign of Ashley or Marcus. Ethan still couldn't risk being spotted by them, and kept an eye out all the way back to Ashley's car.

He'd left the car a good walk out of town, but he finally made it back. He started up the car and headed out of Ustumah City. He was heading to the last place he ever would have thought to have looked for the Heart of the Forest. Claire's interpretation of the final lines of the poem had seemed like random guesses. But Ethan knew that it didn't work that way. What she'd said had made sense to him. Ethan had noticed that the Heart had a flair for the dramatic when it spun it's tales into reality. It only made sense that the key to finding it was in the last place he'd ever look. The place that had been under his nose the entire time. The Chekhov Cabin.

Ethan was speeding down the road. He hoped that local law enforcement would be more occupied in town than watching for speeders. The redwoods around him blurred as he sped by.

Back at the cabin, Ethan parked the car. He got out and walked around to the back. The entire time he'd been in Ustumah he hadn't been behind the cabin once. If the Heart of the Forest was anywhere, it was there. The small fence that surrounded the cabin had a small opening on the backside of the cabin.

Ethan went to the opening and noticed an overgrown trail. Someone had used this trail once, but it had been a long time ago. Ethan followed the trail into the forest. It was short and only took a couple of minutes of walking before it abruptly ended.

At the end of the trail there was nothing but redwood trees. One tree, however, was different from the rest. All the other trees were vibrant and full of life, but this tree was old and rotting. It was much thicker than any other redwood Ethan had come across, and he couldn't even imagine how old it must have been.

The old rotting tree was nothing but a shell at this point. At first glance it seemed like nothing but an old husk, standing out like a sore thumb among the beauty of the forest. But as Ethan approached it he saw it for what it truly was. It was the most beautiful thing in the forest. From it's dead bark new life was sprouting all around it. There was something satisfying about how its death was giving way to new life. The beauty of the forest's circle of life was captured in this one dead tree like a photograph. Ethan walked up to the tree and placed a gentle hand on it. Is this the Heart of the Forest? He asked himself as he ran his hand along the tree. As he did, he heard something move on the other side of the tree.

Ethan froze. Whatever was moving sounded big. Like a person, or worse, a wolf. The movement stopped after a second, and a foreboding silence took over as Ethan worked up the courage to look at the other side of the tree.

"Hello? Is someone there?" Ethan asked as he began to circle the large tree.

There was no response except for more movement. Ethan froze again, and the movement stopped. Whatever it was, it seemed to be methodically moving away from him. As he wrapped around one side of the tree, it did the same. Ethan decided that it wasn't just some forest animal, it was smarter than that.

"Hello?" Ethan called out again as he began moving around the tree.

Again there was no response but movement. Ethan began to pick up his pace and could hear whatever he was chasing do the same. He moved from a brisk walk to a jog, then to a run, until he was sprinting around the huge tree.

"Stop! Who are you?" Ethan demanded as he circled the tree over and over.

Ethan must have run around the tree fifteen times before he began to tire and stopped. As he did, so did the sound of movement on the other side of the tree.

"I just want answers. Please don't run," Ethan called out from labored breaths. When there was no answer, he called out again, "Are you there?"

"Yes, I'm right here," an oddly familiar voice said from directly behind Ethan.

Unsure of how he had not heard the person sneak up on him, Ethan whipped around to face them in a startled frenzy. As he faced the person, his blood went cold. And for a moment he stared in disbelief.

Standing only a few feet in front of him was someone that looked exactly like himself. The features were identical aside from a cocky smirk on the face of the other him.

"What the hell?" Ethan said. "Who are you?"

The other him laughed. "I'm you, isn't it obvious."

Ethan wasn't sure what to think. He had seen a lot of strange things since he'd arrived in Ustumah, but this took the cake. "Then who am I?" he asked. It felt like a stupid question, but he didn't know what else to say.

"Well, you're you. But I'm also you," the other Ethan responded. "I don't understand," Ethan admitted. "Am I going crazy?"

Again the other Ethan laughed. He seemed to be thoroughly enjoying Ethan's confusion. "Everything that has happened, and this is the thing that makes you think you may be crazy?" he said, feigning disappointment. "I really thought you'd recognize me. I'm a little offended you don't."

"I… uh… I'm just…" Ethan tried to say something but couldn't make out the words. The whole thing had scrambled his mind. There was something so unnerving about conversing with himself.

"Here maybe this will help," the other Ethan said. "Hmmm how about… 'She doesn't find you interesting. Nothing you say interests her.'"

Ethan looked on in confusion, and the other Ethan began laughing hysterically. He bent over and held his sides as if to make a show of how hard he was laughing.

The other Ethan stopped laughing long enough to speak again, "How about this one, 'It's all a lie. She could never truly love you. This kiss feels great to you, but she's straining to enjoy it. All because she feels bad for you. Pathetic.'" He started laughing hysterically again. "Wow, 'Pathetic,' that was such a good one," he managed in between laughs.

Ethan finally realized who he was speaking to. It didn't seem like it could be real, but anything was possible with the Forest's magic. Ethan snapped out of his confused stupor and took a tone more appropriate for who he was speaking with.

"Why are you here? Is this the Heart of the Forest?" Ethan asked.

The other Ethan stopped laughing with one final chuckle. "I'm here because you're here. And come on, you and I both know this isn't the Heart. God, you are stupid. You'll believe anything if there's even a shred of hope. You really are pathetic," he said. Then he started laughing again. Harder and harder.

Ethan marched up to his doppelganger and gave him a hard shove. "Stop fucking laughing. None of this is funny," Ethan shouted.

The other Ethan stopped laughing and looked at Ethan with surprise. "I did not expect that. But still, don't pull that tough guy act on me. I know you. You can try to act tough, but you're the furthest thing from it."

"You don't know anything about me," Ethan yelled back, "You've always thought you did. But you just make up lies and try and make me believe them."

"Lies?" the other Ethan said smiling. "I tell you the truth that you're too afraid to hear. You're weak. You'll never be strong, but I can at least tell you the things you need to hear. Maybe then there'd be a chance."

Ethan shook his head, "No. You're the one who is weak. You're afraid of what will happen when I realize I don't need you."

There was a flash of fear in the other Ethan's eyes, but only for a moment. He shrugged and smirked back at Ethan, "Think whatever you want. No matter what you think, you will lose your girlfriend, you will lose your best friend, and you will never find the Heart of the Forest... Seriously, how many times do you need to be 'so sure' that you're in the right place, only to find out you were wrong. Just give up. You're a sorry excuse for a person. If anyone was going to go up against an ancient magical force, it wouldn't be someone pathetic like you." Then he raised his hand to his mouth and giggled.

Ethan narrowed his eyes at the man standing across from him. Some of the things he said were true, but they were just lies hidden in half truths. Lies that it was using to control him. Even knowing that, the things it said were hard to ignore. But standing across from it really helped give Ethan some perspective he'd never had before.

"You know what," Ethan said, "I'm glad you're here. Screw the Heart of the Forest, this is so much better."

The other Ethan looked surprised. "What do you mean?" he asked, his smirk disappearing.

"You've been in my head for so long, and even if I don't always listen to you, you at least plant a seed. You've had so much power over me my entire life."

The other Ethan smirked again and was about to say something, but Ethan interrupted. "But now I see you for what you really are. Here in the physical world I can see that you're the one that's pathetic."

There was fear in the other Ethan's eyes, but still he gave a giggle at the mention of the word pathetic.

Ethan continued, "You laugh at your own jokes because you know nobody else ever will. You desperately cling to your cocky facade because otherwise people would see you for what you really are, and that's the last thing you want. You make up lies because you think it's easier to assume the worst than find out the truth. You're afraid. You... Are... Pathetic."

The other Ethan began thrashing around the forest like a child throwing a tantrum. "No, no, no!" he yelled, "I am not afraid. Not afraid. Not afraid!"

"Yes you are. You're terrified," Ethan said," And you're pathetic."

"No, you're pathetic!" the doppelganger screamed back.

Ethan walked over to his other self and grabbed him. "Stop!" he shouted. The other Ethan looked at him with tears in his eyes.

Ethan spoke to it calmly. "It's over. Stop acting like a child. I know now, and there's no place for you anymore. Take it like a man," he said.

The other Ethan seemed to seriously contemplate his words, and then he looked at Ethan and nodded. Ethan released his grip on him, and the doppelganger took a few steps back.

"I was wrong," the other Ethan said, wiping tears from his eyes. "I'm sorry. Be better." That was the last thing he said, and then he was gone.

Ethan felt a huge weight lift off his shoulder, one he'd never even realized was there. And then, he smiled. It was the biggest smile he'd remembered having in a long time, and he couldn't make it go away. He walked back over to the large dead tree and put another hand on it.

"Thank you," he said. Then he walked back up to the cabin.

Inside the cabin, Ethan turned on his phone and called Ashley. She picked up on the first ring.

"Ethan are you alright?" she asked as soon as she answered.

Ethan was silent for a second and then he just said, "Yeah. I'm sorry."

"I'm just so glad to hear your voice. I was so worried about you. I didn't know what to do.

Marcus and I have been trying everything." Ashley said. Ethan also heard Marcus say something inaudible in the background. "Where are you?" Ashley asked.

"I'm at the cabin. Again, I'm sorry. It was selfish of me to make you worry like that," Ethan admitted. "I'll come pick you guys up."

"No!" Ashley yelled. "We'll get a ride back to the cabin. Just wait for us there. We can talk about everything when we get there ok? I'm just so glad you're alright."

Ethan fought back tears. "Ok, I'll wait here. I love you, Ashley," Ethan said. "I'll see you soon. I'm so glad you're alright," she said as they ended the call.

CHAPTER 27

When Marcus and Ashley arrived back at the cabin they both hugged Ethan. Marcus admitted to Ethan that he'd told Ashley everything. Marcus had been worried Ethan would be upset, but he'd been thankful. Ethan admitted that he should have told them both the truth since the beginning. He apologized to both of them multiple times, but they didn't seem upset with him. They were just happy he was alive.

Marcus did take a moment to talk about the Heart of the Forest. "I know I said you should just let it go, but I'd rather be out there helping you than wondering if you got yourself killed," he said.

Ethan nodded, "You're right. I shouldn't have done that. But luckily everything turned out ok."

"Did you find the Heart of the Forest?" Ashley asked.

"No," Ethan admitted, "But this time I'm really close."

Marcus rolled his eyes. "So you're not giving up then?" he asked.

"No. But this time I'm telling you, this is all coming to an end," Ethan explained. He went on to tell them about Claire's poem and how it told the story of his search for the Heart. Ethan admitted that he wanted to put it all behind him, but explained that being this close meant he couldn't just give up.

"Everything that happened will have been for nothing if I give up now. Maybe I should have given up earlier, but it's too late now," Ethan said.

Marcus and Ashley looked at each other. They seemed to share an unspoken conversation.

Then Ashley looked to Ethan. "We'll help you. We'll do this together," she said.

Marcus nodded, "One last time, Ethan. If this doesn't work out, then you have to promise to let it go. You gotta put this goose chase behind you, for your own good."

Ethan agreed. "One last time. Trust me. I know this is the end." Ashley asked, "So what do we do?"

Ethan chuckled. "I have no idea. Yet," he said. "We can figure it out tomorrow, I think it's been a long day for all of us."

All three of them seemed satisfied with that. Marcus got up and went to take a shower.

Ashley sat with Ethan and asked him about his day. He told her about everything, except seeing her and Marcus at the cafe, and running into himself behind the cabin. Ethan apologized again for everything he'd done, and Ashley assured him that she wasn't mad anymore. She told him that he meant a lot to her, and nothing mattered but his well being. After their conversation, she said she was going to take a shower and go to bed early. Ethan told her that he'd be right behind her.

When Ethan was alone on the couch, he closed his eyes and relaxed. He told himself how lucky he was that Marcus and Ashley had been so forgiving, and willing to continue supporting him. He tried not to think about the Heart of the Forest, and decided it would work itself out tomorrow.

After resting his eyes for a bit, Ethan stood up to join Ashley in the bedroom. Ashley's open purse caught his eye. The manuscript that his young fan, Lance, had given him the day before was still there. Ethan smiled and grabbed the manuscript. He sat back down on the couch and started reading.

Lance's writing etiquette could've used some work, but his story was pretty good. It was a story about a father who moves into a new house with his wife and daughter. It turned out that the house was haunted by a spirit. At first the spirit's influence was subtle. A cabinet would randomly close downstairs. When the characters would check on the cabinet, a door would slam upstairs. As the story progressed things became more pronounced and strange. There would be writing on the wall eerily relevant to the character's insecurities. At times the characters would hear each other's voices calling out to them, only to find nobody there. Ethan thought it was an interesting and welcome take on the horror genre. The entire story went on without the spirit endangering anyone or directly revealing itself in any way. At least, not until the end.

At the end the father found himself face to face with the spirit. Except it wasn't a spirit. Standing before him was a man that looked and spoke just like him. The spirit mocked the father over and over, continuing to poke at his insecurities. In the end the father was able to put his insecurities aside, "defeating" the spirit. It was never seen again. The ending left the reader wondering if it had even existed in the first place or if the father had been having a break with reality.

Ethan wasn't sure what interpretation Lance had hoped for his readers, but Ethan knew the interpretation that the Forest had taken. Ethan was surprised to realize that it had been Lance's manuscript that had been the topic of his last encounter. He was surprised, but he didn't care. If anything he was happy. His earlier encounter had left him feeling free. Not just from the burdens he had placed on himself, but of the Forest as well. It only had one play left to make before the poem was over. Tomorrow he would finally and truly end it. No second guessing. No more.

Ethan set the manuscript down and stood up. He grabbed his phone and sent a quick text to Lance, "Great story. Needs some serious editing mechanically, but you know how to write an amazing plot and relatable characters. Don't stop writing. You'll be a great writer one day."

Then Ethan went to his room and got into bed where Ashley was already sleeping. It had been a long stressful day and she'd probably fallen asleep waiting for him. It'd taken him a long time to read Lance's story.

The next morning Marcus, Ashley, and Ethan decided to get breakfast in town. It was the last day of the festival and there was hardly enough food in the cabin to make a meal for all of them. They packed up their things before getting in the car. They decided they would head home that night rather than spend another night in the cabin.

In the car they discussed what they were going to do with their day. "We missed the results of the contest last night. I looked it up.

Do you guys wanna know, or wait until we get into town?" Marcus asked.

Ashley and Ethan agreed to hear it then.

"First place in poetry was Claire Donaghue and 'The Human Journey,' and first place in fiction was Robert Mitchelson and '*The Pack*,'" Marcus told them.

"Good for Claire," Ethan said excitedly. Then he looked to Ashley to gauge her reaction. He was genuinely happy to hear Claire had won. He just hoped Ashley wouldn't take it the wrong way.

"I never actually read her poem, but I'm sure she deserved it. But I do wonder if she bribed the Book Club members like Robert did," Ashley said.

The car was silent for a moment until the conversation seemed to pass. Then Marcus spoke up. "So, Ethan. What's the plan today? You said you wanted to take one more shot at the Heart of the Forest," he said.

"I still don't know," Ethan admitted, "But I think it will be clear once we're there."

Ashley chimed in. "Well, if you don't have a plan, can I suggest something?" she asked. "You boys have been having all the fun, but you may have already solved this if you'd come to me sooner."

Marcus laughed, "You're probably right."

"What were you thinking babe?" Ethan asked.

"Deaven," Ashley responded. "From what you guys told me, he is clearly involved in this. If we don't know where to look, he's our best bet."

Ethan and Marcus exchanged a quick glance. "I don't know. He's dangerous," Marcus said.

Ethan tilted his head, "Well, if we can find him in town in the middle of the day, then we shouldn't have anything to worry about. And Ashley's right. We don't really have anything else to go off of. It makes sense."

"I don't like it, but I guess you're right," Marcus said, rubbing his forehead.

"Just like that we have a plan. See what happens when you include a woman. This is why we need more women in government," Ashley said.

Marcus and Ethan shared another look and smiled at each other.

"Our first stop should be at the museum then," Ethan suggested, "If he's most likely to be somewhere, it'll be there."

They all agreed on that and a short drive later they were parked outside of Ustumah City.

They got out of the car and headed toward the museum. Surprisingly, the town was the emptiest it had been since they arrived. There were still plenty of people, just no where near the amount from previous days.

The seventh day of the festival was Writing Appreciation Day. Though the entire festival was themed around appreciating writing, the final day was meant to celebrate it more formally. Many non-profit organizations, like the World of Writing Foundation, took center stage in town. There were stands for things ranging from writing workshops to bake sales. And of course there were plenty of stands selling books. It was like the first six days of the festival all wrapped up into one. At the end of the day there was to be a huge banquet to close out the festival. At the banquet, poets, authors, and Book Club Members would be honored. Ethan wasn't looking forward to that, and wondered if Sarah would even care if he left beforehand.

Ashley, Marcus, and Ethan avoided all of the attractions and made their way straight to the museum. The museum was open but it was a ghost town. There were no visitors. All the tourists seemed to be preoccupied with other things. Apparently anyone who cared about Ustumah City's history had already left.

Ethan looked around the inside of the museum for any sign of Deaven. Finally he called out, "Anyone here?" There was no response.

"Seems sketchy to me," Ashley said.

"Maybe he's out at his cabin," Marcus suggested.

Ethan shook his head. "The museum would probably be closed if he wasn't here," he said. Marcus shrugged and looked around, "Well, I don't see him."

Ashley walked over to the section of the museum about the Ustumah Tribe and turned back to Marcus and Ethan. "I never did get to check the museum out," she said, "Gives us something to do while we wait and see."

Marcus agreed and joined her at the Ustumah Tribe's section. Ethan decided to give the Unknown Poet's works another look, and headed over there. He looked it over for a few minutes and didn't see anything new that caught his eye. He was about to go join Marcus and Ashley when he heard the museum's bathroom door open and close. Ethan looked over and saw a teenage girl staring at her phone as she walked out of the bathroom.

He moved toward her to ask if she knew where anyone else was, but she was so engrossed in her phone that she walked right past him like he wasn't even there.

"Excuse me," Ethan called out. That grabbed Marcus and Ashley's attention, but the girl kept walking with her phone.

"Excuse me Miss," Ethan said louder.

At that the girl's ears perked. She looked away from her phone to Ethan. "Yeah, what," she said as if he had seriously inconvenienced her.

Ethan blinked. "Yeah, hi. I was just wondering if you knew where the museum curator was?" Ethan asked.

The girl rolled her eyes at Ethan. "You mean Deaven? He's not here today, so I have to watch the place. It's whatever I guess, it counts as community service hours," she said.

Ashley snickered in the other corner of the museum, but Ethan ignored her. "Do you know where Deaven is?" Ethan asked.

Again the girl rolled her eyes. "Oh, you're like, really not from here," she said. "What do you-" Ethan started, but the girl continued.

"Deaven is like the only really good chef around here. He's getting ready for the banquet tonight down at his restaurant. He cooks like all the food for it pretty much by himself," the girl explained.

Marcus and Ashley had moved over to join them. "He runs the museum and a restaurant in town? How does he manage?" Marcus asked.

The girl looked to Marcus even more annoyed than she had at Ethan. "Dude, I don't know. Go down there and ask him yourself," she said. Then she put her phone back up to her face and sat at the museum's front desk.

Ethan and Marcus looked at each other in disbelief. Ashley was smiling. They made their way out of the museum to follow up on the information the girl had just given them.

"Thanks for your help," Ethan said on the way out, and the girl gave no response. She hardly noticed them leave.

Ashley laughed again as they left the museum. "What's so funny?" Marcus asked her.

"It's just funny," Ashley said, "She kind of reminds me of me when I was her age. Makes me laugh to think of how much of a pain in the ass I was."

"I'm surprised, I never thought of you as the rebellious teenager," Ethan said.

Marcus laughed at that. "I'm not surprised at all. That's actually exactly what I would picture when I think about a young Ashley," Marcus said pointing back toward the museum.

Ashley winked at Marcus while simultaneously flipping him off. "I guess you know me too well," she said.

Ethan ignored the subtle flirting and changed the subject. "So which restaurant is Deaven's," he asked.

"Let's just walk down Main Street and see. It's mostly cafes and there are only a few restaurants in town. We should be able to figure it out," Marcus suggested.

Ashley and Ethan agreed, and the three of them continued on down Main Street. They passed some of the cafes they had visited over the week, relatively certain that none of them was the right place.

Marcus stopped outside of the next restaurant they passed, "Mama Palmer's." He turned to Ashley and Ethan. "This is the place. Deaven signed the check out sheet at the courthouse as Deaven Palmer. This has got to be it. Mama Palmer's," Marcus said.

"Alright. Let's see where this goes," Ethan said leading the way inside.

As the group entered the restaurant they noticed that it was surprisingly empty. Only a handful of tables were filled. Soon after walking in they were stopped by a man standing near the door.

"Sorry, do you have a reservation?" he asked, looking concerned.

"No, do we need one?" Ethan said. He made a point to look at all the empty tables. "Unfortunately today, yes. The owner is using most of the kitchen space to prepare for tonight's banquet dinner. Due to our other chefs having limited space, we are only accepting a limited amount of reservations today," the man explained.

Ashley interjected. "Actually we're just here to see the owner," she said.

A look of surprise flashed on the man's face, "Mr. Palmer is far too busy today. Unless he's expecting you. But I'm sure I would've known if he were."

With impeccable timing Marcus' stomach growled, reminding them all that they had not yet had breakfast. "Is it possible to make a reservation right now?" Marcus asked.

"I'm afraid not. Every year on the final day of the festival Mama Palmer's is reserved for the Ustumah City Book Club Members and their guests," the man said, becoming impatient with their questions.

"Well, I'm Ethan Garland. I was one of the eight authors invited to the festival by the Book Club," Ethan said.

The man was unmoved, "I'm sorry, but if your name isn't on my list then I can't help you."

"This is ridiculous. Come on, if he can't get in who can?" Marcus demanded.

"Someone on my list," the man said pointing at an open notebook in front of him. The conversation was beginning to cause a scene. One of the guests noticed and left their table to approach the group. Ethan was unsurprised to see that it was Claire. At this point he expected coincidence.

"Excuse me sir. These are my guests actually. Could we pull up a few chairs for them?" Claire said looking from the man to Ethan.

"Oh of course Ms. Donaghue. I had no idea that you had more guests coming. I'm sorry for the inconvenience," the man said as he hurriedly motioned for some other employees to make the arrangements."

Claire looked at the three of them. "Good to see you all again," she said. She looked at Ashley and smiled cautiously.

Ashley moved slightly closer to Marcus. Almost not noticeably so, but she did. Then she smiled back at Claire. "Good to see you too. And congratulations on your win," she said.

"Yeah congrats," Ethan and Marcus said in tandem.

Claire shrugged. "Thanks. Honestly, I'm just glad it's over. It would have been a blessing in disguise to get it over with on day two," she said nodding at Ethan. "This whole 'Oh of course Ms. Donaghue' thing is just not me. But I can't complain. This will give me a chance to get real serious about writing now."

"You deserved to win. It's nice to see that count for something. Maybe this whole thing isn't all about bribing the book club," Ethan suggested.

"You'd have to talk to my publisher about that," Claire said, frowning. "But hey, let's continue this conversation at the table." She motioned them over and started toward her table.

To Marcus and Ethan's surprise, Ashley caught up to Claire and stopped her. "Real quick Claire," she started.

Claire turned around and she was blushing. "Yeah?"

"I just wanted to say sorry. I hope I didn't make you feel uncomfortable. You seem like a really nice girl, and I've been kind of bitchy. Maybe I was a little jealous. That was stupid. I'm sorry," Ashley said.

Ethan was completely thrown off. He looked over at Marcus and saw that he was equally surprised.

Claire didn't say anything for a moment, but she was blushing even more than before. "Don't worry about it," she finally answered, "I can honestly tell you I don't make a big deal about the past. Seriously, don't worry about it."

Ashley relaxed a bit and said, "Thanks. I just needed to say something. I felt bad."

"Don't," Claire said, "Let's just sit down together and have some breakfast." Then she rubbed her hands together and continued toward her table. Ethan, Marcus, and Ashley followed right behind her.

There were three others seated at the table. Trent Richards, the poet who had written "No Escape." Keith Sanders, the Ustumah City Book Club Member. And Pamela Hurshman, another Book Club Member.

As they sat down the others greeted them. Pamela was happy to see Ethan again, and eagerly began asking him about his time at the festival. Trent recognized Ashley and Marcus from his poem reading and happily began to chat with them. Keith made a point to take up most of Claire's attention.

They all conversed for a few minutes before the waiter appeared, bringing menus for Ashley, Ethan, and Marcus. "The rest of the table just ordered not long ago. I can put your orders in whenever you are ready," he said politely.

They looked over the menu while the others continued conversing. Keith and Pamela kept going out of their way to make sure that everyone at the table knew they'd been instrumental in Claire's victory. It was a bit awkward for Trent and Ethan, who had both been eliminated.

As Ethan scanned the menu, he noticed the back page was dedicated to "Known Poets and Authors Writing Festival Specials." There was a different special for every day. But it was the seventh day, Writing Appreciation Day, that particularly stood out to him. The special was "Mama Palmer's Famous Jamaican Red Herring." The first part of the description read,

"Prepared by Mama Palmer's very own son, Chef Deaven, enjoy this signature dish served every year at the Known Poets and Authors Writing Festival's Writing Appreciation Day Banquet."

An important realization clicked in Ethan's mind. Ethan was no closer to discovering the secrets of the Heart of the Forest. But he had just eliminated a lead that would have surely led nowhere, and that felt like a win to him.

When the waiter returned Ethan ordered something else entirely and continued conversing with the rest of the table. It was an odd mix, and Ashley and Marcus would have been out of place had it not been for Trent remembering them. Even still, it turned out to be good company. Their food arrived not long after ordering, and they all enjoyed breakfast over more conversation. When Ethan asked, Trent shared his poem with him for the first time. When Trent was finished Ethan praised him, but also took a moment to look at Marcus and acknowledge their encounter with the dark shade in the forest. Marcus gave Ethan a knowing look and they moved on. When the Book Club members gave Claire a chance to breathe, Ashley and Claire ended up getting along like old friends.

Near the end of breakfast Pamela spoke up to all of them. "The festival is truly a special time here in Ustumah City. The only negative thing I can say about it, is that it is too centered in the city. It really doesn't give people a chance to enjoy the beautiful redwood forests we have around us. If I can make one suggestion to you all, it's that today you just pick any ol' trail and go for a hike into the forest. Trust me, it'll be worth it," she said.

Everyone seemed to take her suggestion to heart. But Ethan did more than that. He made it his mission. As far as he was concerned, Pamela had just given him the answers he needed.

As the breakfast came to a close, Keith insisted on paying. They all thanked him as they got up from the table. Keith made off to pay the bill, Pamela said her goodbyes, and Trent thanked them all for a great morning before heading off. Then it was only Claire, Ethan, Ashley, and Marcus remaining.

"Thanks for that, Claire," Ethan said, "That was a nice way to start off the day." Marcus and Ashley agreed.

"Of course, anything for a friend," Claire said smiling at Ethan.

Ethan took a moment to appreciate Claire. Her encounters with their group had not exactly been something most people would think of as the start of a friendship. But Ethan knew she meant what she said. Claire just seemed like one of those people who saw the best in others. Her belief alone seemed to have the power to bring it out in people. He hoped they could remain close after the festival was over.

"I hate to do this, but I do have to get going. My publisher will have my head if I'm late to this meeting. Even though most of the people have left the festival by now, this is the biggest day of sales for the festival winners. But to make those sales, I gotta be there I guess," Claire said, seeming honestly reluctant.

She held out a hand to Ethan and he shook it, "We'll see you around."

Claire nodded. "Of course. Here, let me give my number to Ashley so we can meet up afterwards," she said.

Ashley was surprised, but she eagerly took out her phone and handed it to Claire. Claire entered her number into the phone and returned it to Ashley. Then she took a few steps forward and hugged Ashley goodbye.

"I'm glad we got to know each other and make some second impressions," Claire said as she hugged her.

"Me too," Ashley said, hugging her back.

Afterwards Claire turned to Marcus and shook his hand. "Marcus," she said, nodding her head, with a masculine tone that sounded almost mocking.

Marcus responded with a similar tone and nodded his head back, and they shared a quick laugh. Then Claire gave one more wave goodbye to the three of them, and she was gone.

"We should get going," Ethan told Ashley and Marcus.

"What do you mean? What about Deaven?" Ashley asked. Marcus looked confused as well.

Ethan shook his head. "Deaven has nothing to do with this. He was always just a distraction," Ethan explained.

"Ok, that's a big change from what you had in mind coming in here," Marcus said. "Did the bacon speak to you over breakfast?"

"No, but the menu did," Ethan said.

Ashley and Marcus shared a look, not much different than the one they had given him when he'd told them that he feared *In Despair* was coming to life.

"It showed today's special. The big meal that Deaven is preparing for the banquet tonight," Ethan said.

"And?" Ashley asked, still confused.

"It was Jamaican Red Herring," Ethan said with confidence.

Again Ashley and Marcus shared a look. "Ethan you're a little ahead of us. Can you catch us up?" Ashley asked.

Ethan realized that he wasn't making much sense, and that he had gotten ahead of himself. "Sorry," he started, "I'll explain. In writing, a red herring is a clue that takes the reader and/or the characters in the wrong direction. It's usually something that seems critical to solving the mystery of a story, but its only real intention is to divert attention from the real issue."

Ashley was nodding. "Ok. So you're saying that Deaven is our red herring? And you're sure of that just because of a meal he's serving?" She asked.

"Yes," Ethan said with as much confidence as he could, "I know it sounds crazy, but I know it. Right as we're coming to the end of Claire's poem, the end of all this, we're looking into Deaven. And the signature dish of the festival, served by him, is a red herring. That is no coincidence. Coincidence went out the window when this whole thing with the Heart of the Forest began."

Ashley and Marcus looked as convinced as they were going to get. "Then where do we go now?" Marcus asked.

"Glad you asked," Ethan said, "Because Pamela already gave us the answer. We just pick any hiking trail we want, and head out into the forest. I don't know what's going to happen, but I can tell you that all of this is going to come to an end."

Ashley looked hesitant. "I don't have any other ideas, but I feel like this might be grasping," Ashley admitted.

"Maybe, but it's worth a shot. Just remember your promise Ethan," Marcus said.

Ethan had been wrong so many times in the past week, but he had never been more sure he was right than he was in that moment. "I remember. If this doesn't lead to something, I'll drop it," he said.

"Alright," Marcus said, "Then I'm on board. Pick a trail."

That was exactly what Ethan did. He brought out his phone and looked up nearby hiking trails. He picked the closest one to town and the three of them made their way to it.

CHAPTER 28

The trail Ethan had picked was far enough from town to justify driving, but the group decided they'd done enough driving. The trail was also close enough to justify walking. They bought some supplies in town for the hike, and then they were off. It took a little under half an hour to walk from the outskirts of Ustumah City to the trail.

They had just arrived at the trail, but they were already sweating. They hadn't dressed for a hike, which looking back on it had been an obvious mistake. A part of Ethan always knew that this day could only end in the forest.

Marcus was the best dressed for the occasion, with jeans and a tight-fitting shirt made of lightweight breathable material. Ashley rolled up her pant legs and removed her jacket before tying it around her waist. Ethan removed his blazer, folded it, and tossed it over his shoulder. Then he undid another button on his shirt.

"Well, here we go," Ethan said with a sigh once they were all ready to continue. He started down the trail, and Ashley and Marcus followed.

As they went, they discussed Claire and Ashley's recent exchange. "That was a real change of heart," Ethan said to her.

"Well, I just realized she's a nice person. She didn't really do anything to deserve how I treated her. None of that was her fault," Ashley explained.

"No, yeah. I just think that was really mature of you. A lot of people never would have said anything," Ethan said.

"A lot of people weren't about to share breakfast with her either," Marcus said laughing.

Ashley laughed and flipped him off. "I wanted to apologize to her. Thankfully, running into her gave me the opportunity," she said.

"Either way, I'm glad you guys were able to work it out. She could make a good fourth to our group, she seemed to really like you Ash," Ethan offered.

"Yeah. I actually liked her a lot too. It'd be nice to hang out with her again," Ashley said.

Marcus held up a finger. "I will say, I can't tell if she likes me or not. You know, like if she was messing with me at the end there."

"Well, you guys didn't talk much," Ethan said, "That was probably her way of trying to let you know she considered you a friend."

"Maybe. She doesn't give off the same vibe I'm used to getting from girls like her," Marcus said.

"That's because when most girls like you, they really like you," Ashley said.

The comment seemed strange to Ethan, but he reminded himself that Ashley wasn't exactly talking about herself.

"Oh c'mon I have plenty of girlfriends that aren't into me," Marcus said defensively.

The next ten minutes turned into a humorous conversation where Ethan and Ashley pointed out how every girl Marcus tried to use as an example, was secretly, or not so secretly, into him.

"Fine, fine," Marcus finally conceded. "I guess I'm just oblivious." Ethan and Ashley laughed at him.

"So how far are we going to go?" Ashley asked.

Ethan thought for a moment. "Until something happens," he said.

"Yeah, something usually happens eventually," Marcus agreed. "And what if something doesn't happen," Ashley asked.

Marcus had no answer, and Ethan thought about it. "This trail ends eventually. I guess we'll just go until we get to the end. But that won't happen," he said.

"Well, I admire your confidence," Ashley said, and they continued on.

Fifteen minutes passed as they went, and nothing out of the ordinary happened. Then half an hour with nothing. Then an hour. An hour and a half. Two hours. A drop of doubt found its way into Ethan's mind, but he wiped it away. There was still time. Based on their rate of travel, he figured they wouldn't reach the end of the trail for another forty-five minutes.

"Does it usually take this long?" Ashley asked, stopping. She was huffing and puffing. "Sometimes," Ethan said, "It just depends."

"Well. I need a break. Maybe even a cigarette," Ashley said digging into her purse. "That's really not going to make this easier," Ethan said.

That seemed to seriously piss Ashley off because she didn't even say anything. She didn't smoke a lot, usually one or two cigarettes a day. But she hated it when Ethan gave her a hard time about her habit.

"Ah, we've got time. It'll happen when it happens," Marcus said to Ethan. "Come on," he said beckoning Ethan over as he moved toward Ashley, "We could all have one. It'll be relaxing."

Ethan agreed, if only to appease his friends. Ethan usually only smoked if he got very drunk, and Marcus was more of a social smoker. It wasn't often the three of them smoked together.

As they smoked their cigarettes in the middle of the forest in Ustumah County, it somehow felt oddly like they were back in college. Ethan realized that had been the last time they had smoked together. At first the feeling was nostalgic and comforting, but a strange feeling started to creep up on Ethan as he thought about old times. It was the feeling that had been haunting him the entire trip. The feeling that had been driving him to seek answers from the Heart of the Forest. He felt it more strongly in that moment than he ever had, and he was able to better place it. It was a feeling of being lied to. He couldn't explain it, but somehow his life felt like a lie. He felt like there was some kind of untruth right in front of him, but it was just out of reach.

Ethan ignored the feeling and pushed it aside. He'd have the answers he was seeking soon enough, and there was no point dwelling on it while he was so close.

The group finished their cigarettes and continued on down the trail. Again, minutes upon minutes went by, and nothing happened. Every minute they drew closer to the end of the trail, and every minute Ethan's heart sank a little. Theres still thirty minutes left, Ethan told himself. Then twenty. Then ten. Then five, four, three, two, one, and they were at the end of the trail. The trail ended abruptly and the area around them was dense with foliage and trees.

Ethan turned to Ashley and Marcus. Marcus looked disappointed. He had likely been expecting something to happen, just as Ethan had. Ashley looked sad. Not an internal sorrow, but more like pity. Pity for Ethan. She'd seen how much this meant to him, and here it had turned out to be nothing.

"No," Ethan said stubbornly. "No, this can't be it. I'm telling you guys, I'm sure something will happen."

"What do you want us to do now?" Ashley asked.

"Well, normally we weren't on a trail. It just happened in the middle of the forest. We have to go out into the forest," Ethan said nervously.

"And how long do we go into the forest for Ethan?" Ashley said. "Until something happens," Ethan said.

Marcus walked up to Ethan and put a hand on his shoulder. "What if nothing happens. Or what if something happens and it just leads to more questions? Where do we draw the line man," he said.

"I draw the line when we figure this out," Ethan said, starting to sound upset.

Marcus shook his head. "That may never happen. That's what is fucked up about this whole thing. That's why I wanted you to promise that we could draw the line somewhere. Otherwise it could just become an obsession that never ends. That's why we made you promise that this would be the end, no matter what happened. Or didn't happen," Marcus said.

Ethan realized there was some truth in what Marcus was saying. So far his search for the Heart of the Forest had been a sort of obsession, and every time he had thought it was over it just kept going. What Marcus and Ashley weren't understanding was that this time was different. Even now, after nothing had happened, he knew that it was coming to an end. He was just too close to give up now.

"I'm sorry, but you don't understand," Ethan started.

"No Ethan, you don't understand!" Ashley yelled back at him. "This is a pattern with you." Ashley's outburst had been so unexpected that Ethan was speechless.

"I'm starting to think this is how you'll always be. I wanted to believe it was just a phase, and things would get better. But they're just getting worse," Ashley said.

Marcus was completely silent, and couldn't look Ashley nor Ethan in the eye.

Ethan felt a deep fear and sadness well up inside him. "What do you mean Ash?" he asked.

Ashley looked away and thought for a moment. Then she turned back and took a deep breath. "What I mean is that I feel like you don't really care about this relationship," she said.

"Wha-" Ethan attempted, but Ashley held up her hand.

"Let me finish. I need to say this," Ashley said. And Ethan listened.

"When things are going good, they're great with us. But as soon as it gets hard, you look to something else. You find something that you can spend all your attention on so that you don't have to deal with our problems. You leave me to try and fix it all by myself, and I can't do that. You did it with your book, and now you're doing with this. I can't be the only one trying to make this work full time. You're part time, and it's not enough," Ashley said. She looked like she might cry.

Ethan felt the pit in his stomach growing. He knew what was coming, but he still had hope that he could fix it.

"I do want to make things work with us Ashley. But you're right, I haven't been there as much as I should. I've been running away from having to try. But I'm ready to stop that now. I just need you to believe in me this one last time. Once this is over I'll be there full time," Ethan said. He felt himself holding back tears.

"Ethan." Ashley let just his name linger in the air. A strange combination of love and pity. "I want to believe you. I want to believe that if we just go off into the forest with you for the next month, that something will happen. You'll get whatever answers you seem to need you think so bad. And that then everything would go back to being perfect. But even if I did that, it's not that simple," she said.

"What do you mean it's not that simple?" Ethan asked.

At that point, Marcus turned away from them both and was holding his head.

"There's something I have to tell you," Ashley said with so much guilt, Ethan already knew what she was about to say. "I was trying to fix everything on my own. You were becoming distant, and I didn't know why. And Marcus was there for me. He was there for you too, but you weren't there. And then you became even more distant. You started writing your book and it seemed like that was all you cared about. One night it just happened. I was just emotional, and Marcus was too." She stopped then.

It seemed to Ethan that she may never speak again. The words lingered and he couldn't take it anymore. "Just say it," he said.

"We hooked up." Her words seemed to echo through the forest. Marcus still refused to face either of them.

Ethan didn't say anything. He was struggling to understand the flood of emotions he was experiencing.

Ashley continued, "And I thought that would be the end of it. Just a one-time thing. But it wasn't. It kept happening because it was the only thing that made me feel better. I know that was selfish of me, but it's the truth."

"This whole time?"

Ashley swallowed. "Up until about four days ago, yeah. We stopped though. I wanted to give you and me a chance, and I knew that wouldn't happen if it didn't stop. And Marcus agreed."

"He can speak for himself," Ethan said glaring at the back of Marcus' head. Marcus still said nothing.

"The thing is Ethan. I'm sorry. I do care about you, but I'm realizing that my feelings for Marcus are real. I can't do this to myself anymore. I want to be with someone that I feel like I actually belong with. This just isn't working anymore," Ashley said. Tears were starting to run down her face.

"Say it," Ethan said, shifting his glare to her.

More tears started and Ashley looked at him like her heart was breaking. "I do love you Ethan," she said shakily.

Ethan just shook his head. "Just say what you're doing. Just say it so it's over," he said.

Ashley was shaking her head and sobbing. "I'm sorry," she managed. "I have to end this. It's not healthy for either of us."

Ethan began nodding like he'd just had some sort of victory, though he felt far from it. "Well, there it is. I'm sorry it's so hard for you. I'm sure it's going to be real hard to have someone else to fall back on. That's probably why you started this whole thing in the first place. You wanted to make sure you had a sure thing before you left me. I know how you are," he said.

Ashley was still sobbing but she scowled at him angrily. "That's not fair. You know that is not what this is," she said.

"That's exactly how this is. You're a slut. Plain and simple," Ethan said back. As soon as the words left his mouth he regretted it. No matter how angry he was, there was nobody he cared about more than Ashley. He hadn't even meant it, the words had just come out. A part of him was screaming to take the words back, but his anger was still in control and he was too stubborn.

Ashley's crying calmed slightly and she just stared at Ethan. Marcus finally turned around. "Ethan! I know you're pissed, but don't say that shit. I know you don't mean it," Marcus said.

Ethan quickly turned to Marcus. "Shut the fuck up. I got a whole lot more to say to you," Ethan shouted.

Ashley spoke up. "You're not in a good place. I know you must feel so wronged right now, but for your own good, I'm leaving. I do care about you, and I don't want it to end like this. We can talk later when you've calmed down."

"Yeah, whatever, run away," Ethan said, waving her off.

Ashley scoffed and turned to Marcus. "Are you coming?" she asked. "I'll catch up," Marcus said.

Ashley looked at Ethan once more and he continued to glare at her. She turned and started walking back up the trail. Marcus walked up to Ethan.

When Marcus was close enough, Ethan punched him in the face. Marcus didn't respond. "How could you do this to me?" Ethan asked. "You were like my brother. You knew how much I loved her."

"I'm sorry man. I love her too, and this relationship was just hurting you both. I still love you like my brother," Marcus said.

Ethan laughed. He sounded almost maniacal as he did, reminding himself of the doppelganger he had encountered in the forest. "Easy for you to say. I didn't betray your trust. Do you really think things can be the same between us?" he said.

"I guess not," Marcus responded. "I am sorry man. I've always had feelings for her, but I put them aside for you. I decided you deserved a chance to be happy. Maybe I was losing out on the love of my life, but it was worth it if you could be happy. But then you weren't. How long am I supposed to put your well being before my own when you're not even trying to help yourself? I still care about you. I'm just done putting effort into a bottomless pit. You need to take your happiness into your own hands for once."

Ethan pushed Marcus as hard as he could. Marcus stumbled backward but held his ground. "You're just being selfish and using all that as an excuse," Ethan shouted.

Marcus frowned. "You're probably right. And I'll have to live with that. But it doesn't make it any less true," he said.

Ethan didn't say anything. He just looked at Marcus with a blank stare. They stared at each other for minutes, waiting for the other to say something. When neither did, Marcus finally turned and started walking back up the trail.

"We'll wait for you at the car if you want," Marcus said. Ethan turned away. "Don't bother," he said.

After a while Ethan turned back and watched Marcus walk off, leaving him alone in the middle of the forest. Ethan realized that Ashley and Marcus' affair had been the answer he'd been looking for all along. That itch at the back of his mind that had made him so uncomfortable in his relationship hadn't been nothing. It was subconscious suspicion. It had been right in front of him the whole time. It *should* have been especially obvious this past week, but he'd been so distracted. First by the festival contest and second by his obsession to find answers at the Heart of the Forest.

Ironically, here he finally was in the middle of the forest and he'd finally gotten those answers. He felt like the butt of some cosmic joke, and for a moment felt sorry for himself. That self-pity was quickly replaced with anger as he realized the truth. He was the butt of a joke. A joke being played by whatever magical entity was controlling the narrative. It loved the irony of it all, and it took joy in his suffering.

Ethan looked up at the trees around him. "Are you happy now?!" he shouted hysterically. "You've ruined my life! You've taken everything from me. My friend, my girlfriend, and whatever pride I still had!"

He ran to the closest redwood and punched it with all his force. The tree, ancient and powerful, took little notice of his punch. His wrist and knuckles, however, were not so indifferent to the punch. When Ethan pulled his fist away his knuckles were raw and bloody, and his wrist throbbed with pain at the slightest movement. Ethan let out a primal scream as he kicked the tree.

"Fuck you!" he yelled out into the forest. He was met by nothing but silence. No wildlife. No fiction coming to life. Not even a slight breeze wandering it's way through the trees. The forest gave no response to him.

Without thinking, Ethan began wildly sprinting through the forest in every which direction. "What do you want from me?" he yelled out as he went. "Tell me what you want! Do something!" He continued on like that for what could have been anywhere from two to twenty minutes. Time wasn't something he was paying attention to anymore. He was broken and hopeless. He was out of options. Yelling and running was all he felt he could do anymore.

He kept on like that, aimlessly sprinting through the forest, no longer aware of where he was. He would have kept on like that until he could no longer run, if it weren't for what happened next.

As he was running he took one step onto what looked like a small bush presumably on solid ground. That was not the case though. Ethan's foot fell through the branches of the bush and well past where the ground should have been. He stumbled and tried to catch himself, but the momentum of his movement was more than he could handle. Instead, he fell forward and felt the branches of the bush scratching at his face as he went down. Past the bush he continued falling. Down and down he went. It all happened in a flash, yet he felt like he was falling for hours.

Then he hit the stone ground hard. His arms, legs, and torso took the brunt of the fall. But as he landed Ethan's head made a quick and violent bounce on the ground and everything went black.

CHAPTER 29

When Ethan woke his head was pounding and he was sprawled out on the stone floor of a subterranean cave. It was dark and he could hardly see a thing while his eyes were still adjusting. A small amount of light trickled down from above and through the brush that had concealed the opening Ethan had fallen through.

Ethan stood up and grabbed his aching head. The world was spinning slightly and he hoped he hadn't injured himself too severely. He couldn't stop blinking, and when he looked up at the light his head felt like someone was drilling into it. He felt something wet on his hand and moved it in front of his face. His hand was covered in blood. Fuck, I might seriously be hurt, Ethan realized.

He fought through the pain and looked up at the light pouring down. He needed to get out of the cave and get to a doctor, and that meant climbing out. He could see that climbing wasn't going to be easy, but that it would likely be manageable. The only thing he could say for sure was that it would take him some time to do carefully.

Ethan moved toward the nearby cave wall to start climbing. The pounding in his head began to calm and the world started to return to a stillness. As it did Ethan's eyes began to adjust to the darkness of the cave. At the same time, his sense of smell must have kicked back in because he gagged at the first sign of a foul smell. It was a cold, heavy, nauseating, and rotten smell. Ethan had to fight not to throw up.

In search of the source of the smell, Ethan began frantically scanning the cave around him through the darkness. It only took a few seconds for him to spot the crumpled mass on the ground only a few feet away. Ethan covered his nose with his shirt and approached the mass for a better look.

As Ethan got closer he was able to make it out. It was the decomposing body of a young girl. The body had clearly been there for some time, and the girl was hardly recognizable. Even still Ethan knew he was looking at the body of Ella Schaeffer, the girl whose picture he had seen in the Missing Girl poster on his first night in Ustumah City.

The sight of the girl sent Ethan over the edge, and he began violently vomiting. He was on his hands and knees heaving for minutes. Despite the stench around him, he finally caught his breath and regained composure. He looked back at the girl and frowned. Ethan could only think of the missing girl from his book, Margaret. He had written her fate, and now Ella had shared it.

"I'm so sorry I did this to you."

He grabbed her arms and gently placed them over her chest. Then he straightened her out her legs which had been contorted and likely broken from her fall into the cave. The more Ethan thought about it, he hoped she had died on impact. It sickened him to think of a poor innocent girl crying for help and dying alone in that cave. He took a long moment of silence to honor the dead girl's memory.

Afterwards Ethan's eyes had fully adjusted to the cave. He could see that it led deeper away from the entrance, but not far. The cave was probably about the size of a small house. On the far wall Ethan could make out some kind of drawings or words. He couldn't tell from where he was. He stood up and made his way over.

When Ethan reached the other side of the cave, he was able to make out some old cave paintings. The paintings were in a very similar style to those he had seen at the Ustumah Tribe exhibit at the museum. The cave paintings were not the only things he noticed. To the side of the painted wall there was a worn piece of paper with writing on it. Next to that there sat a leather-bound journal. And beyond that there sat a stack of printer paper held together by a paper clip.

Ethan stopped and took in the moment. He was finally here. It had been nothing like he had expected, but it was the Heart of the Forest. A nervous sensation took hold in his stomach, and he could feel his heart pounding. He swallowed and looked at the paintings on the cave wall.

The paintings seemed to tell a story of great warriors with unheard weapons arriving in a land of beauty. Other people lived in the land, and seemed upset about the arrival of the outsiders. The others attacked the warriors. The warriors fought back, and wiped out the others that had been there before them. Then they enjoyed the land of beauty to themselves.

Ethan bowed his head and placed a hand on the cave wall. He had another long moment of silence, this time in memory of an entire people. Afterwards Ethan turned his attention to the nearby worn sheet of paper. Ethan knelt down and picked it up. He started reading.

"I, Dallas Sutter, have set out on this venture in hopes of changing my luck. For many days now I have searched in vain for the sweet gold which I desire so. It was the last of my savings which I have used to fund this venture. There is nothing awaiting me back at Doe Creek, and I will not return until I have found my ticket to a better life.

That is, there are only two ways for my story to end. I will either discover the most amazing of treasures and live out the rest of my life as a rich man, or I will die in this forest. I do admit, however, that I have no intention of dying yet.

This place in which I find myself seems to hold a certain power that I cannot describe, yet I can feel. The paintings on the wall tell a story, and they hold a dark feeling behind them.

I leave this page behind in this place, this Heart of the Forest, in hopes that I can turn its power in my favor. Perhaps I will, or perhaps I will not. My fate is in its hands now, but as I have said, I have no intention of dying a poor man."

As Ethan read the page he could feel a sort of presence around him. It was everywhere in the cave, but also nowhere. The power Dallas had written of was as real today as it had been then. Ethan did not welcome the energy, but he also did not fight it. He merely accepted its presence.

Ethan set down the page and moved on to the small leather-bound journal. He carefully picked it up, opened it, and began to read.

"My name is Elizabeth Green. I am a poet. I have had the privilege of enjoying the beauty of Ustumah County most of my life. If you are reading this, then it may be too late. There may still be hope, but you must read carefully.

The Heart of the Forest will not so easily allow for it's secrets to be revealed. But I have found a way to cheat it. Within this journal I shall leave clues, or better yet, warnings. These will be my first line of defense in trying to spare others my fate. This journal shall be my last stand.

The Heart is looking for writers. It hungers for their stories. It is a force of nature with only one purpose, and it will move toward that purpose with all its power. Once the Heart takes hold of your life, it is only here that you can make a stand. The first clue will be left somewhere so that it will only be found by a writer already caught in the grip of the Heart.

The heart of the woods, fiction is reality,
there your answers lie.

Next are the warnings. They will be open for all to find. Though they will only make sense to another wrapped up in the magic of the Forest.

We all have stories that we'd like told,
But it's the world that decides which ones take hold,
Though when they come from the Heart we can still shape our fate, We just have to do so before it's too late.

It will not always be that there is time to fix your mistakes. When that is the case, a different warning must be heeded.

Warning to the fool, Magic uncontrollable, Best to leave it be.

Last but not least are the warnings of my failures. Yet, these are not just my warnings. They are also my fate. They will be the last thing I write, and they will be my salvation.

All fear the lover,
Most dangerous beast of all.
Its greed knows no end.

A writer with ambitions for the world, Discovery of a power untouched, Now temptation takes hold,
Curse self inflicted by work rushed, Innocents now pay the debt of this mistake, To bring back balance the writer must atone, To set things right, a choice they must make, The price to be paid: to have never been known."

Reading the last words of Elizabeth Green sent a chill down Ethan's spine. Whatever she had done, the Forest had beaten her. She had tried to at least spare others the same fate, yet here Ethan was all the same. It was a dreadful realization. Ethan began to dread what surprises the stack of paper at the other end of the cave held.

Ethan looked around the back of the cave again. At the cave paintings. At the worn page of Dallas Sutter's diary. Down at the Unknown Poet's journal. And over to the stack of papers to his side. It was a legacy of people trying to control an ancient magic. None of the stories of the people that had been there had happy endings. And now Ethan found himself standing in that same place. He was worried what his fate would be.

Ethan moved toward the stack and stood over it. As his eyes focused, he began to make out the contents of the top page. It was a title page with only six words on it. "Nothing But Words, By Ethan Garland."

Ethan's heart felt like it had stopped. He was frozen with fear as he stared at the page.

Whatever the rest of the pages contained, Ethan knew it wouldn't be good. He could feel it in his gut.

It took everything he had, but Ethan finally worked up the courage to pick up the stack of papers. The exact moment his hand touched the paper his mind was flooded with memories. They were years of memories from another lifetime. In the blink of an eye, he had remembered living a completely different life.

CHAPTER 30

The last thing Ethan wanted to do that night was go to a party. He was tired and had a midterm the next day. But what Ethan wanted didn't matter to Marcus. He practically dragged Ethan out with him.

After a few drinks Ethan started to relax. Though he was still worrying about school, a part of him was glad Marcus had convinced him to come out. At some point in the night Marcus had disappeared with the girl that had invited them to the party in the first place.

Ethan was left with a party's worth of people he barely knew. He did his best to make small talk and meet some new people, but none of them grabbed his attention quite like the dark haired beauty he had bumped into on the dance floor.

"Oh, sorry," Ethan had said when he'd bumped into her. He awkwardly stood there with his drink in hand, as everyone else, the girl included, danced around him.

She had just smiled at him and yelled over the music, "Are you just going to stand there? Or are you going to dance?"

The moment she smiled at him, Ethan was smitten. He smiled back and let out a nervous chuckle. "Dance I guess," he said as he started dancing.

The girl laughed at him and moved closer. They danced together for a few minutes before Ethan leaned in. "I'm Ethan by the way," he said. He pulled back hoping that she had heard him over the noise around them.

She flashed her smile at him again and leaned in toward his ear. "I'm Ashley," she said. As she did, her breath hit Ethan's ear and he felt the hair on his arms stand up straight. He knew nothing about Ashley, but he already knew that she was someone very special.

They spent the rest of the night together, and it had been one of the most amazing nights of Ethan's life. They just clicked. He'd never gotten along with someone as easy as he had gotten along with Ashley. More than a few times, Ethan had wanted to kiss her. He never did though. He felt that he'd have plenty of chances in the future.

Ethan had been partially right. After that night, Ashley became one of Ethan's best friends. The three of them were always together.

Ethan and Ashley never kissed though. He just never felt like it was right. He felt that they had a special connection, but they were just friends. They never flirted or anything like that. Not like she and Marcus would.

Despite all that, Ethan felt that he was missing out on being with the love of his life. Ethan had always had self-confidence issues with girls. Throughout his life, girls were always likely to be more interested in Marcus than him. Ethan became convinced that it was that lack of confidence that was keeping Ashley and him from being together.

One night, years into their friendship, Ethan decided that he was going to tell Ashley how he felt. His heart couldn't stand to be just friends anymore, and he had to at least try.

Ashley, Ethan, and some of their mutual friends had decided to go out to a bar. Ethan was working up the courage to tell Ashley, but realized he needed another drink. He ran to the bar and ordered the strongest thing he could.

Ethan finished his drink. It did little to calm his nerves, like he'd hoped it would.

Nevertheless, he made his way over toward Ashley. She was sitting at a table with some of her and Ethan's friends. Ethan couldn't help but notice how beautiful Ashley looked, and it only served to make him more nervous.

Ashley noticed Ethan as he made his way over. "Where'd you head off to?" she asked.

"Uh, sorry. I needed a drink," Ethan said. Then he paused awkwardly. "Actually, I was hoping we could talk about something. In private." He said the last part a little louder than he'd meant to, and everyone turned to look.

Ashley seemed concerned. She looked at all of their friends, "Be right back guys." Ethan made his way to a quiet corner of the bar and Ashley followed.

Thinking Out Loud by Ed Sheeran began playing from the jukebox. "I hate this song," Ashley said, shaking her head. "So what's up? You're acting weird."

Ethan just went for it. "Ash, I'm so glad that we're such great friends. Every day we've spent together since we've met has been amazing. No matter what, I will always appreciate our friendship. There's a part of me that is so worried that what I am about to say is going to ruin all that, but if I don't say it, I'm not sure I'd ever forgive myself," Ethan said pausing briefly. "Ashley Hollins, I love you. I want to be with you. I think we should be together."

Ashley didn't say anything. She just looked at Ethan for a long time, and finally he spoke up. "Say something," Ethan said, his heart beating like crazy.

"Ethan, you're one of my best friends. I really care about you, and I know you really care about me. But saying I love you is nothing but words. It doesn't make us in love. It doesn't turn our friendship into this romantic thing. I don't know what you want me to say," Ashley said. "I'm sorry."

Ethan didn't know how to respond and he sat there for a while thinking. While he did, Ashley continued. "Don't make this weird. I still want to be friends, but you need to know I just don't feel that way. I don't want you to hang on to this idea that we'll be together someday or something. I have to be honest with you. And if I'm doing that, I should tell you that I have feelings for Marcus. I'm so sorry Ethan, I have no idea what to say. I'm probably saying all the wrong things."

"No, it's okay," Ethan told her. "You're right, I shouldn't have brought this up. We should just be friends. I'm okay with that," he lied. That was the end of the conversation.

Ethan's heart felt shattered after that night, but that was only the beginning. Admitting to Ethan how she felt about Marcus must have given Ashley some needed courage. Within a week she told Marcus how she felt and they started dating.

Ethan realized that Marcus and Ashley had always had a spark between them. Something more real than he ever could have had with her. He just hadn't seen it because he'd been so involved in his own fantasy.

Marcus and Ashley's relationship became exponentially more serious as time went on.

Everyone that knew them saw them as the perfect couple. People could feel the energy between the two lovers whenever they were together. It was abundantly clear that they each cared about the other more than they cared about themselves. They were often called the "match made in heaven" or the "golden standard for a successful relationship." Some people wondered if it only appeared that way on the outside, thinking that clearly no couple could be so perfect. However, Ethan knew the truth. They were perfect for each other. He was their third wheel and he saw everything. Both Marcus and Ashley knew how Ethan felt about Ashley, but it never became a problem. In the beginning of their relationship, the three of them sat down and had a serious talk about it. Afraid of losing his two best friends, Ethan lied. He told them that he had moved on, and that he was happy for them.

As time went on Ethan's lie became further and further from the truth. His feelings for Ashley seemed to become even stronger, though mostly out of jealousy. Eventually Marcus moved out of Ethan's and his place to move in with Ashley. Feeling alone and excluded, Ethan began to resent them both.

Finding himself in a deep pit of despair, Ethan began writing a novel. He had always been a writer by hobby, but one day he hoped to be a famous writer. He began to spend less and less time doing anything but write. As he did, his feelings of loneliness only increased his resentment toward Ashley and Marcus.

In a little under a year, Ethan finished his novel "In Love and Despair." It was about a man who found the love of his life, only to lose her. She met someone more attractive that only wanted her for her looks. The man ended up alone and miserable, but learned a valuable lesson about love. Ethan sent the book to multiple publishers, but none of them ever responded.

After a little over a year of living together, Marcus proposed to Ashley. She said yes, and they were engaged. The news broke Ethan's heart. Straight away Marcus asked Ethan to be his best man. Ethan, over emotional from the news, blew up on Marcus and refused. Ethan told Marcus that he'd stolen Ashley from him. That he was now to blame for all of Ethan's pain.

Marcus had not taken it well, and the two had an argument that ended their friendship. Afterwards, Ashley refused to talk to Ethan.

Ethan was lost, and didn't know what to do. He spent a few months doing nothing in particular. One day he came across an ad for the world famous Known Poets and Authors Writing Festival being held in Ustumah City, California. Ethan had always wanted to go. After reading many blog posts about young authors sharing their work at the festival and receiving publishing deals, Ethan was set on going.

He took time off work and packed a week's worth of clothes and his manuscript for "In Love and Despair." Then he was on the road to Ustumah City.

Upon arriving, Ethan was blown away by the amount of people gathered in the small town for the famous festival. Ethan spent his first day struggling to find a vacant hotel, before he finally found one on the outskirts of town. Not sure what to do on his first day in town, Ethan visited the local museum.

At the museum Ethan learned about the history of Ustumah City. Mostly though, he spent his time appreciating the works of the Unknown Poet. Ethan was reading one work in particular when a woman approached him.

"All fear the lover. Most dangerous beast of all. It's greed knows no end," she said. "There's a real cryptic beauty about the Unknown Poet's work that grabs the reader's interest."

"I couldn't have said it better myself," Ethan said, turning to face the woman.

Ethan was immediately stunned by the woman's beauty. She was a gorgeous blonde with a slender body. Her glasses, outfit, and demeanor gave off a staggeringly sexy intelligence.

"I'm glad you agree. Some people don't appreciate the Unknown Poet's work. They find it 'overly complicated.'" the woman said.

Ethan shrugged. "Yeah well some people just don't get art. Screw 'em," he said.

The blonde laughed at that "It's nice to meet a like-minded individual. They're hard to come by, even here at the festival."

"Thanks," Ethan said, "I'm Ethan by the way." Ethan held out a hand. The blonde eagerly grabbed his hand and shook it. "I'm Claire."

"Well, it's nice to meet you Claire. Is this your first time at the festival? It's mine," Ethan told her.

"Well, welcome," Claire said excitedly. "This is my fourth time actually, but it's my first time as a contestant."

As she said it, Ethan realized who he was talking to. He had seen her on the festival's website. She was Claire Donaghue and she was one of the eight poets invited to the festival. She'd written a poem called "The Human Journey."

"Wow, I'm so sorry. I didn't recognize you at first, you're Claire Donaghue," Ethan said excitedly.

Claire flashed an honest smile. Her smile rivaled Ashley's and Ethan could already feel himself falling for her. "Don't apologize. It's nice to talk to someone about writing without them treating me like some kind of goddess of the trade. I wrote one good poem, that's it," she said.

Ethan shook his head. "I'm sure your other poetry is great. But it's probably good you are a little hard on yourself. We can't have you developing a goddess complex."

Claire laughed, "Yeah, you won't have to worry about that."

From there the two launched into a conversation about all things writing. Claire was a famous poet and Ethan was a nobody, yet that made no difference. Claire and Ethan shared a similar point of view on almost all things writing related. The conversation went on so long, they took it to a small cafe up the street from the museum. After fifteen minutes at the museum and almost an hour at the cafe, Claire had to take a quick phone call.

"Ethan, I've really enjoyed this conversation, but my publisher just called. Apparently I've got places to be. Contest crap, I guess," Claire said after she ended the call. "Let's exchange numbers? I'd love to meet up again."

Ethan almost couldn't believe it. Claire was drop dead gorgeous, and he'd just spent the past hour falling in love with her mind. It seemed unreal that she'd ask him for his number. "Of course," Ethan said a little too eagerly.

They traded phones and put in each other's numbers. Afterwards Claire got up to leave. "Come visit me later at the bookstore for the Meet the Writers event. I'm sure I'll be in need of a friendly face," she said.

"Yeah of course. See you later Claire," Ethan said. Then they both went their separate ways.

Claire disappeared into the crowd on Main Street, and Ethan returned to the museum. He wanted to finish seeing all the exhibits.

Back at the museum Ethan noticed another famous author. It was Robert Mitchelson. Ethan had always been a big fan of Mitchelson and his cinematic way of writing.

Robert seemed to be in a good mood. Based on what Ethan overheard of their conversation, Robert was touring the museum with his publishing agent. Ethan pulled his manuscript for "In Love and Despair" from his backpack and clutched it tightly. If he was ever going to have a chance to get his novel noticed, now was it.

Ethan swallowed nervously, gathered his courage, and approached Robert. "Excuse me, Mr. Mitchelson," Ethan called out.

Both Robert and his publisher turned to face Ethan. "Yes, can I help you?" Robert asked. "I am a huge fan," Ethan started. "I can't believe you're standing here in front of me. I was just hoping for a second of your time."

The publisher looked annoyed but did his best to hide it. Robert, however, smiled happily at Ethan. "I can always make some time for a fan," he said.

Ethan laid on all of the typical ramblings of a fan, and Robert repaid him with the same modest thank you's and niceties that he would expect. When they were past all that, Ethan offered Robert his manuscript.

"I was hoping you would read it. I write as a hobby, and that's the first story I've ever been proud of," Ethan said. "If you could tell me how to improve on it, or give me any kind of praise, it would really help me in my journey to being in your shoes one day."

Robert took the manuscript without a word and began to read it right there. Ethan was shocked and didn't know what to say, so he just remained silent. After about ten minutes Robert stopped. He looked to his publisher and said, "You need to read this." He handed it to the man and then he started reading. Another ten minutes passed before the man handed Ethan back the manuscript.

Robert looked to his publisher and asked, "Well?"

"Well… I'd say you have a hell of a sense of humor Robert," the publisher answered. Ethan looked at them both with confusion.

"Handing me that garbage like that. I expected it to actually be good," the publisher said laughing.

Robert began laughing as well. "I'm sorry, I just couldn't help myself. It really gets old, getting handed these stories by these terrible writers. I had to spice it up."

Ethan was speechless. He felt like someone had just ripped his heart out of his chest. He swallowed and tried to speak, but nothing came out.

"Sorry kid, but give up while you're ahead," Robert said, "You're never going to be in my shoes." He patted Ethan on the back as the author joined his publisher and they walked out of the museum together, laughing.

Ethan didn't know whether to cry or chase after them to give them a piece of his mind. In his hesitation he did neither. He just stood there in complete disbelief. He wasn't sure how long he'd been standing like that when a tall man approached him.

"Don't listen to them," he said in a heavy Jamaican accent. "Those writers don't know shit. They're all a bunch of stuck up fucks that think they're better than everyone else."

"Thanks," Ethan managed.

The man laughed and waved a hand in front of Ethan's face. "Wake up buddy. Don't give them that win," he said.

That managed to snap Ethan out of it slightly. "You're right. I'm not saying I'm a great writer, but that was uncalled for. I know it's not that bad," Ethan said.

"That's more like it," the man said. "Now that you're alive again, it's good to meet you. I'm Deaven."

Ethan shook Deaven's hand. "Ethan," he said.

"Alright, Ethan. How about a personal tour around the museum to take your mind off of it?" Deaven asked.

"That would actually be great," Ethan said, surprised by Deaven's generosity. "Do you work here?"

"I'm the curator," Deaven said proudly, "Now come this way. The museum is best enjoyed chronologically. We'll start with the Ustumah Tribe."

Ethan followed and Deaven began an in depth tour of the entire museum. Ethan was completely engrossed in the interesting history of the town. He'd had no idea it had such a rich background. They went through the Ustumah Tribe, to the Gold Rush era, and eventually to the works of the famous Unknown Poet. Ethan and Deaven seemed to thrive off of each other's passionate interest in the history.

"Deaven, that was great. Thank you so much," Ethan said when they were finished.

"No, it made my day. Thank you. It's so nice to meet someone who sees the value of the history of this place," Deaven replied.

"Honestly, I wish I could learn more," Ethan admitted.

Deaven's face grew serious at that. "I could arrange that," he said staring intently at Ethan. "What do you mean?" Ethan asked cautiously.

"All I can say, is that if you're serious, meet me here later tonight after the museum has closed. I live here in town, but I have another place out in the forest. I'll bring you there and really teach you the history of this place," Deaven said.

A part of Ethan felt defensive. He wasn't sure he could trust this man he'd just met, especially after he'd just begun acting so strangely. But ultimately he felt that Deaven was harmless and truly wanted to share some interesting secret with Ethan. They'd just shared a great couple of hours together, and Ethan felt that Deaven was a stand-up guy.

"Alright, I'll come by after you close," Ethan said.

"See you then," Deaven said, "For now I should get back to the rest of my work."

"Of course, thanks again," Ethan said. Then Deaven waved goodbye and Ethan left the museum.

CHAPTER 31

Ethan spent the rest of his day exploring the festival. It was essentially nothing but an overcrowded book fair for adults. He did enjoy himself, though his mind kept wandering to Robert's comments on his story, as well as to Ashley and Marcus. He did his best to shake those thoughts when he could.

As the small town fell to night, people migrated to the Ustumah City Bookstore for the Meet the Writers Event. Ethan made his way over as well. Not just to check out the event, but to say hello to his new friend Claire. He wanted to make a quick appearance before he went to meet Deaven.

The inside of the bookstore was the very definition of hectic, but Ethan was able to get a good spot in line for Claire's booth. He stood in line for twenty minutes, before he finally made it to her.

"Ethan!" Claire said excitedly. "You came!"

She ran around the side of the booth and hugged him. Ethan nervously hugged her back.

"Of course. I said I would," Ethan said.

Claire released him and went back behind the booth. "Well, do you want a copy of my poem with a personalized signature?" she said, holding her pen in the air dramatically and smirking at Ethan.

"Why else would I come?" He said awkwardly.

Claire laughed and signed a copy of her poem, which had been printed on a beautiful piece of parchment paper. She handed it to Ethan. "There you are. Have you read it yet?"

"No, but I'm excited to now," Ethan admitted.

"Don't be too harsh. If you really don't like it, maybe silently judge it for now," she said, winking and pointing to the rest of the people in line.

"Oh of course," Ethan said. Then he read the poem, and after, Claire's signature.

To my friend Ethan, a kindred spirit and fellow writer. Claire Donaghue.

It was just what Ethan had needed to warm his spirit.

Claire was looking at Ethan with anticipation. "So?" she asked.

"To be honest, I don't read much poetry. Usually because I just don't get it. I'd rather read a good story," Ethan began. Claire looked concerned, but Ethan continued, "But this is really damn good Claire. I'd probably read more poetry if you wrote all of it. There's obviously a reason you're here."

Claire rolled her eyes at him. "You had me for a second there," she said.

"Sorry, couldn't help myself," Ethan admitted. Then he took a second to check the time on his phone. He only had a few minutes to get to the museum before it closed.

Claire sensed his urgency. "It's alright if you have somewhere to go. I've got a whole line of people to get through. But before you leave, I have two questions for you," she said.

Ethan nodded, "Sure."

"First, brunch tomorrow?" Claire asked.

Ethan couldn't believe it. First she'd asked for his number, and now she was asking him to brunch.

"Of course. Text me in the morning," Ethan said trying to play it cool.

"Great! Second," Claire went on, "Now that you've read something I wrote. It's my turn to read something of yours. Bring something tomorrow if you can."

Ethan hesitated, but then he reached into his pack and grabbed his manuscript. "I've actually got something here. But it's a bit longer of a read," Ethan said nervously.

Claire snatched it from his hands. "Looks like I have a night of reading ahead of me!" she said happily. "Now go on, get to wherever it is you have to be. I'll see you tomorrow."

Ethan looked at his phone again. The museum was closing.

"Thank you, Claire," Ethan said waving as he left. Claire waved back as the seemingly endless line of fans moved forward by one person.

When Ethan got to the museum, Deaven was waiting outside.

"I wasn't sure you were coming," he said.

"Sorry, sorry," Ethan said hurrying over. "I had to stop and see a friend."

"No worries," Deaven said, "But I should warn you. It's quite a hike to where we are going. I won't take offense if you decide not to come."

Ethan hesitated, but he nodded his head. "No. It's a bit strange but I'm interested." Deaven nodded and led Ethan to his car. They got into the car and drove for a short while.

Deaven pulled the car over on the side of the road, and parked it behind some trees where it would be difficult to spot. Then he got out of the car and pulled out two flashlights from the trunk. He handed one to Ethan.

"Stick close. It can be easy to get lost out here, and reception is spotty," Deaven warned.

Deaven led the way into the forest. There was no established trail, however there was a slight foot path that Deaven followed. He had clearly come this way plenty of times and knew exactly where he was going. Their flashlights did little to illuminate the darkness, but they were enough to see where they were going.

They hiked for almost two hours before arriving at their destination. Ethan spent most of it wondering if he had gone for a walk with a serial killer. He passed it off as paranoia. A cabin sat before them in the middle of the forest.

Deaven turned around to face Ethan. "This is a special place. Or at least I used to think it was. I don't know anymore. Come inside, I'll explain."

Ethan followed Deaven inside the cabin. Deaven started a generator out back and the cabin came to life with light. The cabin was a cozy habitat filled with books. One wall of the cabin had been completely dedicated to some sort of collage of papers.

Deaven briefly explained that the collage was his life's work. He had dedicated himself to finding a place called the Heart of the Forest. When Ethan began to ask questions, Deaven stopped him.

"Perhaps it will make more sense if I explain from the beginning," Deaven said. Ethan nodded and prepared himself for what he could tell would be a fairly long story.

"When I was a young boy back in Jamaica, my father got involved with some bad men and wound up getting himself killed. Well, these men felt that me and my mom had to pay off my father's debt to them," Deaven began his story.

"They made our lives a living hell. Luckily my mom had friends. Good people who wanted to help us. And they did. They helped us get away to America. The bad men had a far reach though, and moving to a new land did not keep us safe for long. We had to go on the run, moving from place to place for years. Until we ended up here in Ustumah City," Deaven went on.

"Nobody found us here, and we finally started a real life. My mom was a great cook, and she had been teaching me to follow in her footsteps. I listened and learned dutifully, but cooking was never my true passion," Deaven continued.

"Every year writers would come from all around to the Known Poets and Authors Writing Festival. I read all of the work that came through. The writers were my idols. The way they brought words to life was something I found so amazing. I knew that what I really wanted to do was become a writer."

"I continued working as a cook with my mom, but on the side I wrote. I saw myself improving in everything I wrote, and I was proud of my works. Other people didn't see it that way. Every writer, poet, and publishing agent told me that it was junk. Some even went so far as to tell me that I would never have a career as a writer and should just give up. But I didn't."

"Years later my mother's old age caught up to her. She died peacefully in her sleep after living a long life. I miss her everyday. That woman sacrificed so much for me. I can never repay that debt," Deaven said. He paused and squinted as if he were holding back tears. "I inherited her restaurant as well as her duties to the festival. I had less time to write than even before. But I kept on anyway. I wrote a fiction where the main character was a courageous woman inspired by my mother. When I finished it, it was a masterpiece. But yet again, every writer, every poet, every agent, all of them said it was no good. They tossed my passion piece aside like garbage, but paraded each other's mediocre works around like they were written by God himself," Deaven continued.

"I grew to despise the people who came to the festival. I saw them for what they truly were. Liars with giant egos, and nothing more. Even the esteemed Ustumah City Book Club didn't pick the best book or the best poem at the end of every festival. They picked the works that were written by those who flattered or bribed them the best."

"One year, I came across some works from the Unknown Poet stored in the records at city hall. I had known about the Unknown Poet, but I had never read these works. One of them in particular stood out to me," Deaven said. Then he began reciting the poem from memory.

"'A writer with ambitions for the world, Discovery of a power untouched, Now temptation takes hold, Curse self-inflicted by work rushed, Innocents now pay the debt of this mistake, To bring back balance the writer must atone, To set things right, a choice they must make, The price to be paid: to have never been known.'"

"The poem told a story that I believed to be the story of the poet themselves. The first two lines were what really grabbed my interest. They sparked my investigation into a power. The history of Ustumah was filled with mention of a power so great it could bring stories to life. Some call it the Heart of the Forest. Since then I have dedicated my life to finding the Heart of the Forest. When I do, I will change my story. With the Heart, I will literally bring words to life," Deaven finished. He then looked to Ethan for his reaction.

"You have a very interesting story Deaven. But I have to be honest with you, I'm not so sure about all this magic stuff," Ethan admitted.

"I know it sounds crazy. While I wholly believe it to be completely true, there is at least some truth to it that can not be denied. Let me explain," Deaven said.

Deaven began talking about Ustumah's history, delving far more deeply then he had at the museum. Deaven had hard factual evidence of a Heart of the Forest, or something similar by a different name, be referenced over and over again by key figures in Ustumah

County's history. By the end, Ethan was convinced that there was at least some truth to the Heart of the Forest.

"Knowledge that such a thing exists, can be more than enough to drive someone. With such a power, we can change our lives for the better. What goal is worth pursuing more than that," Deaven finished.

Ethan thought about that. At first, he wasn't sure he completely agreed. But as he thought about his failures as a writer, the idea of changing his life became more tempting. Even more tempting was when Ethan thought about Ashley. He still felt as if they were meant to be together. If only that night at the bar had gone differently. My life would be so much better now, Ethan thought. Suddenly, Deaven's words rang truer than anything Ethan had ever heard. What goal is worth pursuing more than that, Ethan told himself.

"Why are you sharing this with me?" Ethan asked.

Deaven nodded. "That's a fair question," he started, "You have to realize that I have spent years of my life trying to find the Heart. I am starting to believe that maybe I'm just not worthy. And, I don't know, but today at the museum when I saw you with that stuck up author and his asshole publisher, it reminded me of myself. Then we began talking about Ustumah's history and you showed a passion that I had not seen in anyone but myself. I just knew somehow that sharing this with you was the right thing to do. Maybe I'm not meant to find the Heart, but perhaps you are."

Ethan let those words sink in, and his mind wandered to Ashley. To him and her together. He saw himself as a famous author. They were happy.

"I'll at least give it a shot," Ethan told Deaven. "I won't let you down."

Deaven said nothing, but nodded and smiled. They talked for a long while after that about Deaven's past attempts to find the Heart of the Forest. Deaven hoped that Ethan could find some success in looking at his own failures. They talked long into the night, until Deaven finally offered to take Ethan back into town. Ethan agreed.

Three hours later Ethan was back at his hotel. He hurried to get to sleep so he wouldn't be completely exhausted when he met Claire the next morning.

Ethan woke up the next morning to a text from Claire. "Mama Palmer's 9:30. Apparently it's the best breakfast in town, see you there," it said.

It was eight o'clock and Ethan had plenty of time to get ready. He got dressed and spent a long while fussing with his hair. He wanted to look good for Claire. At nine-fifteen Ethan headed out toward Mama Palmer's restaurant. When he got there Claire was already waiting.

She checked her watch. "You're early, nice," she said smiling at him. "You're just so excited to see what I have to say about your story huh?"

Ethan had almost forgotten he'd given her his manuscript. His talk with Deaven about the Heart of the Forest had been all he was thinking about. He was interested to see what she would say though.

"Your opinion would mean a lot," Ethan admitted.

"We'll talk about it inside. C'mon, I already have a table," she said leading him into the restaurant.

At the table they ordered their breakfast. When the waitress left, Claire pulled out Ethan's manuscript and placed it on the table.

"Alright. So I read a good chunk of the first part," Claire started. "You're a really good writer Ethan. With the right kind of focus I think you could write something really special."

Ethan was ecstatic. Praise from a writer like Claire really meant something. Maybe his dream of being a famous author wasn't so far off after all.

"But," Claire continued, "I don't think this is it. This story isn't the right kind of focus." All of Ethan's joy deflated. "What do you mean?" he asked.

Claire frowned. She seemed to feel guilty about having said anything. "Like I said, you're a really good writer. But this story is just so preachy. I couldn't help but feel like it was so personal," she said.

"I see," Ethan said looking down.

Claire sighed, "Don't take it like that. I really do think you have potential. You can't be afraid to move past this story."

"No, you're right. I really appreciate the feedback. It's just hard to hear," Ethan explained.

Claire gave Ethan a half smile. "Listen, if I'm out of line just say so. But I feel like somebody hurt you. And, that left you with some serious negativity. It seems like with this story you're somehow trying to right that wrong. But it doesn't work that way. Especially if you channel all that negative energy to do it," she said.

Ethan looked at Claire with astonishment and respect. He wasn't sure if he was just that obvious in his writing, or if she was just that good at seeing it. Either way he was impressed she had discerned all that from reading just part of his story.

"You're right. I did get hurt. And I think I was trying to make myself feel better with that story.

I don't know how I expected other people to want to read it," Ethan admitted.

Claire sighed again. "Just keep writing, alright? And I'm always ready to read anything you're willing to show. I'll even finish this story if you want," she said.

"No, it's probably best if you don't. And thank you Claire," Ethan said. Claire smiled. "Let's talk about something else."

So they did. They talked about Claire's morning, and how she had found out who she was competing against in the first round of the festival's voting. They talked about Claire's history as a poet. They talked about what had happened to Ethan at the museum with Robert Mitchelson. They even talked about Ashley and Marcus. Claire had a gentle and caring way of talking about things. When she talked about herself, Ethan felt like he'd known her his whole life. When she listened to what he had to say he felt comfortable, like he could tell her anything. So, he did. He told her everything about Ashley and Marcus. And after that he even told her about Deaven and the Heart of the Forest.

Claire thought all of the magic was clearly nonsense. But she was very interested in the coincidences, as well as the constant references to the Heart in Ustumah City's history. "I'm not going to go on some witch hunt with you. But I'll give you a hand looking into it. It could make a good book someday," Claire said at one point.

They ended the breakfast on that. Claire had responsibilities to her publisher and the festival, and had to leave. She and Ethan made plans to meet up later that night, or the following day.

After she left, Ethan decided to start his search for the Heart of the Forest. The first day of his search was mostly spent researching the writings that Deaven had mentioned.

On the second day he decided to head out into the forest. Deaven had thought that the Heart was in the center. He had even tried both the current and past center points, even building his cabin at the latter. Ethan decided to revisit the center, and encountered strange entities that he could only attribute to fiction becoming reality.

Ethan, slightly worried by the events of the day before, spent the third day enjoying the festival. He even got as far as deciding to start writing a new story. The decision was as far as he got; all he was left with was some blank printer sheets held together by a single paper clip. He kept the paper with him in his pack just in case inspiration would strike.

By the fourth day, Claire had agreed to take some time away from the festival to join him. Ethan brought her with him to Deaven's Cabin, and along the way they found themselves in a dangerous situation that defied logic and reality. Afterwards, Claire's opinion on magic had changed significantly.

The fifth day of Ethan's search was similar to the others. He ventured out into the forest with Deaven on a hunch, something strange and dangerous happened, and he survived. But he did not find the Heart.

On the sixth day, Ethan felt like he may give up. He met up with Claire, who had just won the title of the festival's best poet. He congratulated her and they caught up, as they had not seen much of each other since their trip to Deaven's cabin.

"I'm going out into the forest today," Ethan told her. "I don't know what's going to happen, but I'm giving it another shot. I was hoping you'd come."

Claire shook her head. "You know I want to help you. But this whole thing is way over my head. I'd prefer to leave ancient magic to itself, and you should too Ethan."

Ethan looked away. "It's not that easy. I need to find it. It's the only way to make things right," Ethan said.

Claire frowned and took Ethan's hand. "Ethan, you're a great guy. You don't need to find some ancient magic so you can set things right with Ashley. Trying to change that doesn't seem right. Maybe you guys just weren't meant to be. You can find someone else," she said in a soft caring voice.

Ethan looked Claire in the eye and she stared back. A part of him couldn't let go of the idea of Ashley, but the other part knew that Claire was right. And when he looked in her eyes, he knew she was that someone else. He leaned in and kissed her.

Their lips had barely met before Claire pulled away. Ethan's heart stopped. "I'm so sorry," he said, "I thought… I thought that… I'm sorry."

Claire was waving her hands back and forth. "No, no. It's my fault," she said quickly. "I should have told you. I just figure people know, and I forget that it can be confusing for guys sometimes."

"Wh-what do you mean?" Ethan stuttered.

Claire let out a long sigh. "Ethan, I'm gay."

Ethan just blinked. The thought had not crossed his mind once. He had thought that she was interested the entire time. She'd seemed so comfortable with him, he'd thought that was the only explanation. But now that he thought about it, it made sense that she could be comfortable with him. She had no interest in guys, so there was nothing weird to her about making close friends with one.

"I really hope this doesn't make things weird. I really think you're a cool guy. I want us to be friends," she said.

Ethan was so embarrassed that he couldn't think straight. All he could manage to say was, "Sure. But I should probably go for now."

Claire looked disappointed, but she didn't argue. "Okay. I understand. See you later?" she asked.

"Yeah, of course," Ethan lied. And then he left.

Whatever part of him had believed what Claire was saying had left. He had never been more certain that the only way to make things better was to find the Heart of the Forest. He had no idea how he was going to, but he knew he would. He picked a completely random part of the forest and started walking.

The deeper Ethan got into the forest, the more certain he became. He could feel a sort of presence tugging at him. Not in any particular direction, but more like it was pulling at his soul. Something had changed. The Heart wanted to be found, and it was leading him. He continued walking.

Eight hours passed. Ethan was completely lost, and he was lucky if he could get any reception on his cell phone. He would have worried that he was going to die lost in the forest, but each passing hour the feeling tugging at his soul became stronger and stronger. Finally, Ethan was walking when he had the strangest feeling that he was being watched. He turned around to look, but saw nothing. Nothing watching him at least. The direction he'd felt the presence coming from revealed the opening of a small underground cave. The entrance was covered with brush, and he wouldn't have spotted it if he hadn't been looking at it from that exact spot.

Ethan was sure that this cave was the place he was searching for. The Heart of the Forest. It was a slow and cautious climb down into the cave, but Ethan managed. It took awhile for his eyes to adjust to the darkness, but once they did, he made his way to the far end of the cave.

He'd spotted something interesting.

Cave paintings lined an entire wall of the cave. There was a small piece of paper and a leather bound journal as well. Ethan read them both and digested their contents. This was the Heart of the Forest, and it's power was most certainly real.

Ethan barely took a moment to consider his options. He opened his backpack and grabbed out a pen and the blank paper he had been keeping on him. He sat down in the cave and started writing. Time to change my story, he told himself. And he began writing a new manuscript.

CHAPTER 32

Nothing But Words, By Ethan Garland

Ethan finished his drink at the end of the bar. His one last bit of liquid courage before he had the conversation that would change his life forever. Ashley Hollins sat at a table across the bar with some of their mutual friends. Like most nights when they went out, Ashley's beauty made her stand out like a gem among stones. Ethan stared at her, taking in all her beauty. Not just her looks, but her being. His final reminder of why she meant so much to him. He didn't hesitate any longer, and he moved across the bar straight toward her.

She noticed him as he made his way over and happily waved him on. "Where'd you head off to? We missed you," she said as her perfect smile made its appearance.

"I needed a drink," Ethan said. "Actually, I was hoping to talk to you about something. Alone." He said the last part quietly to avoid the others hearing.

Ashley was surprised but not concerned. She turned to the rest of the table, "Be right back guys. Don't do anything fun without me," she joked at the rest of their friends. Then she stood up and followed Ethan to a quieter corner of the bar.

As they settled in, Chamber of Reflection by Mac Demarco began playing throughout the bar. "I love this song," Ashley said, closing her eyes for a moment and nodding her head to the beat. "So what's so important you had you had to drag me away from everyone else, big guy?"

Chamber of Reflection was Ashley's favorite song. For it to start playing like that, made the moment that much more special. It gave Ethan the courage to say what he had to say.

"Ash, I'm so glad that we're such great friends. Every day we've spent together since we've met has been amazing. No matter what, I will always appreciate our friendship. There's a part of me that is so worried that what I am about to say is going to ruin all that, but if I don't say it, I'm not sure I'd ever forgive myself," Ethan said pausing briefly. "Ashley Hollins, I love you. And the thing is, saying it isn't good enough. Saying 'I love you' is nothing but words. I want to show you. I want to show you how I feel. I want to give you how I feel. I don't think just being friends is going to cut it for me anymore."

Ashley was absorbing everything Ethan was saying. And for a moment, his nerves got the better of him. He took a deep breath and finished what he had to say. "I guess what I'm trying to do is ask you if you'll give me the opportunity to show you how I feel. I'm asking if you feel the same way. I'm asking if you want something more than this. Because I think we could be amazing together."

There was a silence of anticipation after that. Ethan's heart was beating a million times a minute as he waited to hear what Ashley would say.

Ashley's mind was racing. A million thoughts a second. She had never seen Ethan as anything but a friend. She loved their friendship, and she didn't want to endanger it. But as they stood there together with her favorite song playing around them, she felt this deep romance that she had never experienced before. There was a spark of realization. A realization that she loved him back. Their friendship had clouded that fact from her. She cared for him more than most people in her life, and she knew that he had always felt the same way. She realized that they had always had something special, but that if they weren't together they would never realize its potential. Ethan had said that being friends wasn't going to cut it for him anymore, and she realized that she felt the same way.

Ashley didn't say anything, she just stepped forward and kissed Ethan. As they shared their first kiss the bar seemed to disappear around them. All of their time together before that moment seemed to come together and fill the moment with even more passion. It was the beginning of something amazing.

Ashley and Ethan's relationship was the envy of all their friends. They were perfect together.

Ethan experienced emotions in a way he never had before, and was able to write a masterpiece. He became a bestselling Author and was invited to Ustumah City's Known Poets and Authors Writing Festival.

Eventually things continued on as they were meant to be from that point forward. Ethan's story was just beginning, and it was going to be marvelous.

CHAPTER 33

Now Ethan stood in the dimly lit cave holding that very same manuscript. He'd blamed the Forest for everything that had happened to him. But it had never been out to get him. It had just been interpreting his own writing in the way it thought best. He'd written a story that lacked any consequences, but he'd been foolish enough to write it in a way that was open to interpretation. Eventually things continued on as they were meant to be from that point forward, Ethan thought. A single sentence that undid all his effort. Not how he'd meant it, but that didn't matter. The Forest had twisted his story until it was something more real. Something with consequences.

It was at that moment that Ethan realized the truth. He wasn't the protagonist of his own story, desperately trying to hold on to the girl of his dreams. He was the antagonist of a tragic love story between Ashley and Marcus. An unwanted third in an adverse love triangle. A selfish fool that had discovered a potentially limitless power, but had instead used it to break up a perfectly in love couple. All for his own selfish chance at happiness. Even then, he had failed miserably. The power itself had turned his own pathetic story against him.

Ashley had been torn apart emotionally. The magic of the Heart had forced her to love Ethan, while her own heart knew to love Marcus. Ethan's guilt rose up in his stomach. He could only imagine the pain it must have caused her. The mental battle she must have fought trying to be the girlfriend he'd written about, while trying to remain true to her own feelings, must have been exhausting. Same for Marcus, trying to be the loyal friend, all the while knowing the love of his life was with the wrong man.

Ethan finally saw himself for what he really was. Pathetic. He was an entitled fool that thought the world owed him everything, while he did nothing to earn it. He refused to accept his own mistakes, and even when he did, he found a way to repeat them all over again. He was too weak to handle rejection, taking it out on others, rather than accept his faults. He'd loved Ashley, but it had never been anything but a fantasy. They just weren't meant to be together. It made him sick to see just how far he'd gone to try to impose his fantasy into reality.

Despite everything, he found himself in the cave once again. He wondered if the events of the past week had just happened to lead him to this moment, or if the power of the forest had lured him there for a second chance.

A shot at redemption, Ethan thought. But even as he did, other thoughts of temptation gnawed at the back of his skull. *Maybe this time I can do it right. Ashley and I could be happy,* the thoughts whispered as he fought to shake them away. As his desire to fix his mistakes struggled against his selfish urges, Ethan couldn't shake the feeling that the forest was testing him. Twice now he had read the contents of this cave, this Heart of the Forest. He had the mistakes, of not just himself, but those who had been before him, to learn from. If there was anything he knew, it was that this was all just a story in the eyes of the Forest. What Ethan did next would be the defining moment of his character arc in the story the Forest was telling. He could carefully write a new story. Each word, sentence, and paragraph would be crafted to ensure there would be no room for the Forest to twist the story to its own ends. He would undo what he had done and redeem himself. Maybe I can still be the protagonist after all, Ethan thought. But that was easier said than done. That was a happy ending with little given in sacrifice, other than the suffering that had been endured up to that point. If Ethan undid all of that, he knew it would count for little. The Forest would not allow such a happy ending so easily.

In the cave he held power over the Forest. But neither he, nor the Forest could defy the rules of what makes a story feel real.

He could always choose the other path, writing a more airtight story of Ashley and his happily ever after. Maybe Marcus and he still had a falling out, but Marcus' life turned out better for it. Perhaps Marcus would meet a girl that would make him as happy as Ashley had. It was easy. Ashley would live a happy lie, and Marcus a happy truth, just not the one he had wanted. The villain wins despite it all. A bittersweet ending that seemed to match the Forest's taste. Am I really the villain, Ethan asked himself, is that really what I want?

Ethan scoffed. Even with everything he knew about this supernatural power, he couldn't let himself make everything about writing. He wasn't just some character at a fork in his development. The choice he made would affect real people. A sad writer lost the two best friends he would ever have. A happy couple now lived with regret for choosing their own true love over a selfish friend. And a real mother was out there grieving for her daughter who'd been rotting in this cave for over a week. All of that and more, because Ethan had hastily scribbled a sorry excuse for a story onto some pages in a cave. Ethan felt a single tear slide down his left cheek. He closed his eyes and swept it away. He knew what he had to do.

Ethan pulled the remaining blank pages apart from "Nothing But Words." He grabbed a pen that had been lying nearby, and he started writing. He thought of everyone who had been a part of all this. Ashley, Marcus, Claire, Deaven, Ella Schaeffer, and her mother Elisa. He wrote about all of them. They deserved to be happy, and he had the power to make it so.

He wrote and he wrote and he wrote. Finally he was nearing the end of his story. It was both a happy beginning and ending for everyone. Everyone except for Ethan. He had left himself out of the story up until that point. He'd been focused on his realization about stories and consequences. The story he'd written seemed happy on paper, but the Forest would find a way to manipulate it. There had to be consequences, and so far he hadn't written any. That was why he had saved himself for last. If anyone was going to pay the price, it should be him.

Before, he had written like his hands were on fire. Now that it was his turn, he couldn't finish one sentence. "As for Ethan," was all he had managed. He wasn't sure what should happen to him. How he could make amends. Not just that, but he was scared. It was not an easy thing to decide your own fate when it was unfavorable. He stared at those three words, "As for Ethan," for a long time. He thought of a thousand endings, but none of them felt right.

He was still thinking, when he heard a voice call out to him from above, "Hello!" As it did the brush that had been covering the cave entrance began to rustle. The brush was pulled aside and light flooded the cave from above.

The light revealed the decomposing body of Ella Schaeffer and the voice above said, "Jesus Christ."

Ethan said nothing. So far back in the cave he would not be visible to whoever was standing above. However, he got a good look at them as his eyes adjusted to the light flooding in. It was Officer Riley, and he'd taken his gun from his holster.

"I know you're in there Garland. Come out with your hands up. Let's do this peacefully," Riley shouted into the cave.

Still Ethan said nothing. There was no way Riley could have known he was there.

"For fuck's sake Garland! I followed you and your friends out here. I knew you were up to something. I saw you run off into the forest. I lost track of you for a bit, but now that I've found this I don't know where else you'd be," Riley said.

Ethan considered going to Riley, but he had to finish the story. He just didn't know what to write, and Riley was a distraction that was making it even more difficult.

When Ethan didn't respond, Riley called out again. "I don't know what kind of sick ritualistic shit you've been doing out here," he said gesturing to Ella's body, "but either you're coming to me, or I'm coming down there. And if I have to come down there, I'm shooting on sight. Don't give me an excuse Garland."

Fuck, fuck, fuck, Ethan thought. He'd have to convince Riley to let him finish the story. He didn't have enough time to think of an ending before Riley could get down. "Okay, I'm coming out with my hands up," Ethan called back.

"About fucking time," Riley said. "Slowly. Hands way the fuck up."

Ethan put down the manuscript and pen. He raised his hands high above his head and started walking into the light. Riley got eyes on Ethan and pointed the gun at him.

"I knew you were behind this you sick fuck. Was it all to try and sell more of your book? Or some other weird shit?" Riley asked.

Ethan shook his head. "You don't understand. It's not that simple," Ethan said.

"Fucking explain it to me then. I'd love to hear what kind of story your writer ass will come up with for this," Riley demanded.

Ethan told Riley the truth. It was all he could think to say. No lie was going to get him any further.

When Ethan was done Riley just laughed. "You expect me to believe that some magic shit took your story and killed Ella with it? Fuck off. Start climbing up here. And if you make a move I don't like, I'll shoot your ass. God knows I want to."

"I can't do that," Ethan pleaded. "You don't understand. If you just let me finish writing, I can fix all of this. It'll be like Ella never died. You and I want the same thing Riley."

Riley shook his head. "What kind of cop would I be if I let you go back in there and finish whatever kind of serial killer ass ritual you've been working on? You make one move that's not toward this wall to start climbing, I'm shooting."

Ethan hesitated. He could go with Riley, but he'd never be able to explain the truth. The only way was to finish the story. He looked Riley in the eye for a fleeting second, before making a dash for the back of the cave.

"Damn it, don't!" Riley yelled. Then three deafening gunshots rang through the cave rhythmically.

Ethan felt three small stings in his back, and he grunted. He kept up his dash until he reached the manuscript. He fumbled with the pen as he brought it back to the paper. He could hear Riley cursing above and starting to climb down into the cave. Ethan didn't have long.

He sat there again staring at the paper. "As for Ethan," stared back. As for Ethan, as for Ethan, as for Ethan, he thought to himself frantically. Then the pain kicked in, followed by the acknowledgment of the three bullets that had just hit him in the back. He felt the pain in his chest and his gut. He looked down and there was blood everywhere. He could feel himself getting lightheaded.

Ethan realized he was going to die there unless he wrote something. Anything is better than being dead, Ethan told himself. But as he did, the answer came to him. He felt like he was about to die, and he realized it was fitting. It was the highest price he could pay. Nothing else made sense. Even still, he didn't want to die. He wouldn't do that to himself. But he had the answer he needed. He wrote furiously. Every moment he could feel his consciousness leaving, but he held on to finish. He wrote the last word and placed the last period. As he did a drop of blood fell from his chest onto the paper. He thought of Ashley's smiling face one last time, and everything went black.

CHAPTER 34

Setting Things Write, By Ethan Garland

1 - The Happy Couple

Ashley danced to the music like she was the only one around. It had been a great night so far, and she didn't think it could get any better. She couldn't believe how wrong she was. She wasn't watching where she was going and she accidentally bumped into fellow party goers. She stumbled, but the man she'd just run into caught her in his strong arms.

"Hey, watch out," Marcus said as he let go of her. "It'd be a shame if the prettiest girl at the party hurt herself." Ashley smirked at him. He wasn't too bad looking himself, but she wasn't about to let him get away with that cheesy pick-up line.

"How often does that line work for you?" she asked. Marcus laughed. "That's my first time with that particular use. But other variations work often enough that I haven't stopped," he admitted.

Normally Ashley would have found that cockiness to be off putting, but there was something different about this guy. She felt like she already knew him. He seemed honest, and his cockiness seemed to have more to do with his humor than anything else. So she let it slide. But that didn't mean she was going to make things easy for him.

"Well, thanks for catching me, but it's not going to work tonight," Ashley said as she started to make some distance.

"Ahh c'mon," Marcus called back to her. "At least dance with me."

Ashley stopped moving away, and Marcus eagerly awaited her response. He'd been to a lot of parties in college, and he'd hooked up with his fair share of girls. Normally he'd let a girl leave. He'd just find another one that was interested later. But something about this girl seemed different. He'd just met her, and he couldn't say what it was, but she made him want her like no one else ever had.

"Alright, I'll give you one dance," she said.

Marcus' eyes lit up. They danced and it felt so right. One dance turned to two, then three, then more. It wasn't long before they left the party together. They went back to Ashley's place and stayed up late into the night getting to know each other. Surprisingly to both of them they managed to not even kiss. But that changed the next morning. Ashley thanked Marcus for a great night and he did the same. As he was getting ready to leave, Ashley hugged him goodbye. Then it just happened, their first kiss.

Marcus didn't end up leaving that day, and from then on he and Ashley were inseparable. They were the happy couple everyone else wished they were. They dated for a while before they moved in together. Then it was only a matter of time before they were engaged. Their wedding was both modest and amazing. It was only the beginning of something truly magical.

All relationships take work. Some marriages can't handle that and they fall apart. Others find a way to live with it, but they're never happy as they were. But every so often there's a couple that is as happy together at the end as they were in the beginning. The couple that finds true love. Ashley and Marcus were that couple. They lived a long happy life together, before passing away in their sleep the same night.

2 - A Mother's Love

Elisa Schaeffer watched her daughter Ella playing in the yard with their dog. Nothing brought her more joy that her daughter did. She was thankful for every moment she got to share with her. As she watched her daughter play, she swore that she would never let anything happen to her. Ella lived a happy life, and Elisa kept her word. Nothing bad ever happened to Ella.

Eventually for Elisa old age came like it does for us all. She passed on, but even in death she watched over her daughter. Ella went on to be a mom of her own, and just like her mother before her, she protected her daughter from everything. The Schaeffer family was always protected from tragedy by the all-powerful magic of a mother's love, passed from generation to generation.

3 - Pride and Poetry

Claire had been writing poetry professionally for years. It was honest work and she enjoyed it, but it hardly paid the bills. Her luck changed, however, when her poem "The Human Journey" was recognized by the Ustumah City Book Club and they invited her to the Known Poets and Authors Writing Festival. Claire enjoyed the festival, but she found herself stressing over the contest portion. She knew the truth behind the festival. It was driven by the egos of the book club members and nothing more.

Claire's publisher knew that truth and used it to their advantage. Claire made it to the final round of the contest and ended up winning. Being voted the festival's best poet meant a bright future for Claire. She could write poetry for a living, and she could live well. Her works would shape the work of future poets, and she would always have a place in the history of the writing community. But that wasn't enough for Claire.

Writing meant everything to Claire. She saw it as a way for humans to express themselves in the purest forms. As far as she was concerned the Known Poets and Authors Writing Festival was a stain upon that purity. It did nothing but keep good writers down, and encourage lazy writing among those with the means to bribe the book club.

Claire used her new prominence in the writing community to eventually blow the lid off the lies of the festival. Quickly attendance to the festival in Ustumah City fell every year, until they stopped hosting it all together. Claire continued on with her success knowing she had changed the writing world forever. She was a poet that would be remembered for a long time coming.

4 - Man of Heart

Deaven had been a struggling writer for many years. He cooked for a living, but he wrote on the side. Much to his disappointment, nothing he wrote was ever recognized as worthy of being published.

Deaven's dream was to be a writer, but it wasn't just about himself. To him, it was about his mother, and honoring her life. That was why one day Deaven decided to write the story that meant the most to him. His own story. An autobiographical recounting of his journey. It was a true story that had it all. A gang of criminals trying to extort an innocent family. A tale of immigration and struggle. An ode to a mother who sacrificed everything so that her son could have a better life. And a story about a young man who never stopped following his dreams.

After sending out the story, Deaven received offers from more publishers than he knew what to do with. He took the offer from the publisher that seemed most interested in his story, and not in the money. The book was published not long after, and swept the nation. It was an instant bestseller. Deaven eventually decided that there must be others with similar stories that needed to be told.

He moved on to writing even more books about those other people's stories, and they were equally as successful as his first book.

Deaven took his earnings and turned his mother's restaurant into a successful nationwide chain. He proudly ran the company for the rest of his life, before passing it on to his own children. He was always remembered by everyone who knew him as a true man of heart.

5 - Writing the Wrong

As for Ethan, it was as if he had never existed at all. Ethan had tried to play god, living in a story of his own creation. Only one punishment could fit that crime. He would no longer have a story.

His story ended. A price to be paid so that the stories of others could begin again, free of the influence of the Forest. Free of despair.

About the Author

Dustin Hoiseth is a new author who has always had a love for storytelling. His first novel, *Nothing But Words*, started as an idea that had him making notes late into the night. From there it turned into conversations with himself as long car rides turned into some of the stories most climatic scenes. Within a year the first draft was complete, and Dustin began work on the newest idea keeping him up at night.

Nothing But Words did not go forgotten, and Dustin was soon revising the first draft with a fresh pair of eyes. Dustin believes that the best stories are the ones that never forget to focus on real people and real problems, even if magic always somehow finds its way into the plot. *Nothing But Words* is one of Dustin's proudest accomplishments, but he looks forward to sharing even more of his stories with the world.

9 781737 883241